Shadowy Natures

Stories of Psychological Horror

Edited by Rebecca Rowland

www.DarkInkBooks.com

ISBN: 978-1-943201-35-8 (pbk.)

Library of Congress Control Number: 2020933545

Cover Photo "Birds" Copyright: Phil Fiddyment licensed under CC BY 2.0, Share Alike

This is a work of fiction. Names, characters, places, and incidences either are the product of the author's imagination or are used fictitiously, and any resemblance to actual persons, living or dead, is entirely coincidental.

First Published by *Dark Ink Books*, Southwick, MA, September 2020

Dark Ink Books is a division of *AM Ink Publishing*. *Dark Ink* and *AM Ink* and its logos are trademarked by *AM Ink Publishing*.

www.AMInkPublishing.com

for Frank the man and Frank the cat,
both of whom loved unconditionally

"The boundary line between instinct and reason is of a very shadowy nature"

-Edgar Allan Poe, *Instinct vs. Nature—A Black Cat* (1840)

Contents

Mandibular Fixation
Lee Rozelle

On the digital x-ray screen my daughter's skull became a bad traffic jam, a pileup in some crowded city where cars of ivory tailgated, rear-ended, pushed against one another, backed into each other, and edged in sideways from all directions, all trying to exit through narrow intersections of bone. Jagged, gapped lines of baby teeth crept forward as rows of large, serrated permanents squeezed through the gums from behind. Incisors emerged in crooked columns from the bottom of her eyeholes, down from the nasal septum, up from the chin and jaw, all coming and going nowhere. Her skull was a jack-o-lantern carved by the devil himself.

"Is this unusual Peter?" I asked.

"Not for around here," chuckled the gaunt orthodontist.

"Will there be a lot of pain?"

Turning from the screen, Peter grinned. Pointing at areas where the teeth seemed most knotted, Peter explained that Ally's case was rare because not one row of permanent teeth was squeezing to get out, but two.

Before I go further, I must admit that I'm a bit of a wimp when it comes to the oral cavity. Slurping, drooling, licking, smacking…they always make me nauseous. A bit of mayonnaise on an old man's lip or a drooling baby and I'm getting vertigo, and it takes every bit of my strength to pucker on the rare and always public occasions that I am forced to kiss my wife. So as I stared up at the screen at my daughter's twisted teeth my knees buckled for a second, the air in my lungs got coppery and brownish haze floated in front of my eyes. I was literally passing out.

"Are you prepared to lead?" Peter uttered as if asking himself a question.

"What?" I stamped my loafered feet to shake off the dizziness.

"I said are you up to your responsibility? As head of the household?"

"Of course, Peter. Yes."

Peter explained that Ally would need braces to pull her front teeth aside so that the irregular clusters from the back might push through. In the years to come, Ally would need a second and perhaps third set of braces, a retainer, and a series of unfortunate forms of headgear consisting of wire and screws and rubber bands. The entire lower jaw would be stressed for months, maybe years, as Peter would slowly drag my daughter's teeth bracket-by-bracket along the jaw line. Gums and roots would open and bleed. Teeth would be excised by the fistful. My daughter's oral cavity would be a web of raw nerves, torn many times before her smile would match those of her private school friends. Peter said it just had to be done.

"Guatemala?" In his half-whispering monotone, Peter had said something about Guatemala. Peter was an elder in our church, and running makeshift dental clinics on Latin American mission trips was his thing.

"You should come with us again," he licked his dry lips. "It's been a long time."

"Just be in the way," I uttered, short of breath.

"Think about it, *deacon.*"

With a series of well-practiced gestures, Peter maneuvered me from the examination room into the hall. I glanced for a moment at Peter's hallway lined with photographs of our church members on missionary trips. I was in a few of those photographs. I didn't look.

At home, my wife's face stiffened when I told her about Ally's visit to the orthodontist. Thumbing through the mail, Rachel dropped breast cancer donation requests and credit card offers one-by-one into the trash.

"Peter asked me to go to Guatemala," I said.

"Oh?"

"Of course I can't go."

"Oh." Her face darkened.

"Don't be so disappointed."

"Guess you know," she glared, "about Leila."

"Leila?"

"Leila. Leila your ex."

"No."

"No?" She arched an eyebrow.

"No." I stared down at envelopes and uneaten egg yolk in the trash.

"Last night she died."

"What are you…?"

"She drowned."

"God, what happened?" I staggered backward to a chair.

"Bridge was wet. They say she just flipped her car off Tallapoochee Bridge."

"Oh my God. *Leila.*"

"They say the car went down instantly, and you know how deep it is."

"Leila…"

"But here's the thing. When they pulled her car out of the creek, only *some* of her body could be found."

"Some?"

"Just skin and hair. Most of her, you know, her epidermis was right there in the seatbelt, still wearing her clothes, but her skeleton and organs were just gone. I've been a doctor for ten years and I've never heard of such a thing."

"Can we pray?" I dropped to my knees.

That night I was nauseous, eardrums buzzing, the wife's ugly casserole like wormy knots in my stomach. In the dream, my wife ran into the office screaming that Ally had been taken by kidnappers—*Mexicans! Illegal Aliens!* she howled—but I was still on the treadmill. I only had thirty seconds left on the blinking machine and needed to finish my workout. Rachel hit and kicked at me during cool down, slapped and screamed, struck my sweaty body with what looked like that repugnant casserole running from her upturned nose. Her face ballooned in maternal terror as she screamed for me to get off the treadmill, to go "save our daughter." I felt the urge to raise my hand, to slap her disappointed face, but instead I apologized, reassured her, took charge, fulfilled my abhorrent responsibilities as head of the household.

Then I was all alone. It was pitch black and I found myself stumbling in yoga pants through an abandoned building that had this reek of burnt oil and rotten onions. The stark odor of human grease, unwashed clothes and thick black flies spiraled upward in a confusion of staircases as I ran in the direction of

Ally's screams. Black bags of half-eaten food blocked me as I gaped into each rotten door up and down the ill-lighted hall, shuffling around like a lost rector through one doorway then another as roaches skittered in a black mass along the ceiling. Ally cried for me upstairs, under the floor, around the far corner.

Turning, backtracking, I found her alone in a dirty room sitting on a narrow bed, and when I reached out to touch her I saw that something was wrong. My daughter's eyes smiled but her mouth was pulled wide, so ugly, a jumble of teeth jutting every whichaway from her mouth like yellowed dominoes and nails, lips crusted and cracked, tiny metal wires tied in thick knots from mouth to hands and eyes, a tongue of chewed rubber straps. I pulled at wires coiling and extending from her teeth and hands and began putting the wires and brackets into my own mouth. Bugs poured like black paint down the walls.

"Daddy you did thith," she said.

Tomorrow, I woke with startled eyes. *Tomorrow I'll call the elders.*

In the second nightmare, I was on some street corner south of the border, my cupped hands full of little packs of gum the wetback babies used to sell to keep from going hungry. Wormy chickens in the park, the metal smell of hog blood and grilled organ meat, stark raw-boned men in front of a concrete wall, plastic garbage turning end-over-end along the street. Peter was yelling at me from the other side of the Zócalo as Pastor Chuck stood on top of a car pointing at what looked like alien ships on the horizon. Pastor Chuck was wearing a wooden Aztec mask, and Peter's arms quivered and shook, his legs still, hair aluminum. The dead girl Leila rode a bicycle right between us, bouncing rings of red hair, a face of flowers and dense braces. Wearing a yellow sun dress, she passed by the mob of Mexicans clustered outside the store. They were in my face trying to tell me something, sell me something, pointing, shouting, fists and opened palms and crooked Mayan calendars. Stumbling backward tripping righting myself I could see desert hills, hear the buzz of foreign voices. Dogs in the distance stood on the hood of my car and howled. The space ships were coming closer. Staggering into the alley, I saw ceremonial masks in dust-caked shop windows and eyes. I knelt under wrestling posters taped to the whitewashed wall. Men in shiny masks making muscles. *Lucha libre.* The wrestling event of the year. Santo, Dr. Wagner, Rayo de Jalisco. Wrestlers glued to the wall recognized me, beckoned me down into the alley, down in the dark with Peter and Pastor Chuck.

I woke again. My wife was curled up facing the wall dead to the fucking world as always. Someone was standing in the hallway.

I got up and walked in the dark toward Ally's room hearing crying.

"Baby?" I said through the door and knocked. "You OK?"

"Daddy?"

I opened the door. From the blade of yellow hall light I could see Ally sitting up in the bed in her robe, her arms clutching her knees, her face red and swollen.

"Sweetie," I leaned down to look. "What's the matter?"

"My mouth," she said and rubbed her cheeks. "It hurth."

"Let me see, honey."

Ally opened her mouth and I felt my throat tighten, felt the room go brown. Teeth like thorns and devil horns stuck through my daughter's gums in tight rings around her remaining baby teeth. I remembered something Pastor Chuck said about the devil, how the devil can root himself inside. I offered a reassuring grin and said things a dad should say. I gave her Vicodin.

Brown clouds from the paper plant crowded Lake Guin on the day my daughter got her braces. From the side kitchen window I watched a skinny Hispanic man with a dead face, clearly the runt of the landscaping litter, as he clipped one of the pair of long privets that ran down our rock driveway. Wearing ear buds and a sleeveless shirt, the man stooped over the clippers, his mind elsewhere. He was making my hedges all crooked. Putting a white bathrobe over my pajamas, I walked out the door down the hill to where the young man clipped. I took a knee and cocked my head toward the hedge. The boy's neck tightened, and he looked over his shoulder at another man at the edge of the road working a weed eater. The men exchanged blank stares.

"Morning." I sported a stiff, wealthy grin.

The aged boy pulled out his ear buds and lifted his chin.

"Can I see those clippers for a second?"

Glancing over his shoulder again, he handed them to me and stepped back. With care I clipped across the hedge, forward and back, forward and back. After a minute, the section I worked on was right, and I moved my hand over the perfectly leveled space.

"That's what I'm talking about," I said. A couple of unsightly sprigs bulged up just out of my reach, so I leaned down and clipped a bit more. "That's what I'm..." My knees were now wet with dew, my face sweating. I wanted to show him again. Snip, snip, snip. Snip, snip, snip. I showed him. Snip, snip, snip. I showed him.

"*Dad?*"

Ally stood at the door, her voice abrasive. I realized that I had been in the yard for over an hour. She looked different, with an older girl's slouch, and somehow larger. She was grinning down at me, grinning with those ungodly teeth. She wanted to embarrass me, parade her corrupted mouth in front of the whole neighborhood. The boy with the ear buds cringed at that hideous maw and turned from us with an uncomfortable clearing of the throat. Beaming at no one with my best church face, sharp clippers in my hand, I stood and glared at the front door. Ally had disappeared back into the house.

The surgical suite was an open bay with a low, angled ceilings and stark lights. Five dentist's chairs jutted from the room's center in the shape of a star, five outstretched children with heads together like Siamese quintuplets, all of them with lip and cheek retractors in their opened mouths that pulled the bottoms of their faces down into distorted gawps. All those little teeth and eyes in the starkness, my Ally one of those stretch-faced children. After seeing what they were doing to one fat-faced boy with a pair of forceps, I decided to hide in the bathroom for a while.

Sitting on the tile floor, I dug into my jacket pocket and pulled out my Santo mask. Given to me by the elders, my wrestling mask was silver and smooth to the touch. When I put it on I could feel God's power. I could forget about all those little mouths laid bare, their pink gums and stretched lips open to Peter's stainless steel tools. Spotlights turned children's faces a ghoulish yellow while young dental assistants with flawless smiles and rubber tubes sucked drool from gaping mouths attaching brackets and twisting strands of wire. Children's small bodies lay flat, their little eyes darting around like confused spider monkeys. Peter flittered from patient-to-patient pulling arch wires, testing brackets, and leaning into pincers. Looking into the bathroom mirror, I took off my shirt and made a few muscle poses then took off the mask and stuffed it back into my pants. When I walked by the bay, I saw Ally's eyes trained on me.

"You look sick," Peter gleamed after the procedure.

"It's messed up," I said. "What you do."

"These children...they're my flock," his eyes glittered, "as you are."

I walked into the hall and scanned photos for a glimpse of myself and the woman who drowned. Jowly, sunburned and dressed in sweaty t-shirts, most of the missionaries in the pictures looked out of place in sunshine. There was Pastor Chuck, a face of grooved wood and cobalt eyes that sucked out the sky. And there was Peter, detached and bony with God knows what on his mind. And there between them was Leila. My Leila. The dead, beautiful Leila. The girl I should have let rescue me when I had the chance. Memories of the elders in a circle wearing tight masks burst into my head.

"I can't concentrate," I said to Peter, "even in church. I keep thinking about her…"

"When's the last time you've had *your* teeth checked?" Peter leaned in, his face becoming a sharp, yellow incisor.

"Get away." I covered my mouth and nose like a terrified child.

Turning in the hall, I righted one of the well-polished frames. It took me a while, but I found the photo I sought around a dark corner on the top row. Leila and I stood together at the edge of a crowd of haggard mission workers under a squat mango tree. Most of the sweaty faces in the picture looked sunburned and grim, ready to get back to air conditioned 'Bama, but Leila and I were smiling. Leila was always giggling and making off-the-wall comments that nobody really got. She played the guitar so beautifully, and her green eyes took your breath away. People at church said she was "outspoken," which meant she'd best keep her metal mouth shut. But our slender bodies and braces matched, and she adored me, wrote me sprawling letters. But when it came down to it Leila just wasn't right. Pastor Chuck explained that Leila was the type of girl you could play stink finger with at camp, not present to father across the bay with his state senators and seedy TV preachers. Not a good match for mother with her cut glass and bald Pilates trainers and tight-knit prayer circles. Leila just wouldn't have made the cut. Especially after what happened. You don't get engaged to a girl who's been kidnapped and raped by Mexicans. You don't tell them men in wrestling masks kept her for hours and made her do degrading things, removed her wisdom teeth with a set of dirty pliers, manipulated her body with rudimentary 3D printers. I never could have a child with someone like that.

That night Rachel was on call. Just after dinner, she had to perform a face lift. As Ally took her bath, I turned on the porch lights and stared at the pair of privets that dropped into darkness down the hillside. The space in the privet that I had done, the part I had clipped perfectly, now looked as jagged as my kid's mouth. I walked around the house staring at the tainted water of Lake Guin with images of Leila clouding my mind.

"Daddy, read to me?" Ally stuck her shining choppers out of the patio door in her pajamas.

"No." I rubbed my temples.

As I squirmed that night in tortured sleep, I thought I heard a pleading scream. It sounded like my Leila. I felt the presence of the elders, the secret world of the deacons, of the Gospel and our apostolic mission. I covered my ears with a pillow but heard another scream. Now awake I realized that it was Ally. I sat up in the empty bed, too petrified to go to her, and as I listened through the wall it sounded like more than one person in her room. Down the corridor I could hear girls not crying but what sounded like giggling. I clamped my eyes shut, put the pillow over my face, and wormed in gutters of sleep until the girlish laughter stopped. Finally, when the house was silent, I put on my robe and tiptoed to Ally's bedroom. Opening the door just a sliver, I saw that Ally was sitting up in bed, alone.

"Ally?" I said. "I thought I heard someone."

"You're supposed to knock."

I closed the door and tapped with my knuckles.

"What do you *want?*" Her high voice fouled the air.

"I thought something was wrong," I said through the door.

"My teeth are growing everywhere, Daddy."

"Do you want me to look?"

"No," she shuddered. "Get out."

I went down the hall into the laundry room, got the hedge clippers, and slid on my Santo mask. Pastor Chuck says to live a Godly life, fathers must accept their responsibility as leaders. Fathers must make the hard calls. Fathers must stand firm. Holding the clippers behind my back in the Santo mask, I went to her door and tapped again. When she didn't answer, I opened the door just a crack. Lying flat as a board under the covers, she appeared to be asleep. I tiptoed closer and could see that her eyes were clamped and quivering, her mouth pinched tight. She was faking sleep. Lying to her father. I shook her shoulder, but she remained as still as a corpse.

The following morning, as my family sat down to a rushed meal, Ally at the breakfast table wiggled some of the numerous teeth that had not been captured by the braces, the pancakes and fruit on her plate left untouched. I tried not to watch. Cutting into an undercooked egg, I could hear Ally slurping with her unwashed hands in her mouth. The smacking sounds made my sensitive stomach twist.

"*Stop.*" I stared out at the lake.

Ally rolled her eyes and continued to twist and pull her teeth making that revolting sound. Rachel sucked at her smoothie and checked the time as I fingered the clippers in my robe pocket. Taking a drink of cold coffee, I looked into my daughter's enflamed face, at the tiny lines of blood on her fingers as she tugged at her deranged teeth making guttural groans. Jesus, the smacking. Jesus, all those teeth. Finally, as I felt chunks of egg coming up in my throat, she pulled a tooth from her bloody gum.

"Get it away from the table," I waved my arms. "Put it under a pillow." She showed the bloodstained tooth to her mother as if it were a misshapen jewel, and then with Leila's mischievous grin she turned and held it up to me.

"Look at it, Daddy," her snaggled face rancid. "Look."

"*Get it out of my face!*" I shoved my daughter backwards with both hands. I didn't push her that hard, just enough to get her away from me, but her head snapped back with a loud pop as she hit the floor. More shocked than hurt, I'm sure, she crawled over to her mother screaming like she did when she was a screaming screaming baby. Clasping our daughter, Rachel just looked at me not saying a word, but that crushing look, that vicious frown I had grown so used to making those crusty makeup craters around her scowling mouth.

Pathetic, her face said. *Unemployed*, it said.

"*Let the woman learn in silence with all subjection!*" I brayed and stood with outstretched arms. Ally and Rachel turned to look at each other for a moment with wide eyes, and then they both burst into laughter.

I woke early. No dreams, thank the Lord. Putting on my robe I went downstairs into my dusty corner office and locked the door behind me. Fumbling around in my locked file cabinet, the one I've had since I was an Omega Lam, I found the thick white envelope I had hidden from myself for so long. But now I needed to look. I had to. I was called to bear witness on this great getting up morning. There were dozens of pictures of Leila, so young, and me never more alive, our braces shining in the sun. Gently I slid out the stack of letters held together with rubber bands. Leila's love notes held traces of feeling that I just couldn't fathom anymore. Water from my eyes stained the browning paper. It had taken a lot of moral strength to do what the elders did to Leila. What they were chosen to do.

I'll go burn these letters in the barbecue pit because the elders will soon arrive. After the ordination, I will be a deacon, and I will see the temple's inner chamber. I will learn the codes. Chokeslam. Cutter. Piledriver. DDT. I will master them all. I still hear Ally and Rachel bumping around upstairs. I hope they're not in too much pain. After I burn these letters, after prayer and hand washing we will put on masks and go upstairs for fellowship, and after the liturgy we will administer to the women. Pastor Chuck and the elders will take my women and conduct the procedure, the ordination, the operation. Call it what you want. Cast stones if you want.

Father accept this offering from your whole family and from the one you have chosen.

Drifter
C.W. Blackwell

Central California, 1850

"'Sure do appreciate the company," Hoyt said to the dead man.

The corpse lay bound and folded over the saddle of an old painted mare, stiffly bouncing as they crested the last of three large hills. A sprawling cypress tree leaned to the lee of the hill, sculpted in the cold breath of the Pacific Ocean.

Hoyt tied the mares and tapped his boot in the dirt.

"It's dry," he said. "I'd sure hate to see a fire spread. No tellin' how long it'd burn for." He clicked his tongue and walked a circle around the old mare. He considered the dead man and shook his head in pity, insects blackening the air in a cloud of winged ecstasy. "Damnit, Morris. Must've picked up every critter from here to Sacramento. Betcha never thought yourself a popular man till now."

Hoyt untied the rope. The dead man slid from the saddle and crumpled in the dirt. He dragged the corpse to the trunk of the cypress tree and tried to settle the head, but it slumped to one side or the other like some ghastly drunkard. He fetched the rope and tied it around the tree across Morris's forehead so that he sat forward, the head pinned and centered. The eyes had festered deep into the sockets and his black mouth hung slack as if he had died screaming.

Hoyt waved his hat in the air to disperse the flies.

"Beautiful out here, ain't it, Morris? *God's country*. Closest thing to the Garden a couple of greasy old bastards like us will ever get. But you ain't a religious man anyhow, right Morris?"

The flies had settled again, parading into every fleshy chasm.

"We'll get someone to speak over your grave, friend," said Hoyt. "Gonna have to put you in the ground soon." He was still waving his hat, but it was more to ward off the stench than the flies. "Eight days is plenty in your condition. And this heat. *Lord, this heat*. My companion up north travelled ten days before she was requirin' of a burial. Of course, some nights she'd freeze through on account of the chill. Reckon it kept her fresh enough. Seen all manner of weather in the company of friends."

The sun was now low in the sky, a roiling cataclysm soon to dissolve into the great Pacific. Hoyt foraged for tinder in the half-light and when he returned, he dug a pit and laid a small fire. He had shot a hare just an hour before and he fetched it from the saddle and cleaned it with a large Bowie knife. He whistled as he freed the meat from the pelt.

"Bet you're wonderin' about the girl," said Hoyt. "You remember the girl. She called herself Agnes. I never liked the name, though. I'm not above teasin' a body about their name and Agnes was no exception. Lord, I teased her good."

Morris's forehead began to split under the rope's abrasion, and the rope made a gradual slide up to the hairline, pulling the skin with it. The face creeped an inch in Hoyt's direction.

"I knew you'd perk up when I mentioned Agnes. She was you're predecessor, after all. She weren't no whore neither. At least it weren't her primary occupation." The hare pelt lay folded over the end of the blade and he held it in the air as if affording Morris an opportunity to admire his butchery. "Pacheco was my companion when I found her curled on the road like a sleepin' dog. Just a poor raggedy thing. Part of some failed caravan on the Oregon Trail. It's a tough country, Morris. I took good care of her. After a few days she was strong enough to help bury Pacheco. She even knew a few good prayers. I asked if she'd like to be my new companion and she said that she would, but I don't think she understood what that meant."

Morris's rotten scalp finally pulled away from the skull and the rope slid off. The head dipped and the body slumped.

"Don't do that, Morris. Damnit. Ain't got no right to judge me. You done most of the work puttin' her in the ground, after all. I didn't put a single bullet in her. And I didn't run her through like I done you. Just a dip in that ol' Snake River till she quit fussin'. Just a quick, merciful dip. I done right by her."

Hoyt now had the look of angry child. Lips tense, eyes squinting in mute enmity. He stood over the dead man, the hare leg smoking at the end of a cypress skewer. With his free hand he yanked at the unhinged scalp, tearing it from the skull until it caught just above the nape. Hoyt dropped the hare leg in the dirt and pulled the Bowie from a sheath in his belt and worked the final inch loose.

"*Judge not lest ye be judged, Morris.*" He shook the rotten scalp in the air like a dead bird and pitched it into the campfire. The fire protested the offering with a wild sputtering and a fit of smoke. "I'm done with you. Just done. And if you continue your disrespect, well." He lifted his revolver and settled it over the dead man, slow and ceremoniously like a religious rite. He rocked the hammer with his thumb and licked his lips with a maddening stare until the moment emptied.

Hoyt went to his saddlebag and freed a half bottle of whiskey and twisted the cork with his chewing teeth. After a hard pull from the bottle, he returned to the campfire and found the cooked hare's leg in the dirt and stomped into the darkness.

It was well after dawn when Hoyt returned to camp, half-drunk with redwood needles tangled in his hair. The horses stepped and snorted as he drew near.

"Settle down, ladies," said Hoyt. "It's only me."

Hoyt froze when he saw Morris.

The corpse lay a dozen feet from the cypress tree, face down and encircled by a haphazard ring of shredded linen.

"Oh lordy, Morris. Look what they done to you. Coyotes, looks like. Thought I heard 'em cacklin' somewhere."

Hoyt kicked Morris over and covered his mouth. There was a terrible wound in his stomach where the shirt had been torn away. A black wash of entrails spilling into the field grass.

"Poor bastard. Looks like they got your liver. Maybe more. Lordy I'm sorry for misbehavin' last night. I feel downright awful about all this." There were tears building in the shelves of his eyes. "If it weren't for you, they'd've eaten the mares. Then where'd we be? You saved us, Morris. Offered yourself to the hungry beasties of the night." Hoyt caught the corpse by the armpit and hauled him up in an awkward embrace and kissed the bald erasure where his scalp had been. "Come on, friend. Let's move on."

Hoyt found a southern coastal trail that wound through swathes of bush lupine and seaside daisies. The night fog was dissolving over the shoreline, ragged vapors subtracting to the saw-toothed sea. The trail angled down a sandstone wash before opening to a wide beach crowded with bull kelp and dark stains of magnetite. The tide was out. In the distance, Hoyt saw a figure stooping in the tide pools.

Hoyt called to the figure, but there was no response.

He rode closer.

It was a young man, barefoot and shirtless. Not more than fifteen. He was scraping mussels off the wet limestone with a wooden spade and tossing them in a sack.

"Hidy there, young man," called Hoyt.

The boy stumbled back, startled. Eyes big and wild-looking. He lifted his nose to the air.

"I apologize for the stench," said Hoyt. "My companion's been dead awhile. Attacked by coyotes. Reckon them creatures in your sack smell better'n him. Speak any English?"

The boy nodded slowly, eyeing the corpse. "Yessir," he said.

"That's good. You got a name?"

"William. They call me Billy. Or Bill."

"Fine name for a fine young man. They call me Hoyt. Just Hoyt. And this here's Morris. You come from a town, Billy?"

"We got a ranch up on the hill. Nearest town is Santa Cruz. 'Bout a half-day ride."

"And which direction might that be?"

"The town or the ranch?"

"The town."

Billy pointed.

"Well," said Hoyt. "Might have to head that way for whiskey and supplies. Maybe some female company if I can find it. Say, you any good with that spade, Billy?"

Billy looked at the spade. "Reckon so. Not much to it."

"Well, that's good. 'Cause I got a piece of silver for the youngern that can dig ol' Morris a decent grave." Hoyt wagged a coin in the air. "Sound like a fair price?"

Billy nodded quickly. The wind had picked up and he was shielding his eyes from the blowing sand. "Just that I'll need to tell my ma. She's waitin' on these here mussels."

Hoyt clicked his tongue. "It's a pressin matter, son. See them buzzards circlin' overhead?" The kid looked. A pair of turkey vultures wheeled in the sky. Maybe there were three. "They been huntin' us all mornin'. Bet they wanna finish what them coyotes started. I need your help here, Billy."

"The ranch ain't far. Them buzzards'll leave you be."

"Tell you what. For all the trouble we'd cause your dear ma, reckon I could pay you double. But you gotta work fast."

"Double?"

"That's right."

"Two dollars?"

"I ain't no professor, but I reckon that'd be double."

The boy set the sack of mussels in a shallow tide pool and took another eyeful of the corpse. The mare's hide was matted with gore. Sandflies tangled in the mess like shiny burrs.

"Heck, mister. I'd groom up your horse after for that wage."

"That'll be fine, Billy. I like an industrious youngern."

The kid led Hoyt down the beach along bone-colored dunes that spit sand as they passed. Pink verbena sprouted from the ground and lolled in the seawind like eel tongues.

"This is where we bury the farm dogs," said the kid. "The ground's soft enough. Won't take much for a hole."

"Don't need to be deep. Just deep enough."

"Oughta be deep," said the kid. He had already stabbed at the sand with the wooden spade. His voice now had the somber quality of an old man. "Had a yellow dog named Trigger, buried him here a couple years back. Got hisself bit by a lion. We got lions out here if you didn't know it. Some call 'em cougars. It was springtime and ma had me huntin' mushrooms up in the hills all day and I was tired. Too tired to dig deep. I buried the dog right over thataways but it weren't deep enough. You could tell somethin' was buried there. Next day, I came back with my brother Peter and Lord Almighty if it weren't the gruesomest sight anybody ever seen. Somethin' dug up Trigger and there was a dozen buzzards tearin' apart what was left. Might as well've just blown him up with dynamite. It'd almost be more respectable. So Peter looks at me and says *that's what Hell is*. See, accordin' to Peter, in Hell you get torn to hairy little pieces and you feel every last bit of it, and when it's over you gotta do it all again. You get put together and torn apart as day becomes night and night becomes day. Like spinnin' a ball in your hand. No end and no beginnin'."

"Never heard a description such as that."

"Well that's Peter. They say he'd make a good priest someday."

"And what do they say about you, Billy?"

"Me? They just call me a chatter bug. No good could come of it."

"Ain't so sure," said Hoyt. "We could all use good company."

It wasn't more than an hour before the kid was shoulder-deep in the hole. Hoyt helped him climb out and they rolled Morris to the rim, the corpse half-coated in grains of sand. There were gulls screaming from the tops of the dunes and the buzzards were now circling at a lower altitude.

"You know any good prayers?" Hoyt said.

"I know a few," said the kid. "I could call my brother down. What he'd have to say, well you'd get hairs stickin' up on the back of your neck, mister."

"Well I ain't payin' the both of you. Morris weren't much of a religious man anyhow."

"I could say the Lord's Prayer."

Hoyt nodded. Big rotten smile.

"You're a sweet boy, Billy."

By late afternoon, Hoyt had found a logging road that veered to the East, just skirting the town of Santa Cruz. The remains of redwoods lay in a clear-cut over the hillsides, wide as wagon wheels. There were fresh shoots blossoming from the stumps in a rebellious act of renewal. Billy lay bound and folded over the saddle of the old painted mare, stiffly bouncing as they descended into a creek bed.

A trail of flies blackened the air as they passed.

"'Sure do appreciate the company," said Hoyt.

The kid offered no reply.

Taking Out the Garbage
Thomas Vaughn

"I'll take a pack of Kool 100s."

I almost never hear the guy come in the store. It's like his feet don't touch the ground. I've got good hearing and this isn't the type of neighborhood you drop your guard. I turn around and there he stands, a faint smile on his face. He smiles a lot, sort of like he's in on some secret joke. The people in the neighborhood call him Light. I don't know his real name because I've never seen his ID. The dude always pays in cash. He's not a bad looking guy and really soft-spoken. His clothes are a notch above most of my customers so I welcome the high-class trade. I just wish he wouldn't sneak up on me like that.

"You got it, my friend," I reply. "Just one pack?"

"Yeah. Just one pack. And this." He motions to the six pack of beer on the counter. Unlike most of the people around here, he still takes some pride in his appearance. He lives in the house across the street. It's one of those narrow row houses built when this was a thriving neighborhood. Unlike most of the structures, it's in pretty good shape. He keeps the yard clean and the windows are still intact.

While ringing up his order I'm distracted by a commotion on the sidewalk outside. A woman everyone knows as Cleo stands in the middle of the street shouting obscenities.

"You dumb motherfuckers! I'll show you! I'll show every motherfucking one of you bitch-ass motherfuckers!"

She is disheveled and her sweatpants hang loose on her frame. There is no use guessing what provoked her. It doesn't really matter. Her brain is so addled she can't even pick a target for her rage. She just vents against everything and everyone.

"It's a shame what this neighborhood has come to," I sigh, handing Light his change.

"It is what it is."

"It's all the damn drugs," I snap. "All of these crackheads and whores."

Light kind of sits back on his heels and eyes me for a moment, the smile never leaving his face. "I hear you, Patel. But there aren't any jobs. People got to pass the time."

"Bullshit," I spit. "Look at me. I've got a job. What do people like her do? She can't even take care of her children." As I speak Cleo wanders into oncoming traffic, gesturing wildly. A car stops and honks.

"Don't you be honking at me, motherfucker!" she yells, glaring murderously through the windshield.

I pick up my phone to contact the police. I call them three or four times a week, for all the good it does.

"No, Patel," says Light gently, calling me by my last name. "There's no need for that. I'll take care of it."

Then he just sort of glides out of the store and into the sunlight. It's still only ten o'clock in the morning. I watch as he gestures to Cleo who seems to calm instantly at his approach. Light shows her what's in the bag and they exchange a few words. Then he takes her by the arm and leads her from the street, waving to the motorist good-naturedly.

And just like that, the situation is diffused. I crane my neck to track their progress across the boulevard. Light opens the gate to his front yard, smooth and chivalrous. Cleo is all smiles. I shake my head.

"What would a nice-looking man want with a whore like that?" I mutter under my breath.

But then, there is no accounting for taste.

My parents brought my brother and me to America when we were just boys. We opened the store on North Broadway back when it was a thriving neighborhood. You could raise a family and didn't have to worry about walking down the street at night. Then the crack came in. The people began to change before my very eyes. It was like some regressive form of evolution. Their skin became ulcerated and cheeks hollow. It was like watching a slow-motion transformation of humans into reptiles.

Gradually I began stocking different items. I still keep milk and eggs, but mainly I just sell beer, candy bars, and packaged ice cream now. Fruit simply rots on the shelf.

If my parents had known what was going to happen, perhaps they wouldn't have come here. And maybe my brother would still be alive. There were two of them. They came in the store late one night, both high. They shot him three times through the heart when he fumbled while opening the drawer. The policeman said they were lucky shots because usually, tweekers just spray the place. But for my brother, all three bullets hit him right in the heart.

One. Two. Three.

Three lucky bullets.

The boy is no more than twelve. He has a wadded-up five in his hand and asks for those copper Brillo pads. I should really stop stocking them, but they are one of my best-selling items.

"Why do you want these?" I ask. "These aren't something a child should be buying."

"They're for my mama," he replies, his eyes dropping to the floor. I know what the pads are for. They use them as screens in their pipes. Steel pads don't work.

I study the boy. He looks malnourished.

I take the five and change it out for a jar of peanut butter.

"You take this instead," I say. "Don't tell your mom you've got it. Now you show me where you live."

I lock the door and follow him three blocks up the street. Every third or fourth house is abandoned. There is a dead cat on the corner, flattened and covered in flies. He points to a dilapidated shack that smells of human excrement. I know the woman who has been staying there. They call her Jazz. I phone the police and tell them about the drug activity, then walk back to the store, leaving the boy blinking in the sunlight.

It's about time someone started cleaning this place up. The people here smoke right out in the open. They don't even stop when the local pastor walks by. They have no shame.

Just as I look up, I catch his eye. He's sitting on a stoop with some other men. There is a beer on the pavement in front of him. It's like that with Light. I never see him first. Whenever I catch sight of him, he's looking right into my eyes.

How does a man know when and where you will look at him?

"I don't know what the hell the problem is, Patel. All I know is I've got the city inspector breathing down my ass crack." Freddie is a good guy, but he has problems. He runs the restaurant on the corner across the street. They specialize in a combination of Chinese and Soul Food. "I mean, that new drainage system cost me five grand. Now they want me to re-plumb the whole goddamn corner."

"It's bullshit," I concede. "They just look for ways to hassle honest businessmen instead of addressing the real problems around here."

"Extortion," he proclaims, drumming thick fingers on the counter. "It's just extortion. How the hell am I supposed to know where the smell is coming from? I run a clean operation."

The stink has been getting worse as the summer intensifies. It smells like trash and rotting flesh. Strangely, the smell seems focused on the corner around Freddie's restaurant. Responding to neighborhood complaints, the city inspector has been paying him weekly visits, requiring a series of modifications and upgrades. I have been inside his business many times. It looks completely spotless.

"All I know is the stink isn't coming from my pipes. They probably have some dead animals stuffed down in the drainage tunnels or something. That's all I can figure."

Three men have been loitering outside the store for an hour. I watch them through the security mirror while Freddie complains. One finger gently falls to the revolver I keep on the shelf below the register.

I will not end up like my brother.

One. Two. Three.

"What can we do?" I ask. "We're honest men. The world is unkind to honest men."

At least things have been a little quieter on the street recently. It takes me a minute to figure out the cause of the momentary lull. Cleo hasn't been around for a while. I hope she has moved on to another neighborhood, but that's unlikely. Where do these people have to go? Where else will they find so many abandoned houses to smoke crack all day?

The three men finally disperse, each sauntering off to his own uncertain future. I relax just a little when the sidewalk is finally empty.

"Her name is Denise," says the man, holding a picture in front of me. It's a handmade missing persons poster. "You sure you haven't seen her around here?"

I take the flyer and study the face. It's a picture of a woman sitting in a well-appointed living room, beaming at the camera as if she hasn't a worry in the world. At first the face means nothing to me, then I recall a woman I saw around the neighborhood a few months ago. She was a little thinner and seldom smiled, but I recognize the gap between her front teeth.

"Sorry, my friend. I do not think I have seen her. Are you related?"

"Yeah," he says. "She's my mom."

He seems like a nice young man in his late twenties. His button-up shirt and slacks are clean. He strikes me as the sort who would be a dependable worker.

"You check with the police?"

"Already done that. I even asked at the coroner's office. Nothing. It's like the earth just swallowed her up."

"If she was living on the street she could be anywhere. These street people come and go like the seasons."

He shakes his head and exhales. "Denise wouldn't do that," he replies. I am struck by the way he calls his mother by her first name. "She has some problems, but I just don't think she would up and leave without telling anyone. It's not like her."

"People change when they hit the crack. They do things they wouldn't normally do. I sometimes wonder if they are even still human."

His eyes flash for a moment and I know I've said too much.

"Well, do you mind if I put a flyer in your window?"

"Yes, I do mind. I need a clear line of sight out of every window or I will lose my theft insurance. But you may use the telephone pole outside."

I watch him leave the store and staple the picture of the smiling woman to the pole.

It must be hard when it's your mother. But then I think about my brother. He didn't deserve what happened to him. We all must cry, each in our own time.

I hear the sound of breaking glass as I am locking up for the night. It's followed by a thud and a low moaning sound. I tell myself to keep walking, but someone has to watch over the neighborhood. In a place where they steal the copper out of the walls, honest men must stick together. I cross the street, my phone in hand and the pistol in my pocket. It sounds like it might be coming from the back of Freddie's place.

There is a narrow alley between the restaurant and Light's house. I peer into the darkness. At first, I see nothing. Then something moves on the ground. It's a naked woman. She's crying and holding her head. I look up and notice that the second story window of the house is broken. Shards of glass litter the alley. The woman rubs her temples like she has a headache.

"You okay, lady?" I call. "You need me to call the hospital?"

"Thanks, Patel. But we're all right."

He did it again. Honestly, I was looking right into the darkness where he was standing, but I didn't perceive him until he spoke.

"Is that you, Light?"

He steps from the shadows and I see that he too is naked. There is something disarmingly casual about the way he strolls toward me, completely unashamed of his lack of clothes. His uncircumcised penis hangs like a sausage between his legs. He walks like a man who hasn't a care in the world. The woman tries to stand. He helps her to her feet. She leans uncertainly against the wall. It's Jazz, the woman who sent her son to buy copper pads from the store.

"You okay, baby?" he asks the woman. She clings to the wall, like one who has received a blow to the head.

"You still open, Patel? Me and the lady could use another six pack."

The phone is still in my hand, one finger poised over the number for the police.

"I can't sell it to you now. It's past midnight."

He shakes his head. "That's a hell of shame. The party's just getting started over here. Ain't that right, baby?"

The woman groans and sinks to the pavement.

"What happened?" I ask, looking pointedly at the window.

He follows my gaze. "You know how ladies can be." He walks a little closer. Again, I glance down at his penis hanging flaccid between his thighs. I have never been so nonchalant about my own nakedness, even in the privacy of my home. He reaches for a nonexistent pocket, then stops himself.

"Damn. Left my cigarettes in the house."

"Is that lady OK?" I ask, but I know a part of me doesn't want to hear the answer.

"Oh, she got pissed when we ran out of beer. I told that bitch to be cool, but she jumped out the damn window." He looks up, shaking his head. "Gonna have to fix it now. She's drunk—won't feel a thing until morning."

"You sure you don't want me to call the hospital?"

He seems to genuinely consider the proposition, then shakes his head. "No, we can't afford something like that. She'll be fine. I'll look after her."

My finger hovers just above the screen, suspended by a flock of uncertainties. Then I find myself sliding the phone back into my shirt pocket.

"Sure, Light," I say. "You look after her."

I continue up the street. My footsteps quicken because the smell is really strong tonight. I look over my shoulder once, seeing Light and Jazz walking toward his back door. His arm is under her shoulder. She clearly can't walk on one of her legs. I hear him whispering gentle comforts in her ear.

The following night I review my savings. Just two more years and I can retire. I will sell the store and move far away from here. This happens many times a day. I know the bank account like the veins on the back of my hand. It hovers out there like a life raft. Those numbers represent my salvation—the thing that sets me apart from the rest of the people around here. I will leave them all to stew in their own filth.

"I'll take a pack of Kool 100s."

Goddamn him. How does he do that?

I look up and there he stands. He's still wearing that smile, like he knows some joke I don't. He thinks he's better than everyone.

"Yes, my friend," I reply, trying to sound cordial, but the strain in my voice is evident even to my own ears. "No beer tonight?"

"No thanks, Patel. Just the smokes."

I slide them across the counter and take his money. Usually I'm friendly with my customers, but something about the man bothers me. He carries the graveyard stench around with him. The others can't smell it because they live in those sewers with excrement on the stairs, but I can. I can't stop the self-righteous indignation from rising.

"Maybe you've had enough parties for a while." I expect him to retreat because I know his little joke. I know why he smiles like he's better than everyone else. The rumor of it engulfs him like a death shroud.

But he doesn't look frightened. I think about the night before when he stood there with his penis hanging out, a broken whore at his feet. His smile broadens.

"You should come to one of my parties sometime, Patel. I can find you a date too. You bring the beer and I'll hook you up."

"No sir," I say, my back stiffening. My hand drops instinctively to the handle of the revolver hidden beneath the cash register as he uncoils like a poisonous snake. "I am not that kind of man."

"Not that *kind of man*," he scoffs. "What kind of man don't like a good bitch? And I got lots of bitches. I got them in the attic, under the stairs, in the basement. I got that backyard so full you can't walk without stepping on a bitch."

My hand wraps around the handle of the gun. I open my mouth, but no words come out.

"I got so many bitches in that house I lost count. And I'm good at math. Did I ever tell you I was good at math? But I can't remember how many bitches I got stuffed in that place. They're practically coming out of the walls." I hand over the change.

He meets my eyes.

"But for a friend like you? Well, I can always make a little more room. We'll get us a pair of big old hos."

His cackle hangs between us like a cancerous lung.

"I'll call the police," I manage.

"You ain't gonna call shit," he says. His voice is no longer soft-spoken. It drips with contempt. Now he's pure street. "You know why? For the same reason you ain't gonna pull that pistol you're fingering."

That's when his hand touches mine. It happens when I hand over the change. It's just a light graze, but in that moment, I see how cold and worm-eaten his heart really is. It hangs in his chest like a moldy side of beef. I can sense the way it festers as it pulses in steady rhythm to the ongoing decay around us.

There is something else. His heart calls out to mine, like a beacon signaling a ship in the night. But strangely there's no answer. My own heart isn't cold or rotting. Instead, my chest is empty. What happened to my heart?

One. Two. Three.

Then he breaks away, turning toward the door. My body relaxes, as if someone had been subjecting me to an electrical current and suddenly threw the breaker. Just like that, the vision is gone. It had something to do with my chest. But the thought of that empty chamber fades like a meandering echo. I strain to remember it, but the idea resists my efforts so completely it disintegrates into meaningless fragments.

"I'll be seeing you, Patel," he calls over his shoulder as he walks through the door. I watch him cross the street through the security mirror. His feet never touch the ground. He just hovers like a specter until the night swallows him.

I wipe the perspiration from my brow with my sleeve. It's hotter than usual this summer. Then I lock the drawer and hang the closed sign on the door, thinking about the numbers in my bank account. I need to hold out just two more years.

Looking across the street at Light's place I notice that it's starting to fray around the edges. The trim is falling off and the paint chipping. Eventually they will find the source of the smell and it will become a vacant wreck just like all the rest. It's too bad about Freddie spending all that money on new pipes, but that's the price of taking out the garbage.

Seven Days of Dog Walking
Scotty Milder

Day One

When the old couple with the Newfoundland walked by on the other side of the street, Tiger started pulling against his choker. Tiger was a yellow lab, and stupid. He gagged but kept pulling.

"No!" Charlie hissed, and yanked back on the leash. Tiger gave one last half-hearted lunge and then fell back in step. Charlie was gratified to see that the Newfoundland had pulled, too, damn near taking the old lady off her feet. "Beauty!" She reprimanded in stage whisper. The dog gave one gruff bark and then settled. But he and Tiger kept eying one another.

The old man chuckled and shook his head toward Charlie, as if they had already developed a wordless bond. Charlie didn't get it but decided to be diplomatic and laughed too.

"Nice night," the old man said, smiling.

Charlie smiled too and nodded. "Sure is!" he said, and kept walking. The old couple kept going, too. Their short little union was broken.

But the dogs kept sniffing at each other until they were around the corner.

It *was* a nice night. But summers in Colorado were generally always nice, so it was nothing special and Charlie was actually a little annoyed that the old man had brought it up. Small talk made him feel unsure of himself. How do you respond to something like that? Your library of possible retorts is tiny. *Sure is!* Or *Isn't it, though?* Or (if you really wanted to live on the edge) *It kind of feels like rain.* Anything outside those four walls was entirely unacceptable, and Charlie's mind just didn't work like that. Charlie was a verbal person, and his brain always wanted to cough up the most inappropriate response possible.

Nice night!

Just like an octopus!

Or:

Nice night!

But not as nice as your wife's tits!

But he was overthinking it.

He always did.

Day Two

No old couple tonight. Charlie was glad.

The moon was full, and its light was bright and blue and turned everything inky and rich. Charlie liked full moons.

Tiger was limping a little so Charlie stopped. "C'mon, boy," he whispered and inspected the dog's paws. He found a little burr on the bottom of one of them and flicked it away. Tiger was much better after that.

They came around the corner and Charlie debated how much farther he wanted to go. He was tired and so was Tiger, but Christine and the kids were still awake and Charlie liked to get back after everyone else was asleep. Otherwise they would all try to talk to him and he didn't like that. Charlie was a verbal person but he didn't like talking to his wife. It was pointless. They always ended up carrying on two separate conversations, talking over each other even when they weren't arguing.

He looked at his watch. He hit the Indiglo, and it told him it was 9:43. Christine went to bed at ten every night. She was a teacher and had to be at the school by seven. He decided to keep going.

Charlie hadn't noticed how quiet the night was until the silence was broken. At first what he heard sounded like static. Then, as he kept walking with Tiger panting at his side, he recognized it as music. Some sort of generic heavy metal.

He liked generic heavy metal. He stopped and tried to pinpoint the sound.

All of the houses on this street but one were dark and quiet. The one that wasn't was a big two-story brick with a long front path and wide columns and shrubs along the patio. He looked up and saw an open window. The music was coming from in there. He could even recognize the band now; it was Sepultura, but he didn't know what song.

He walked a little ways forward and stopped directly in front of the house. He looked up at the window.

There was a girl in there, and not the sort of girl he expected to be listening to Sepultura. She was tall and thin, with golden arms and long blond hair held back with a scrunchie. She was standing on a stool, back to him, running a tape measure across the ceiling. He couldn't see her face.

She stepped off the stool, started to turn around, and he

kept going.

Day Three

Charlie usually didn't take Tiger out three nights in a row but he was sort of half-hoping he would see the girl again. He felt a little embarrassed by that and at first didn't admit it to himself. But after he was out the door he had to admit it because he was heading straight for her house and he was walking a little faster than usual. Tiger was actually jogging a little to keep up.

He passed a brown-haired lady, maybe thirty, walking her Irish Setter. The two dogs did their usual growling and pulling, and Charlie hissed "No!" and the lady hissed "Stop it!" and then they smiled at each other and the lady said "Nice night" and Charlie agreed and didn't say anything about her tits and quickly put it out of his mind. He didn't dwell on it this time because he was already thinking about the girl. He wondered how old she was—seventeen, maybe, or maybe a little younger?—and then felt embarrassed all over again.

Her house was dark and quiet like the rest. He frowned a little, disappointed, and stopped. Tiger tried to keep going and pulled against the choker until he gagged. Charlie yanked him back absently and fished a cigarette out of his pocket. He usually didn't smoke while he was walking but right now he wanted one.

A voice: "Hey!" It was a whisper.

Charlie looked up sharply. He looked around, saw no one. "Hey!"

It came from the girl's house. He looked and saw her standing on the patio. She was wearing black and the moon was obscured by a thin cloud tonight so that was why he hadn't seen her at first.

"Yeah?" He tried to sound casual but for some reason his voice didn't sound like he thought it would. It cracked a little. He blushed but it was dark so she couldn't see it and he was glad about that.

She came out from under the little awning and walked up to him. She was wearing a long-sleeve Slayer shirt and he grinned because it looked funny on her.

She stopped three feet in front of him, smiling, and he noticed that she was just as pretty up close. Her eyes sparkled, and it wasn't the streetlight on the corner.

"Can I bum one?" She asked. She pointed at his cigarette.

"I don't know," he said. "Are you eighteen?"

Her smile grew but he saw desperation and annoyance in her eyes. "Oh, come on. My parents are gone. You won't get in trouble."

He fished one out for her. "You know this is like a thousand dollar fine or something."

He flicked his lighter. She leaned into it and he saw how long and delicate her eyelashes were. In the flame, they looked silver.

She took a drag and blew the smoke out in a practiced way. He noticed the way she held her cigarette between her pinky and her ring finger. It was weird but kind of cute.

He figured he should keep walking but she didn't seem to mind him talking to her and he didn't want to go.

"So, what are you doing lurking out here on your porch?" He asked.

She shrugged. "Just enjoying the night."

The "nice night" thing again. Only this time it didn't feel like small talk.

"Yeah, it's a nice night," he said, and regretted it.

She shrugged.

"So how old *are* you?" he asked, and regretted that too because it sounded somehow lecherous even though he didn't mean it that way. At least he thought he didn't.

But if it sounded lecherous she either didn't notice or didn't care. "Almost seventeen. Is that all right, *Officer?*"

He chuckled. "It's all right with me." She gave him a look he couldn't quite read.

Tiger whined. He didn't know why they had stopped and he didn't quite know what to do with new people. But he was just going to have to deal.

"What's your dog's name?" she asked.

"Tiger."

"Huh," she said, and looked perturbed. "He doesn't look like a tiger..."

He didn't know what to say to that, almost said *he doesn't look like an octopus, either.*

"What's your name?" she asked.

"Charlie. I live just up the street."

He cringed. Stupid comment. Stupid stupid stupid. *Of course* he lived just up the street. People didn't usually drive across town to walk their dogs.

"So how old are *you*?" she asked, and grinned a little. But she wasn't looking at him; she was looking at Tiger.

He thought of lying and decided not to. "Thirty-two." He didn't say anything about being married.

She nodded as if that was pretty much what she figured.

"What's your name?" He asked and was amazed by how inane this conversation had become. He was usually a verbal person; he didn't know what his problem was tonight.

"Lara," she said, and didn't elaborate.

"I like your shirt," he said. "You don't look like a Slayer fan."

She shrugged. "It was my brother's," she said.

That threw him.

"But—" he stopped.

"But what?"

"Nothing. I don't know. Forget it." He had almost told her he heard her listening to Sepultura just last night. But then he really would seem like a lech.

She shrugged.

"Well, thanks for the fag," she said. That threw him too, but then she flicked her butt into the street and he knew what she was talking about. She turned to go.

"Nice to meet you, Lara," he said, and gave a little bow. She giggled. That was more like it.

"Hey, I like your hair," she said suddenly, and without asking reached up and touched it. "Is it dyed? Yeah, I can see the roots."

His heart was thumping suddenly. "Uh... yeah. I usually wear a hat though."

"It's bushy," she said, and ruffled it.

"I'm, um, trying to grow it out," he said. He was sweating now.

"That's good," she said. Matter-of-fact. "I like guys with long hair."

And then she threw him one more quick smile and skipped back up into her house. She was gone before he realized it.

He stood there for a second, blinking.

Tiger whined.

"All right," he snapped and yanked a little too hard on the dog's choker. Then they were off and up the street again.

Day Four

Four days in a row. Christine was starting to wonder. Charlie just mumbled something at her when he left. Besides, it was good for the dog.

Lara's house was dark. It stood cold and empty, like a used battery, against the starry sky. Charlie stood there awhile and gazed onto the patio, trying to pick her out of the shadows. After awhile, he moved on.

Day Six

He skipped a day. That was only prudent. Christine had started asking him where he was going, said if he wanted a smoke he didn't need to start sneaking around. *Jesus*, he thought. *I'm just walking the goddamn dog.*

They passed the old couple with the Newfoundland again. The old guy didn't bother commenting on the night. To his disgust, Charlie found himself doing it for him.

"Nice night," Charlie said. Tiger growled at the Newfoundland and the Newfoundland growled back.

"Yup, sure is. Looks like she might rain, though," the old man said. He looked briefly at the sky. Charlie followed his gaze. Not a cloud up there. The stars poked through bright and clear, and he could even see the Milky Way. *What the fuck?* He turned to say something but the old couple was already rounding the corner.

Charlie shook his head.

She was there tonight. She was up in her room and tonight she was jamming to Sabrina Carpenter. He knew it was Sabina Carpenter because his daughter was nuts for her. Kids were schizophrenic these days. Charlie could understand Sepultura, but Sabrina Carpenter was not within his realm of comprehension.

He stood there smoking a cigarette and watched her. She was measuring the walls again. Her back was to him. She looked like she was wearing a bathing suit; electric blue, one piece. She had let her hair down tonight and it fell all around her like a silk veil and it bounced whenever she moved. It was longer than he thought it would be.

He thought of going up and ringing the doorbell and then wondered why the hell he would do something like that. There were no cars in the drive; maybe her parents were still gone.

He pitched his butt into the street. Tiger was pulling against the choker, coughing.

"Jeez, man," Charlie whispered. "Okay, we're going. Jeez."

He turned and looked back up at the window. She had turned around and for one exhilarating second Charlie thought she was looking down at him. But no, that was stupid because it was dark out here and the lights were on up there so even if she was looking at the window all she would see would be her own glorious reflection.

And sure enough, she turned back around without even a wave.

Day Seven

She was hanging posters. That's why she was measuring shit. Why she needed to measure shit to hang a few posters he didn't know; maybe she was some kind of anal retentive.

He couldn't make out what the poster said because she was standing in front of it, using thumb tacks and a little hammer to put it up. It was colorful, whatever it was. Red and bleeding something splotchy out the sides.

Just four days ago she had talked to him. Ruffled his hair. Told him she liked guys with—

The old couple with the Newfoundland again. Jesus, they were as bad as he was.

"Nice night," the man said.

Tiger lunged against the choker. The Newfoundland barked.

"No!" the old lady said, and pulled. "Beauty, no!"

"For fuck's sake, Tiger!" Charlie yelled. He yanked as hard as he could and felt something give. He heard a yelp that turned into a gurgle.

The old lady just looked at him, and he saw how white her

eyes were in the moonlight.

She wasn't there, and it wasn't a poster. What was it?

It was all over the walls, red and splotchy. He looked closer and thought he saw a handprint. Was she painting? Doing some kind of abstract mural or something on her walls?

It was on the window, too. The handprint, he saw, was on the window. It was a palm, four fingers and a thumb bleeding out in all directions, and then stretching and trailing off beneath the sill.

What was this?

It was all red. *All* red.

A thought occurred to him. He went up and rang the doorbell. He waited. He rang the bell again. He waited a few more seconds and then tried the knob. It wasn't locked and the door swung open noiselessly.

He looked in. Nice house. Economical, but nice. Not a lot of furniture. All the lights were out except for the one over the stairs.

He leaned in. "Hello?"

He waited.

"Hey, hello? You okay? I—"

Then his nose caught the smell and told him everything he needed to know.

He ran.

Halfway home he realized he didn't have Tiger anymore. He stopped under a streetlight and ran his hands through his hair. Jesus, he was sweating. His hands were sticky with it—

He pulled them away from his hair and looked at them.

The old lady's eyes were so white in the moonlight. White like bone.

How did he know that?

He looked back toward the corner. He thought he heard a bark. Shadows moved outside the reach of the streetlight, but they didn't solidify into anything he could understand.

Where the fuck was Tiger?

He ran back to Lara's house and looked up at her bedroom window. The light was still on, and the red stuff was still spattered all over yellow-white walls. And the handprint was still there, reaching out to him.

The front door stood ajar. He went slowly up the steps and saw the bloody handprint by the knob and his stomach dropped. There was blood on the knob too. Still wet.

He pushed the door open again. Nice house, economical, light on above the stairs, and whatever it was that bled over the walls bled down here too.

And then he saw the yellow, furry thing on the stairs, the lolling head, the wide-open mouth with blood-stained teeth.

Christine had asked him why he was taking the dog back out. Christine had asked him if he was meeting someone. She had started shouting. And then the world had gone about six shades of gray.

The old lady's eyes, wide and white like bone. What had she been looking at? What did she see when she saw him?

He tasted blood all over his mouth, in the back of his throat.

It was not his own.

He heard the sirens and started to laugh.

In Control
Joseph Rubas

"I swear, Frankie, sometimes I think the best part of you ran down the crack of my ass."

They were in the sunbathed kitchen, Frankie at the table and mom at the stove, her head tilted back and her shoulders slumped, looking for all the world like a poor, put-upon wife.

"I'm sorry," Frankie said, "I'll clean it up, okay?"

He leaned over and picked up a shard of glass.

"God, you're so lazy," mom spat. She grabbed a dish towel from the counter and came over. "Just eat your breakfast. You've caused enough trouble for one morning."

Frankie shrugged and went back to his eggs, but inside he seethed. She was always belittling him. Always calling him names. She was never happy. Never satisfied.

Gripping his fork so tightly that his knuckles turned white, he stabbed a piece of egg and shoved it into his mouth. It had no taste.

Muttering to herself, mom picked up the glass and mopped the juice off the floor with the towel. She threw the glass into the trashcan and flung the wet cloth onto the counter. Droplets of juice splattered the wall.

"Your father was the same way," she said. "He'd make a mess and expect me to clean it up while he just sat on his fat ass. The day he walked out was the happiest of my life. The. Happiest."

Blood was pounding in Frankie's temples. Your father this, your father that. Every. Single. Time. And on and on it would go. Standing up for himself didn't work. He'd tried. Once, she was standing in her bedroom, nagging, when he snapped and shoved her onto the bed with all of his might.

She was sweet as pie for a week after, but before long, she was at him again, and, his rage spent, he sat there and took it.

"...while you sit on your ass all day."

"I work nights, Mom," Frankie said around a mouthful of food, speaking with a calmness he did not feel. "You know that."

"That doesn't mean you can lay around the house with no shirt on all day. Get a second job. Or a girlfriend."

Frankie sat his fork down. Now he was *really* starting to get mad. "I've asked you to introduce me to some of the girls you work with. You said no."

Mom was a secretary at the university in Baker. She worked with about a dozen other women, many of them coeds.

"Oh, they're too good for you."

Frankie bit his lip. That's what she always said. *They're too good for you. They're nice girls. They wouldn't want anything to do with a nutcase like you.*

"Then don't complain."

Mom shook her head. "I'm going to get ready for work. Do something today. Go for a walk. Go to the gym. Something. *Anything.*"

Muttering again, she passed him by and went into the living room. When she was gone, Frankie turned around and flipped her off.

Bitch.

It had always been like this with her, though when he was younger, there was the occasional good day. She wouldn't attack him. She wouldn't hound him. She would speak with something approaching tenderness and sometimes, she'd even hug him. When he came out of the hospital for shooting grandma and grandpa, even those rare happy moments were gone.

He remembered being thirteen and thinking he couldn't take much more. He remembered begging Nan and Pap to take him and let him live with them. But Nan was just like her daughter. Constantly complaining, constantly browbeating, emasculating him and his grandfather. One day he snapped, got his grandfather's rifle from the hall closet, and shot the bitch in the back as she peeled potatoes over the sink. The bullet went clean through and shattered the window.

Pap...he didn't want to kill Pap. But Pap loved Nan, and seeing her dead would kill him. So when Pap got back from town, Frankie walked out onto the porch and shot him in the chest.

It was *her* he was killing. He realized that in the hospital. He wasn't killing Pap and Nan; he was killing Mom.

And that depressed him. A boy should love his mother.

Sighing, he got up, crossed the kitchen, and dropped his plate into the sink. He went to wash it, but stopped himself. Let her do it.

In the living room, he paused as Mom came down the hall, looking for something in her purse. A short, plump woman, she had once been slim and beautiful, her hair the color of midnight. Now she was as ugly outside as she was in.

Without acknowledging him, she left, slamming the door behind her.

"Bye then. Bitch."

In his room, Frankie closed the door and went to the window. He pushed aside the curtain and watched as Mom backed out of the driveway and rocketed off down the street.

He hoped a Mack truck hit her.

Letting the curtain fall back into place, he turned around and put his hands on his hips. Small and sparse, the walls an ugly brown and the carpet a deep blue, his room was more like a cell. Books were piled sloppily on the nightstand. Detective fiction. Psychology texts. He didn't feel like reading, though. He briefly considered looking at the *Hustler* he kept between his mattress and box spring, but he was still so angry at Mom that he didn't think he could stomach looking at a woman.

A drive. That's what he needed.

Going over to the nightstand, he sat and opened the drawer. Inside, under an old issue of *Time,* was a .38 revolver. He took it out, relishing the weight in his hand, and cracked the cylinder. The butts of six brass casings greeted him.

Snapping it closed, he got up, grabbed his coat off the back of the door, and dropped the gun into one of the oversized pockets. In the garage, he climbed into his battered '78 Monte Carlo, tucked the .38 under the seat, and backed into the street.

Something about the houses in the neighborhood, so cozy and pretty, made him mad. Though his house was almost identical to all the others, it looked different. Somehow shabbier, somehow colder.

He sighed.

From home, he drove north through downtown, past all the shops, restaurants, and pool halls. Though it was mid-November and chilly, people still crowded the sidewalks.

Outside town, Frankie left US20 for the freeway. He turned on the radio and found a station playing oldies. He thrummed his fingers against the wheel as he drove, his mind already a million miles from the hateful little house on Lewis Place.

Frankie liked to drive. There was something liberating in it. When he psychoanalyzed himself, which was very rarely, as he couldn't stand to see himself, he realized that it was a way for him to revel in his newfound liberty. For six years, he sat in that hospital, his movements watched and restricted. Out here, on the road, with the radio playing and the wind blowing, he was as free as one could get. Soaring like an eagle. To him, driving was a hobby, a passion. He would leave the house and drive sometimes for hours on end, no destination in mind, just going where the road took him.

Occasionally, he would pick up a hitchhiker and take them where they wanted to go. Along the way he would make small talk with them, practicing his laugh and his smile, his interpersonal skills and his humor. By now he was really good at disarming people and making them like him. Just last week, he picked up a skittish girl, and by the time he dropped her off fifteen miles later, she was smiling and relaxed. So relaxed that he could have easily overpowered and strangled her.

But he didn't.

He was in control.

That's what it had become. A demonstration of his control. Especially with women. The gun was under the seat. A folding knife was in his pocket. His hands were big and rough. He could kill anyone five different ways, but he didn't.

Though sometimes he *really* wanted to.

Pushing that thought aside, Frankie left the freeway north of Santa Carla and took Route 12 south through the barren foothills. Though he tried to play dumb with himself, he knew he had come here on purpose. Tillman College, an all-girls school, was nearby, and a lot of pretty coeds hitchhiked.

After six miles, he turned onto Route 8, a narrow, winding highway which passed through Mountain Vista, Paoalo, and Carmichael.

Two miles after turning onto Route 8, Frankie saw her on the side of the road, her thumb in the air. His heartbeat sped up.

When he was closer, he could see her more clearly. Long black hair, slim build, angular face. His throat closed up and his stomach rolled.

Drive by, he told himself. *Drive by and don't stop.*

Swallowing hard, he let up on the gas.

It was girls like that, the pretty ones with black hair, who really tested him.

The ones who reminded him of his mother.

He was in control.

He stopped.

Total control.

She came up to the passenger window and leaned in.

He smiled easily.

"Where are you headed?"

"Rock Springs," he said.

"Could you drop me in Carmichael?"

Fifteen miles.

Fifteen long, jittery miles.

"Sure. Get in."

Thanking him, she opened the door and slid into the seat.

"I've been walking all morning," she said, slamming the door. Frankie pressed the gas and navigated the car back into the right lane. "My feet are killing me."

"I'm not a big fan of walking," Frankie said, "as you can tell."

She laughed. "Neither am I, but my car broke down."

"Oh," he said, "do you need to call somebody? I have a cell."

"No, it's at the shop, but thanks."

By now her smell had filled the car. Sweet. Intoxicating. *Rotten.* He rolled down his window. His hands were shaking.

"Do you go to school around here?" he asked. His voice, at least, was steady.

"No, I'm all done with school."

"What, no college?"

"I graduated ten years ago."

He made a show of looking at her, then to the road, then back again. She was beautiful, but he could see the ugliness lurking beneath. He always could. "Get out of here. How old are you?"

"Thirty-three."

"What? You don't look thirty-three."

She laughed. "I swear."

"Bet you get carded a lot."

"Yeah, sometimes."

He wanted her.

He wanted to *kill* her.

"When I turned twenty-one," he said, licking his dry lips, "I was all excited because I could legally drink, you know? I went to this bar and ordered a rum and Coke, and wouldn't you know, the bartender didn't even card me."

That was a lie. He was still in the hospital on his twenty-first birthday.

"That's a good way to lose your liquor license."

"I guess if you do it to the wrong person."

For a while, they drove in silence, Frankie's tongue clenched firmly, and literally, between his teeth. Whenever he felt like he might be in danger of losing control, he bit down.

Ten minutes later, Frankie saw the Carmichael city limits sign and breathed a sigh of relief. "Anywhere particular?"

"Just drop me in front of the bank."

He pulled to the curb in front of the bank.

"Thanks for the ride," she said as she got out.

"Anytime."

"I'm Michelle, by the way."

"Frankie."

"It was real, Frankie."

Frankie shrugged. "It was 'ight."

Frankie spent the rest of the afternoon driving through the countryside, trying to get Michelle out of his head but failing. He regretted letting her go now. He should have done everything he wanted to do to her, then choked her. She was probably a nag anyway, just like Mom. Most women were when you got right down to it. Bitch, bitch, bitch.

At three, he drove back into town and had lunch at Carl's. Sitting at one of the benches outside, the sun warm but the wind cold, he ate and people watched. At one point, an ugly green twelve seat van pulled up and a gaggle of girls in soccer jerseys piled out. Frankie's heart froze. There were ten of them (he counted, twice), all roughly twelve to fourteen. A few were a little on the mannish side, but the majority were petite and pretty.

Though he had half a hamburger left, he got up, got into his car, and drove away, turning the radio up as loud as it would go. Images still assailed him, though. Horrible images. Exciting images. He closed his eyes and relished them.

He opened his eyes just as the car ahead of him stopped at a red light.

His heart launched into his throat. He slammed his foot down on the brakes, jerking against the seatbelt. The tires locked and shrieked. The front end shook. He braced for impact, but it never came. Mere inches separated him from the other car.

Panting, Frankie calmed his nerves, then took a left on Rosette Blvd, and followed it back to Lewis. He pulled the Monte Carlo into the garage and killed the engine.

You're weak.

No... I'm in control.

Hahaha, you're weak.

He hung his head over the wheel and squeezed his eyes closed. He wasn't weak. He wasn't. He was strong. Stronger than anyone knew.

When he trusted himself to walk, he got out of the car and went into the house, going straight to his room and closing the door. For a long time, he sat on the edge of the bed, thoughts racing through his head. At dusk, he kicked his shoes off and masturbated furiously, but he couldn't keep hard and finally gave up.

Mom got home at seven. He heard her come in. He got up and went into the kitchen. She was putting a pot of coffee on, her back to him. He watched her from the doorway, opening his mouth several times to speak but closing it again. He wanted to talk to her, to connect with her, to *love* her, but he knew where that got him.

Giving up, he went back to his room and lay in the darkness.

* * *

Frankie was depressed that night at work. He went through his daily routine with no heart. At six, when his shift was over, he drove home, the first light of day touching the eastern sky.

At home, or what passed for it, he sat behind the wheel for a long time. Mom would be up, making breakfast and getting ready for work. As soon as she saw him, she would start in on him. Nag, nag, nag, nag. He thought of cruising until she left the house, but instead he got out and went inside. The smell of coffee and bacon seasoned the air.

"I'm home!" he called, closing the door. He shrugged out of his jacket, hung it up, and went into the kitchen. Mom was at the stove, still in her bathrobe. Her back was to him.

"Good morning," he said.

She didn't respond.

"How did you sleep?"

She angrily forked bacon onto a plate and dropped it onto the counter.

"So we're doing this again?"

Sometimes Mom would give him the silent treatment. Hours. Days. Once a whole week. It was nice to not be nagged, but the tense, dreadful silence was just as bad, if not worse.

Throwing his hands up, Frankie sat down at the table. He opened the newspaper and scanned the headlines.

Silent, Mom came over, dropped a plate of food in front of him, and then slammed a plastic cup of orange juice down next to it. "That's so you don't break another one of my glasses."

Rage rose in Frankie. He threw the paper down. "I'm getting really tired of this shit. You have nothing but complaints and criticisms. Constantly. Never-ending. That's why Dad left. He got tired of you."

Mom glared at him. "Why don't you leave too? I haven't been with a man in six months because I have my psycho son in the next room."

"You haven't been with a man because you have a terrible personality, you're old, and you're fat. Now shut the fuck up and leave me alone or I'll knock you through that wall."

Lips pursed, eyes shining with malevolence, Mom turned away and went back to the stove. Frankie didn't feel like eating. He was feverish and his stomach hurt. But he ate anyway. He ate every last bite, got up, and left the room without so much as taking his plate to the sink.

After Mom left, he dozed for a few hours. He dreamed of the incident again and again. Only this time, he pulled the gun out and shot her in the head. It was so realistic it scared him. A red hole appeared in her forehead, then blood trickled down the bridge of her nose. She fell, swiping the skillet off the stove and spilling hot grease all over the floor and herself. Smiling, he put the gun back in his pants and went on with breakfast.

The last time he woke, he was so sure it had actually happened that he went breathlessly into the kitchen, expecting to find her body curled up on the floor, but instead he found nothing.

Still trembling, he searched the rest of the house for her corpse to make sure he hadn't stashed it somewhere. When he was satisfied, he went back into his room, sat on the edge of the bed, and cried. He hated that bitch. He hated *all* of them.

He must have blacked out, because next, he was in the car, driving along the freeway, hills rising up on either side. He was close to the Santa Carla exit. To the college.

He wasn't in control.

He drove the roads around Tillman for nearly two hours, but saw no hitchhikers. By the time he was done, he had calmed down and regained control. He took the freeway back and turned off at his exit. At the bottom of the off-ramp, a woman stood with her thumb held out. Frankie ignored her.

Back home, he closed himself in his room and turned the radio on. The Doobie Brothers sang "What a Fool Believes." They soon gave way to Steely Dan's "My Old School."

Rocking back and forth on the bed, he tried to quiet the hatred within. He hated that bitch. He hated her and every other woman. And wasn't that a shame? She'd ruined women for him. He never saw himself loving a woman, or holding a woman, or kissing a woman. Only cutting her throat and raping her.

Because of Mom. That old, fat fucking stupid bitch. All her fault.

Frankie had never been as angry as he was then. He swiped the lamp off the nightstand and sent it into the wall with a satisfying crash. He then grabbed his pillow and threw it at the window. Blinds crinkled.

The rage slowly turned to sadness, and Frankie sobbed so deep and hard that he thought it would kill him.

At some point, he fell asleep, and startled awake hours later, stiff and disoriented in the dark. He fumbled for the clock on the nightstand, saw that it was 11:02, and dropped it.

Mom was home. Light seeped through the crack under his door.

Fucking Mom.

Gritting his teeth, Frankie got up, used the bathroom, and went into the garage.

From a display on one wall, he selected a wrench and went back inside. At his mother's doorway, he paused, holding the wrench behind his back. She was in bed, playing Candy Crush on her phone.

"What do you want now?"

"To say goodbye."

She snorted. "Are you finally leaving?"

He brought the wrench around and slammed it onto the top of her head. She jerked, the phone flying from her hand and landing on the floor. He pulled back and hit her again, and again. Blood and bits of skull splattered his face.

Panting, he climbed on top of her and wrapped his hands around her throat. She was already unconscious, blood gushing from her nose and mouth.

"You stupid bitch!" he spat, spittle flying. "You did this to me! You did this to me!"

He squeezed so tightly that he felt something crush in her throat. He hoped it was her voice box. It would serve her right.

When he was sure she was dead, he stripped the blanket off the bed and unzipped his pants. Grabbing a handful of her nightgown, he ripped it open, revealing her nude, corpulent body. He slammed into her as hard as he could, baring his teeth. Slam. Slam. Slam. Her pelvis broke and he came.

"There you go," he muttered. He was sitting on the floor, his knees drawn up to his chest. The fire within had turned to ice. "There you go, Mom. How was that?"

He wept.

Hours later, he carried her out to the garage and put her in the trunk of the car. He did this mechanically, coldly. He felt nothing inside anymore. No love. No hate. No lust.

From Lewis Place, he went south, then north, then east, aimlessly driving the streets. At dawn, he backed up onto the sidewalk in front of the police station, got out, and went to the trunk. As mechanically as he put her in, he took her out, carrying her inside. The desk sergeant looked up as Frankie entered, and his eyes widened.

Frankie stopped at the counter and dropped Mom onto the floor.

"I lost control," he stated.

Maternal Bond
KC Grifant

"Hush little baby, don't you cry," Bethany sang between gritted teeth. The baby's crying was a drumbeat in her head, a spike stabbing her temple, over and over, but she pushed past her pain and rocked Wyatt. The first night Rob was gone, Bethany had thought it wouldn't be so hard to take care of their newborn on her own. But by the third night the baby was waking nearly every hour.

"Any chance they'll let you come home sooner than a month? With a two-week-old and all?" Bethany asked when Rob called a few minutes later.

"I tried, love," Rob said. "It's monumentally bad timing, I know. Why don't you invite Alice over to help you?"

Bethany shuddered to think of any of her friends seeing her like this, with bags under her eyes and oversized clothes to hide the still-receding postpartum belly. Their gazes would slide over her body as they commented on how great she was recovering, even as their tone would betray a competitive glee at how Bethany's once-perfect form hadn't yet bounced back.

"Wyatt can't be around people until he gets his vaccines next month," was all she said. "I'm not about to take a chance during flu season."

"What about a walk around the block? Or a drive?" Rob's voice, reasonable and kind, cut in and out through the phone. Somewhere in the middle of Texas, his team was preparing to go on a field survey. Bethany pictured the freedom of roaming in an open space, the sun beating down on her arms and hat, breeze blowing past her skin. She'd take Texas over being enclosed in the house any day.

"Maybe." It seemed like a Herculean effort to get herself and Wyatt outside. She didn't even have time to shower. Instead, Bethany had been spending the first few days of Rob's absence in the living room, the TV droning on in the background as she scrambled to meet Wyatt's every need and tried to remember to feed the cat. *It gets easier!* So all the mommy blogs had claimed.

"Poor Beth. Just sleep when the baby sleeps."

"OK," Bethany replied, wondering how she could sleep when Wyatt's incremental naps were the only chances she had to eat or use the bathroom.

"You sound exhausted. Maybe your mom can fly down and help out?"

"God no." Bethany tensed. That would surely put her over the edge. She cleared her throat, trying to sound more upbeat. "It's fine. I'll manage."

"All right. Make sure you take some time for yourself. We're heading out first thing in the morning. Love to Wyatt."

"Good luck with the field tests. Watch out for snakes."

She tapped the phone off, cradling Wyatt in her other arm. It was a rare moment of peaceful dozing for him. Bethany inhaled the top of his head, the newborn scent intoxicating.

You're so worth it, she thought, admiring his round cheeks and tiny, caterpillar-like fingers that gripped and splayed as he dreamt.

She woke to ear-piercing wails later that night. Wyatt's screams rang hoarse and desperate, as though he had been at it for a while.

"I'm sorry," Bethany cried, staggering out of bed.

Wyatt accepted the bottle and regarded her with his brown-eyed stare while he sucked. At times like this it seemed they were the only ones in the world. Just as Bethany started to relax, Wyatt coughed out milk and began to scream again.

"I don't know how people do this as a single parent," Bethany said to his red face and patted his back, hard, until he burped. His sobs receded to whimpers.

Bethany yanked open the window to see the backyard drenched in fog. Maybe the crisp air would help him sleep. November in San Diego meant the weather was finally cooler. The fog peeled off from the canyon beyond their house, creeping past the yards and forming a cone of fuzzy yellow below her neighbor's porch light, so thick you could cut it.

A yipping rang through the fog and Bethany jumped, startling Wyatt into another cry. Bethany peered out the window and heard the sound again.

Coyotes. Reports of recent sightings had sprung up throughout the neighborhood messaging forums as the creatures ventured out of the canyons looking for food. Just last week her homeowners' association sent a notice that a member's Chihuahua had been snatched right from the backyard. The coyote had hopped over the fence and disappeared with the pet, all in the span of a few seconds.

Don't let kids or pets out of sight, the neighborhood newsletter had warned. *Coyotes are AGGRESSIVE and HUNGRY*.

Now the coyotes' plaintive howls sounded like a cult of wailing humans. As Wyatt continued to bawl, Bethany wondered if the coyotes could hear it, if they ever homed in on the cries of a human baby.

She closed the window and rocked Wyatt, who sobbed for the next hour.

* * *

The mornings were the worst, having to face a new day after no sleep. An aching band tightened around Bethany's temples and her stomach turned and sloshed as she got up to Wyatt's shrieks. Quicksand had been poured into her limbs and a thick humid towel seemed to be wrapped around her brain, slowing the flow of any thoughts.

Bethany hauled Wyatt downstairs, past the first-year memory journal and heap of scrapbooking materials sitting untouched on the kitchen table. Every joint felt iced into place, hard to move. Not to mention the throbbing that plagued her lower half from childbirth, preventing her from even sitting comfortably.

She downed some painkillers and searched for a babysitter or nanny, someone who could give her a break so she could clean up or go out for a bit. But after scanning nanny sites, which depressingly reminded her of online dating, she gave up. Background checks, reference calls, interviews. It was all too much.

Before she could think of a back-up plan, Wyatt began screaming even though he had just downed a bottle. To add to the noise, the cat started meowing.

"You'll survive," Bethany told the cat as she rocked Wyatt. "I don't even have time to feed myself. He comes first."

An hour later, Wyatt still showed no sign of stopping. She had read about newborns' growth spurts and accompanying hunger pangs but this, this constant wailing for no apparent reason, was more than she could take.

"What is wrong with you?"

Wyatt screamed louder in response, piercing her eardrums and giving her headache a fresh boost. She touched the fuzz of hair on his head and considered one of the beige couch pillows next to her. She could use it to mute his wails for a minute, so she could think.

Horrified at the thought, Bethany dropped Wyatt into his bassinet and ran into the bathroom. She let the water run while Wyatt continued to screech. *You're a monster.* The thoughts, in a mean-girl drawl, ran staccato. *Just. The. Worst.* She avoided looking too long at the bedraggled face in the mirror. The put-together blonde who would never let her roots get this bad was distant as a dream.

It takes a few months to bounce back, all of the mommy bloggers seemed to agree. But she was barely surviving a few weeks.

I am a good mother, she told herself. *I am.*

You're not, though. The mean-girl voice was back. *Like, not even close.*

She clenched her jaw. *I am. I can be.* Bethany breathed in and out and thought about how much she loved Wyatt. Even though it had only been a short while since he had been born, the conviction that she would do anything for him filled her heart. She loved him so much.

She emerged from the bathroom and paced with Wyatt until her back muscles threatened to give out. She took a few more painkillers to numb the pain and continued to walk him around the house until his screams turned into sniffles.

"Let's go outside," she said. A little jaunt around the block could only do the both of them good and might help Wyatt sleep.

A shout outside the window stopped her as she reached the door. Through the window she glimpsed kids on bikes making lazy loops down the street, already out from school. What if they got too close to the baby and coughed on him? She couldn't risk it.

She settled for the backyard, using the last of her strength to drag out the portable bassinet and place Wyatt inside. The canyon stretched out, breathtaking in the sharp cerulean sky. The days were so short this time of year; she barely had a glimpse of sunlight some days before nighttime settled in.

As she scanned the yard for the unfinished gardening she had to do—all the plants needed watering—her gaze fell on a dark shape beneath the roses. The fresh dose of painkillers had set in, and she blinked to clear her vision.

Mangled patches of gray fur spread beneath the bush, trailing down to the canyon. A rabbit, maybe? Bethany looked out at the canyon and pictured tossing Wyatt down the steep incline, his tiny arms, unable to coordinate movement, flailing out before he disappeared into the thick brush that covered the grounds.

Bethany tried calling Rob but it went straight to voicemail. Too late, he was out in the field, untethered to her. She wracked her brain for someone else she could call to help ease her rising panic. But what was she panicked about exactly—a dead rabbit? She tried to breathe, rubbing her eyes against the grating blue from above.

That night, she stretched out on the floor next to Wyatt's crib, waiting for him to doze off. She started to drift into sleep when a bark jolted her awake.

She opened the window to see a coyote in her yard, barely visible through the fog that had returned. She had never seen one so close before, tall and thin, like a dog but wrong. It looked at the window, its yellow eyes reflecting the porch light as tendrils of mist raced by like spirits over the pavers.

It smells the baby inside, Bethany thought.

The coyote yipped once and far-off echoes met the sound in unison. A mother, maybe, with babies of her own to feed. Curls of fog swept past, obscuring its legs. It looked as though the coyote floated in a milky cloud.

A little voice came to her, in the upbeat, blog-style narration she had read too much of: *They are hungry! A mother will do anything to protect and provide for her cubs. Moms are amazing!*

* * *

The sight of the coyote may have been a dream, Bethany couldn't tell anymore. Her days and nights and waking and sleeping blurred together, a messy composite against the thickening wall of fatigue around her mind. She had called the county animal services and tried to remember what they said. Snatches of conversation came back: herself yelling, someone on the line saying they couldn't do anything and advising her to stay inside at night.

Another evening settled in and the fog came in quickly, barely an hour after sunset. How many days, how many hours had it been since Bethany had slept? Her skin was covered in a layer of days-old sweat, and occasionally she caught a whiff of her body odor. The baby wailed in the background, a constant drone she had learned to ignore.

Sometimes in moments like this, the baby looked utterly unfamiliar to her, squirming like a worm about to hatch in his tightly bundled swaddle, his face red and gaping as he screamed. Then the feeling would pass and she loved him again. Bethany swallowed a double dose of the pain meds and opened the bedroom window.

They were in the yard. Waiting. Bethany almost screamed when she saw them—three, no four, no five—coyotes standing next to her rose bush and between the thick arms of aloe vera.

Like demons sensing vulnerable souls, Bethany thought, and said out the window, "You can't have him."

One of the coyotes cocked its head as though to say, *Yes we can, momma. We can and we will.*

A scraping at the back door downstairs sent a tingle of alarm running along the base of Bethany's spine.

The coyotes. They were plotting to get inside.

A vision pushed itself into her mind of tufts of down-like baby hair and shreds of a swaddle as mangled as the rabbit under the bush. The coyotes wouldn't leave her alone until she did something.

Bethany gently picked up the baby, who had cried himself to sleep, and crept downstairs, afraid to make any noise. She unlatched the dog door that they hadn't used for years and pushed the cat outside with only a twinge of regret.

An offering. Maybe they would go.

The cat's claws skittered against the pavement as it ran. A yowl, followed by crunching and slurping, like overly done sound effects in a horror movie.

Bethany opened the back door, first a crack and then wider. The coyotes stared, their yellow eyes like car beams drilling into her.

They were still hungry.

Not the baby. That was the one thing she was certain of. She put him down into the portable bassinet and smiled. He really was a sweet thing despite all the crying.

She stepped out into the fog, closing the door behind her. For the first time since the baby's birth, a glimmer of relief came to her. She knew exactly what to do.

The coyotes were still as statues as she crouched next to her wicker chair. She lay down on the pavers next to a large bloodstain and shivered through her yoga pants and sweatshirt.

"Come on," she called, teeth chattering.

It took a few minutes. Particles of fog flitted across her vision as bristles began to scrape her palms. The smell of matted fur and blood filled her nostrils. Maybe it wouldn't be that bad. She closed her eyes to the low whines of the animals and the little tugs at her sleeves and pant legs.

A wet nose pressed against her before something nipped at her cheek. Somehow one had torn off most of her sweatshirt and she was colder than she thought possible. Despite the painkillers, she felt needles sink into her bare ankles and hands, reminiscent of the shock when she had tried—and failed—to breastfeed.

The pain reminded her of labor, an all-encompassing fire that wracked her body and took her breath away as the animals feasted. She called up the visualization she had used to overcome contractions in the birthing room: ocean waves, breaking and receding. *You are far from here, watching the waves go in and out*, she told herself fiercely. In and out. In and out.

It wasn't working. A reflexive scream welled up but she could only manage a gasp. Bethany tried to squirm, to kick, but the coyotes restrained her—she didn't know how many gnawed at her ankles and arms, chest and cheeks. The pain spiked before a blanket ran over her like warm milk.

At least now they won't go after the baby, she thought, drowsy as the pain receded.

Maybe she was a good mother after all.

Ring Rock
James Edward O'Brien

I didn't want a mortgage. I was stuck like a wasp in amber to the idea we could cut ties on a whim. Skip town. Start over.

I didn't want kids. Neither did Gina. She wanted that house beside Ring Rock.

She saw her dream house. All *I* saw was a fixer-upper parked in the sticks that stank of must and mothballs.

I took a leap of faith though, and signed on the dotted line. I mean, who was *I* to stand in the way of G's dreams? I remember thinking this'd be the new life I'd assumed I'd one day skip town for—unaware that our new lives would soon not be like living at all.

Backed-up septic, sealed-up chimney, and a stillborn litter of raccoon kits under the porch. The *dream home* became an unwieldy project. We fought more than usual, Gina stressed over her new position as assistant chair of the geology department at a community college, me looking for work and keeping house.

It was geology—*rocks*—that drew her there. Our property bordered a stone field of *lithophonic* rocks: rocks that rang like bells when struck—a novelty that drew bored bumpkins far and wide. On the opposite side of our property lay a derelict bungalow with the unimaginative moniker "Ring Rock" hand painted on a sign below its mailbox.

According to the realtor, a vet of the first Gulf War—an unfortunate case—who lived off disability and was seldom seen, inhabited the bungalow. Ideal, if you ask me. No potlucks. No idle chatter while mowing the overgrown lawn.

I'd piled a bunch of crap on the table that'd been jettisoned by the previous owners that I'd hoped Gina wanted to trash. At the bottom of the pile was a patina frame that'd hung above the fireplace, the photo inside mealy with water damage, yellowed with age.

The photo depicted a couple. Faces piebald with water stains. Judging by their wardrobe, I'd wager the photo was taken in the eighties. But the couples' posturing was rigid—that awkward formality evident in old-timey photos when everyone wore a sourpuss.

It was taken at the side of the house; Ring Rock loomed behind them. Happier times: lattice fence, bold aluminum siding.

Gina spun her fork in a bowl of undercooked fettuccine puttanesca. "Save the frame," she choked.

She was a packrat. I knew it was coming. A tiny piece of me died nonetheless. "It's trash," I insisted.

"Vintage," she corrected.

I studied the photo in the frame.

"Maybe we should give this place a name," I said. "Like that dump next door."

"Felsenmeer?" she suggested.

I shrugged. "Geology geek jargon?"

She nodded. "You know, if you extracted one of those rocks from the field and gave it a whack, you wouldn't hear jack. It's the frequencies playing off the *other* rocks in the field that make the magic happen."

I rolled my eyes and wished there was more than sonorous rocks to pass the time. Gina taught evening classes at the college every other weeknight. I bought myself a pack of cigarettes and a bottle of whiskey—sinful pleasures to kill the time between prepping dinner and awaiting G's return.

I'd never realized how woods were so simultaneously noisy *and* still come nightfall. I hadn't known much about the woods at all: hoot owls and crickets, night creatures upsetting twigs, fallen leaves—the entirety of it unfurling in a giant belly of darkness. It conjured a feeling of constantly being watched by something that might not even be there.

I kept the porch light on and fired a smoke. The sound of broken church bells resounded from the direction of the night-blanketed *felsenmeer*. Glass shattered. Laughter. Bored high school kids drinking, punishing the rocks for the fact they'd been born into a backwater.

I toyed with the idea of calling the cops, reminding myself that I was bored kid once upon a time. Besides, my phone had shoddy service out here. I was pussyfooting my way around the headache of switching carriers.

The darkness kept me jumpy. I scanned the road on the ridge for G's headlights— no light but the silvery moon peering over piney treetops. I grabbed the whiskey bottle by the neck, like a club, and walked the perimeter of the house to try and prove to myself I was more than a lost, frightened child.

Light shone through the slats of Ring Rock's shuttered windows across the way, easing my nerves. A bit. I toyed with the idea of going over there and introducing myself one of these afternoons—with a bottle of vino, some baked goods—knowing deep down I wasn't the type.

If there was any advantage to our move to the sticks, it's that there weren't people up your ass 24/7. High beams along the road—crackling gravel as the lights drew closer. A fox sprinted across the lawn. All ribs and mange—not at all the sort of thing I pictured from storybooks.

Gina struggled with her car door, spent from her double course load, administrative claptrap.

"Smells like smoke," she said. "You been smoking?"

"No," I lie.

Dinner was cold. G didn't seem to mind but it lit a fuse in me.

"Just shoot me a text when you're gonna be home this late," I pouted. "Just so I know you're not dead in a ditch somewhere."

I poured her a whiskey. She scrunched her nose. G stood her spoon in the coagulated bowl of cream of mushroom soup. I'd made it from scratch.

"You wanna watch something after I clean up?" I asked.

"I've got to run through my syllabus," she apologized.

We fought over nothing. Slept with our backs to one another. The next day I stenciled *Felsenmeer* on a two-by-eight cut of cedar I dug out of the tool shed alongside a rusty chisel and some wood stain: junk jettisoned by previous owners.

I set to work on the porch. I wound up opening the heel of my left hand with the chisel. Blood stained cedar. I called it a day, taking extra care to not fuck up anything else as I cleaned my wound in the cast-iron farmhouse sink G adored.

G texted me ahead of time that she was grabbing takeout––some banh mi shop near the college. She must have felt guilty too.

I slid a cigarette from the pack I'd stashed between the rafters of our covered porch. I smoked it shirtless so the smell wouldn't cling to me.

The moment I spotted high beams I darted inside to gargle mouthwash. I heard car wheels on a gravel road, and then a car door slam, and then the screen door whinnying open. I'd set the table. Uncorked some wine. Lit a candle.

G pecked me on the cheek. Scolded me for the candle wax dripping on her new butcher-block. I slid a tea saucer under the candle.

Neither of us made eye contact. I was the first to try, G's gaze fixed above my head.

"I appreciate that," she choked. Mouth full. "I know you hate that frame. Did the realtor take that one?"

"Take what?"

G smirked. "You're sweet." She gestured behind me.

The patina frame I'd wanted to trash hung over the fireplace. A new photo had been slipped into the frame right over the old one: Gina and me in the foreground, arm-in-arm, squinting against the sun, the house behind us.

The photo was grainy, as if taken from a distance and magnified. "It's not the *worst* photo."

"C'mon G," I said.

"C'mon *what?*" she asked.

"I didn't put that up. But it's *nice*," I lied, trying not to raise her hackles—unsure of what she was playing at—hanging that heinous frame, pinning it on me.

Gina frowned. "You cut your hand."

"Hammering in those warped floorboards," I lied. "Before I repaint the stairs out back." I wanted to keep *Felsenmeer* a secret until it was ready for her.

"Be careful, *please*," she fretted. "I *do* like the picture. That *was* very sweet."

"Wasn't me," I insisted.

Gina winked. "Well, *somebody* put it up there."

Gina fell asleep early. I lay there resenting her for it. I awoke to the sound of G driving off to work, a sink full of dishes from the night prior in the kitchen—another fracture line in G and me's fragile social contract. I didn't so much mind being a house frau—it was the *house* that bothered me.

G's dream house. My nightmare of tedium. I suppose it remained a *dream* to her because she hadn't yet fully occupied it—
—always onto the next thing, throwing herself into the

mundanities of administrative life—stoic and unyielding as the rocks she studied. Hopscotching jobs, hobbies, friends; for whatever reason, I was the only constant.

I needed a day off from all these days off. More booze. Some nocturnal pain-in-the-ass had gotten into the porch rafter and gnawed through my cigarette stash. I decided I'd walk off my shitty mood, restock, and then finish the sign for Gina.

I made for the far side of the stone field where an old Lenape trail ran along the road toward town—"town" being a collapsed granary, a Lutheran church, and a "convenience" store that closed shop at five and shut down entirely Sunday.

A cheese-colored bus full of school kids idled in the lot beside the stones. I quickened so as not to get caught in the stampede of brats, fixing to take hammers to them.

Jagged. Haphazard—a great, gray callus in the center of an otherwise sheltering woodland. I hopscotched from unnavigable rock to unnavigable rock, making it to the Lenape trail just as the school bus unleashed the hounds: a lawsuit waiting to happen even without the hammers.

The walk revivified me—all stripes of birds I'd never seen before flitting amongst the trees, wind rattling half-naked autumn branches. *It wasn't all bad*, I told myself.

The convenience store clerk was slow talking, overly familiar—knowing, somehow, that I'd moved into the place beside Ring Rock, wanting to know where I were from, what I did, and when we'd moved in.

I wanted scotch, but Beam was on sale. I bought two fifths (one for my hypothetical "welcome to the neighborhood" reconnaissance of Ring Rock), an off brand of cigarettes, and a few groceries that tread the line of their best before dates.

I smoked and walked and felt alive amidst the bird chatter and the crisp autumn wind. By the time I got back, the bus and brats had cleared out of the stone field beside our property and a light rain had started to fall. I sat on the porch and smoked another cigarette and listened to the rain hit the roof of the porch.

I noticed a pair of thrown-open shutters across the way— one of the windows facing our place. Ring Rock. I squeezed the paper bag containing the fifth of bourbon between my knees and thought I might as well take advantage of the crappy weather and play happy neighbor while this better-than-crappy mood persisted.

The old bungalow wore a coat of crawling vines, splintered lattice, and peeling paint. The front steps were so creaky I feared I might plunge right through the warped planks. A platoon of brightly colored, fresh-painted garden gnomes was scattered among the overgrown weeds.

There was no doorbell; a knocker rusted off its hinges. I rapped on the door—the only sturdy component of the entire structure. Heavy footsteps inside. More creaking. A gruff voice, a child's voice. Then quiet. A vet, the realtor had mentioned—didn't say anything about a family.

Kids killed grownup fun. Kids killed sipping bourbon on the porch at two in the afternoon. I rapped on the door again. I heard a child's voice again. Then, a door slammed.

I tried, I thought, contented by my unrealized gesture. At least I'd have a couple hours to work on the sign for Gina.

As I turned to leave I was struck with déjà vu—the photo in the frame above the fireplace of Gina and me. The selfsame vantage point, shot from this very spot.

I chiseled on the porch. I'd stenciled the E's in *Felsenmeer* lowercase—an oversight, I realized, once the chisel slipped, and slipped again and I narrowly evaded having a *Fclsenmcer* sign on my hands. I swigged bourbon to steady the hands.

I'd chiseled my way through the final lowercase E when a short, sharp *pop*, sudden and jarring as a gunshot, echoed across the lot. It was the sort of sound a person wouldn't pay any consideration amidst the cacophony of urban life, but out here, couched amidst the birdsong, the lazy applause of branches, it was pronounced. I flinched like a timid fawn.

Hunter, I imagined. I kept below banister level to have a gander, trying not to think about how little protection weatherworn cedar might offer against a twenty-five-caliber bullet. I waited for it—for anything—a second clap, a wounded animal limping from the brush, a camouflaged trespasser—cell phone at the ready, reception little to none. I craned my neck—eyes toward Ring Rock, hoping the noise might have aroused whomever it was who'd chosen to snub my neighborly call.

I breathed deep. It was only a loud noise. *In the woods*. I felt silly, humbled at how the feeling of being nothing in the middle of nowhere could alternately feel so goddamn liberating and goddamn terrifying. The bourbon had gone to my head.

The rain had stopped. The shutters, I noticed, at Ring Rock—a sudden wind, or something, had slammed that shut. That had been all.

I did a set of pushups in the wet grass to try and reclaim my balls. Checked for ticks afterward. I stowed the chisel, the hammer, and the half-finished sign back in the tool shed. I swept the wood shavings off the porch.

Gina returned home that night with news that a child had gone missing.

"There's a checkpoint along Quarry Road," she said. "Surprised they haven't gone knocking on doors. A field trip, apparently, to the felsenmeer."

"No shit," I said. "I *passed* that bus. I schlepped down to that shitty deli down the road for some uh—" *Booze. Cigarettes.* "—*brown rice* before lunch."

I'd attempted a Thai curry. "Too spicy," G griped. She hammered me with the mundanities of her day.

"Hey," I interrupted. "When the realtor took us on the walkthrough before we closed—you remember her mentioning anything about the neighbors having kids? Grandkids?"

Gina shrugged. "Haven't seen any."

"Me either," I said. "Heard one, though."

"Heard one? What? Having a go at the rocks with a mallet?"

"No," I said. "I went next door this afternoon—to make nice. The way neighbors do—*I think.*"

Gina golf clapped. "Well, look at you! The things you get up to when I'm not around."

I excused myself and hit the bathroom for cell reception. I called the county police. Told them that my wife and I had recently moved into the house beside the park where the child had gone missing. I told them that I'd heard a child in the house next door—that it was probably nothing. I gave them my name and number. They thanked me for the info.

Gina retired with a cup of chamomile tea and a stack of student papers—so much for chitchat or a little TLC after my day in solitary. I entertained the idea of lingering round the country store for company. I'd start smoking regularly again—

and the daily walk back and forth would be a halfway passable exercise regimen.

I'd never considered myself a needy person, but the lack of human interaction was doing my head in. I'd sent out ten résumés that week with nary a callback. I actually felt *lonelier* when Gina was around lately—the sickly glow from her laptop in bed an encroaching ghost from her daily grind.

I poured myself a tall glass of whiskey and went on the porch to sulk. I even lit up a cigarette, like some latchkey kid looking to drum up negative attention from a despondent parent.

Police car lights from the road drew closer. No siren. Police car wheels chewed gravel as the cruiser pulled up to Ring Rock. A motion sensor set off an LED porch light that illuminated a massive gnat swarm visible across the property. I stamped out my cigarette.

The cop moseyed up to the rickety porch. She searched for a doorbell. She rapped on the door. Light appeared through the slats of the shutters. The front door whinnied open. The light in the doorway framed a hunched silhouette that loomed crookedly over the officer. I waited for a quarrel, for the cuffs to come out, but there were only voices, low and neighborly, punctuated by laughter.

I was a rat, an under-stimulated, voyeuristic twat who had zero idea of how life worked in a place like this. I slinked beneath the banister, planted my ass on the stoop, below potential eyeshot.

The cop shook hands with the man on the porch, made for her cruiser, and then drove back off down the narrow gravel lane. The figure on the porch lingered in the light until the car was gone.

He stretched like a cat awakening from a nap. He stared into the darkness, straight toward our place. Straight at me, though there was no way he'd seen me. Maybe he'd seen the lit ember of my cigarette before I'd stubbed it out. Maybe he'd been watching all along.

He waved. Flashed a smile. I pulled my knees to my chest and wrapped my arms around my shins. I peeked through the carved uprights of the railing, holding my breath and willing myself invisible like a guilty child. The figure lumbered back inside and killed his porch light.

I didn't sleep much that night. I was tired of going to bed mad. I got up before Gina and made toast and scrambled eggs.

"*Breakfast*," Gina sing-songed through a mouthful of eggs. "That was sweet of you."

I wanted to scream, but only managed a neutered smile. A yellow curd of scramble fell to her blouse.

"I've got to go," she said, scraping her chair legs across the hardwood floor.

"Of course you do," I mumbled.

"What was that, hon'?"

"Home the usual time?" I covered.

"Hope so," she said. She pecked me on the lips.

I was smoking regularly throughout the day. Every hour on the hour to mark the passage of time. I touched up the *Felsenmeer* sign with wood stain in spots where the chisel had chewed into the wood where it shouldn't have. I laid the sign on the railing to dry. It looked like something a special needs kid in junior high might make for his mother in shop class.

"Howdy, *neighbor*." The gruff monotone sent me out of my skin.

Lord knows how long he'd been standing there—a man in soiled, safety orange coveralls a sweat-through camo thermal beneath. The man from the porch. The skin hung from his face like a hound dog mask. It obscured his close-set eyes and gathered beneath his chin like the remnants of a candle that'd burned through its wick—thinning hair combed through with oxblood boot polish. He had a camera round his neck—an old point-and-click, and two tattered paperbacks wedged into his armpit.

"Jesus—you scared me half to death," I said.

The man smiled. "I live next door," he said. He gestured toward Ring Rock.

"I know," I said.

"Good keeping an eye out," he said.

"Eh?" He knew I was the rat.

"People don't look after one another anymore. People from down east buy places out here; throw their money around——won't so much as give you the time of day. Act like their shit don't stink. *I served my country*," he blustered. "Glad you're different."

He eyed the empty bottle of Beam beside the coffee can lid I was using for an ashtray.

"Smoke?" I offered.

He shook his head *no*. He placed the paperbacks on the stair—a birdwatcher's guide and a copy of the New Testament––and planted his muddy work boots on the stack.

"Your wife comes and goes," he said.

"*Goes*, mostly," I said bitterly. "She took a gig at the county college. That's how come we moved out here."

"Well, least she's got you to hold down the fort." He leaned on the stoop, snatched up my cigarette pack, and then plucked one from the pack with untrimmed, blackened fingernails.

"They'll find that kid," he assured me.

"Kid?" I said, playing dumb.

"The runaway—the one they say went missing round the quarry."

"They think the kid ran away?"

The man shrugged. "You know how kids are."

"Was never a fan," I confessed, firing my cigarette. "Even when I was a kid myself."

The man stuffed his cigarette in the breast pocket of his coveralls.

"You got kids?" I asked.

"Me? Naw. No wife. No kids. When Ma was still alive she said I must've used up all my luck in the service. All I had when I got out was what the cancer had left of her—and Ring Rock."

"I'm sorry," I said, hoping he'd leave.

"No need," he said. "Good neighbors are a blessing all their own."

He loped back toward his property.

"Say, I didn't catch your name," I called after him.

"No," he said. "No, you didn't."

"Your books," I called after him.

"I'll collect them some other time," he said.

I made risotto that night—Peruvian asparagus. I positioned the freshly minted *felsenmeer* sign at Gina's place setting. She appreciated it more than the dinner.

"Asparagus makes my pee smell," she protested.

"I met the guy next-door today," I said.

"And?"

"Weirdo. Figure he's some Bible nut. Left behind a copy of the New Testament. Told me neighbors are a *blessing*."

"You always think the worst, don't you? Ever think that maybe he's just *grateful?* Do you really have to be a Bible nut to have a little *faith* in your world? Did a little religion ever kill anybody?"

"You watch the news lately?"

Someone was out in the field clobbering rocks—the night upset by a clamor akin to church bells, their clappers wrenched out like rotten teeth. "Sonuvabitch," I snarled. "It's too late for this shit."

"It's probably only kids."

"Yeah, kids at 9:30 at night—on a Wednesday!"

"C'mon," said Gina. She placed her hand over mine. We seldom touched anymore. "Listen to yourself. You were a kid once."

"Yeah," I said. "And I wish somebody had set me straight when I was."

I pulled my hand away. Dug my phone from my pocket. Dialed the local precinct. No reception.

"Lemme use your phone, will ya, G?"

"Just give it a minute, hon? If they're still banging away once we finish the dishes—"

Above her head, the picture—Gina and me, arm-in-arm, squinting against the sun, the house behind us—a fresh crescent moon had been carved into the photo, right across my face as if a toothy white smile had chomped down on my head.

"That stupid frame fall?" I asked

"You're the one who's home all day," she said.

A slight? I swatted my plate across the table.

"I didn't mean it like that, hon," said Gina. "To be honest, I like you home. I like *us* home."

G turned, eyes drawn to the imperfection in the imperfect photograph. The hammering from the field persisted.

"You'd think differently if *you* were holed up here all day," I snapped. "You like the *idea* of here, but you're somewhere else three-quarters of the day, aren't you?"

"It's my first semester," said G. "Once I get over the learning curve, get all my syllabi hammered out, I can switch to autopilot." G got weepy. "Just stick this out will you, hon? This is *our* dream house, remember?"

"This is *your* dream house, G. You have it. *Be here. Now.* I'm just treading water in somebody else's dream."

Gina started to bawl. She slammed her fist against the butcher-block table. I should've just sucked it up. Spared her feelings. The sound of ringing rock grew frenzied.

"L-look G," I stammered. "I-I'm gonna *murder* whoever's hammering on those goddamn rocks."

I swiped the Mag-Lite from the mantle. Stormed onto the porch. I marched down the stairs and tripped right across the paperbacks that dimwit from across the way had left on my stoop.

A photo slipped from between the beaten covers of the birdwatcher's guide. I shone my light. It was a photo of a child staring out a window with its shutters thrown open, taken from behind—G's dream house through the dirty panes. A blurred figure inhabited the porch. *Me.*

I glanced at my phone. One bar. I sped dialed the police station.

It rang. And rang. A voice. At last. *"—ville Police. —ow —an I be of —stance?"* Shoddy reception.

"I called about the kid—at the quarry. Yesterday."

A garbled response. The phone cut out. I'd call with G's phone once I got back inside. *No kids*, he'd told me.

I clenched the Mag-Lite. Its beam swept brittle grass. I marched toward the felsenmeer. *Clunk. Clunk. Clunk.* I listened for the sound of breaking bottles, pubescent laughter, but there were only ringing rocks above the crickets chirping, autumnal winds through naked branches.

The ground turned brown and bald as it eased downward toward the field of stone. Jagged rocks sprouted further afield, each one intersected by shadowy gaps wide enough to lose a shoe, snag an ankle—take a spill and split one's skull if a person were unwary.

I scanned for trespassers. The light caught nothing but whittled gray crags. The hammering persisted. I hopscotched around the perimeter of the field. Out here, my Mag-Lite a beacon, I was a target for beer bottles, jeers—whatever these pricks had in their arsenal.

"Park closes at nightfall," I growled, sounding like the grumpy old man G had accused me of becoming. Frightened. Obsolete. "People are trying to sleep."

A frenzied percussion of rock was the only retort. I wagged the flashlight wildly, hoping to catch the bastards in the act— still, only jagged edges, shifting shadows.

A sudden flash rendered me night-blind. I cursed, blinked my way back to seeing. My flashlight caught a silhouette in the distance. Hammer in one hand, camera in the other. I shone the light. Hound dog mask, close-set eyes, thinning hair combed through with boot polish.

I thought of the picture tucked away in the pages of his book, the picture hung above our fireplace with my face scratched out. My bowels turned to water.

I fought to stay upright. Knock-kneed. The felsenmeer unforgiving. A man could twist an ankle. Break a neck.

"The wife comes and goes," he crowed over his banging. "She's home now. Saw the car pull in."

He leapt. Almost simian. The claw of his hammer raked stone. His arm that wielded the hammer was otherwise flaccid as a ragdoll's.

I swatted the air with the Mag-Lite. "Cops are on their way," I bluffed.

He fired the camera flash again. "I get under your skin, don't I? Get under your skin a bit and there's not as much distance as you'd *think* between the likes of me and the likes of you all, though—is there?"

He pointed the camera lens, a condemnation. I swung the Mag-Lite to keep him at bay. I slipped on the convex rock face.

He played the stones with the hammer that dangled from his ragdoll arm. My ears rang. I prayed for police sirens to shatter the night. But there was only ringing and the beam of my flashlight.

I roared at the top of my lungs. *"Call the cops!"*

I prayed my voice might rise above the clangor, drift back toward the house—through the window where G was probably curled up with a stack of student papers.

"You said you'd called them already." The man, perplexed. "Now, which is it?"

He zigzagged, and then pounced—a creature suppler than one that might wear a weathered, hound-dog face. The claw of his hammer bit the meat of my calf. Pain razored through my leg. My knee buckled.

I jabbed him in the groin with the head of my Mag-Lite; the brunt of the blow buffered by the sag in his loose-fitting coveralls. He howled. Kicked out my standing leg. When my head struck the rock, the rock did not ring—*migraine red, midnight blue.*

The killer stepped over me. Blue midnight faded to black. I clutched jagged rock with blind fingers. Read the gaps from stone to stone. I crawled toward the blurry migraine light from the porch upon the rise.

As I dragged myself across the rocks, it felt as if they were scraping my insides out, beveling bits of ribcage and bone. I inch-wormed toward the brown, bald rise leading up toward the property.

A rapping in the distance: the wooden handle of a claw hammer against a rickety porch door.

"There's been an accident," he bellowed. "Your husband––"

No response. His rapping grew more forceful—insistent.

I dragged myself to the top of the rise, porch in clear view, good neighbor taking the handle of his hammer to the door like an ice pick.

A light from the rear of the house: our bedroom. I searched the road beyond the hill for red and blue lights, but there was only darkness.

Uncle
Elin Olausson

Uncle says that it was for the best that Mother died. I didn't agree at first but I agree now. She was slow and clumsy, like a slug or cow or some other animal you don't have to be nice to. Her food tasted bland and she was always crying. *Boo-hoo*, Uncle said, then lifted one of her thin braids and spoke with his lips touching her ear. *Boo-fucking-hoo!* He doesn't want me using bad words but it's not the same when it's only in my head. I don't think it's the same.

Uncle is the only man I know. We don't need other men here. Svetlana does the cleaning and I answer the telephone and Uncle does everything else. Svetlana lives in town; she drives here in the morning and leaves at noon. She tried to smile at me in the beginning but smiles don't work on me. I don't despise her, really, but I don't care for her either. Uncle says she's sloppy and wears too much makeup. At least she never cries.

The motel is ours and when Uncle dies, it will be mine. I have a lot of responsibilities. I do as I'm told. The old woman in Room 12 says I'm very clever. She has a strange way of talking; the words come out all stretched and bent. She has stayed for one week already, which is good because there are no other guests. The VACANT sign blinks, blinks, blinks like a shock-pink constellation in the sky. The woman has a big head and a name I don't like, so I think of her as Head. Every day, Head drives off in her rusty white car with her canvas bag. I peeked into the bag on her first night here, when she forgot it in Reception, and saw an old camera and a book. I wonder if Head reads the same book every day or if she has lots of them to pick and choose from, lining the walls in Room 12. I have ten books but I haven't looked at them since Mother went into the tub. None of them have pictures, because Uncle says picture books are bad for children. Mother used to read the stories to me when she was around. I guess you could say it was the only thing she was good at.

I have a secret place of my own below the counter in Reception. I can sit there with my legs outstretched and Uncle doesn't notice, Svetlana doesn't notice, no one notices. It's a lockable hollow space inside the counter, dark and dusty, all empty because Uncle keeps everything important in his office down the hall. Sometimes I fall asleep in there. Other times I spy. I listen as Uncle asks guests for their names and hands out keys. I hear his voice ripple through the air. If the front door is open, which it is a lot because of the heat, I eavesdrop on the conversations on the porch. Those are what interest me the most. Uncle talks to all the guests. Only girls come here, and they are always alone. Their cars break down close to the motel in the middle of the night, or they come wandering from nowhere, barefoot, carrying nothing but their shoes. Hitchhiker girls, runaway girls, girls with pills in their pockets and china doll faces. Uncle tucks their long hair behind their ears and they laugh like a choir of broken toys, shrill and off-key. They ask him to fix their cars or make them coffee or let them stay the night. Uncle twirls their hair around his finger and they melt until the floor is a gooey mess.

There are no girls here now. Only Head. I like it when Uncle talks to her. Their talks are like cigarette smoke trailing through the air, beautiful but not beautiful at all. I don't understand what they talk about but I want to hear it and pretend I am grown like them. Uncle sips the peach-flavored iced tea you make from powder. He buys twenty bags of it every time he goes to town for supplies. Once, I tore open an empty package and lapped at the remaining powder inside. I imagine that real peaches would taste just like that. An explosion of sweetness.

I sit under the counter tonight playing the spy game. Uncle is outside, and Head with her pale eyes and the usual scarf tied over her grey hair. I have made a hole in the counter with a nail. It's small, but if I press my eye against it, I see things. Right now, I see the rickety porch table with Uncle's glass of iced tea, his long thin legs and his hairy arm, reaching for the glass. Head sits at the other side of the table. She drinks from a hip flask. Sometimes it's a thermos, sometimes a water bottle. Uncle has never offered her anything from inside the house and she has never asked. Her bra is visible through her worn white t-shirt. Not like Uncle's girls would do it, to be sexy. Head doesn't know and if she did, she wouldn't care.

"Found anything today?" Uncle asks. His voice is cool as always but there's that sugary note to it that belongs to evenings on the porch. I know that his mouth would taste of peaches if I licked it.

"What's there to find?" Head's deep voice twists the words around slowly. "I won't go inside the place. I can't. The house looks just the same from a distance, though. All worn and sagging, like me." She makes a strange sound, some sort of laugh. "As long as I don't get too close, I can pretend I'm still living there and Bill's on his way home and Charlie's asleep in his room."

"Yeah." Uncle drinks. The hairs on his arm shimmer like gold in the ripe sunlight. "I've had places like that too. Before. I've found that it's best to stay the hell away from them. The past…it eats you."

Head runs her thumb along her cheekbone, as if she's brushing a tear away. "What if I want it to eat me?"

"Well, clearly you do." Uncle doesn't seem to notice her crying. Or maybe it's not a problem when Head does it. "I'm trying to help, that's all. You lost something, I lost something. We all lost something. But some of us don't like being eaten." He laughs. Uncle's laugh is smooth and warm as desert sand at the end of a hot day.

"I took a picture today." Head doesn't seem to want to talk more about eating. "I thought you should see it." She grabs her canvas bag from the floor and rummages inside, then picks up a photograph and shows it to him. Her eyes stay on his face the whole time. I want to know what's in the photo, but all I see is a dark and blurry, white-framed square.

"Not bad." Uncle doesn't grab the picture to take a closer look. It hangs between them, dangling from Head's wrinkly hand. After a while she puts it back in her bag.

"What happened?" she asks, her voice as cautious as a hand reaching into a lion's cage. "To her, I mean…your sister-in-law. I thought she'd be here, I thought she was working for you. Then today I saw that cross, in the middle of nowhere, and I—"

"Nothing happened." Uncle cuts her off without raising his voice. I wish he'd let her talk, so I could learn more about the cross. "She wasn't happy," he continues. "Some people aren't."

I know what you're doing, Mother whimpers in my head. *I know what you're doing to those girls.*

"It must be tough," Head says. "Bringing the boy up on your own."

My chest flares up with excitement. They're talking about me. It's the first time I've heard them talking about me.

"Not at all." Uncle's long fingers trace the rim of his glass. It must be cool and wet to the touch. "It's easier now, in fact."

Head shakes her head slowly. It reminds me of a turtle, or an old tree when a storm grabs hold of its branches. "Even for you, that's damn harsh."

"Blah, blah, blah." Uncle's hand opens and closes in the air like a nagging beak, a yapping dachshund. "You know, I do kind of enjoy your company. Don't ruin it."

"All right, I think we'll just call it a night." Head sighs and heaves herself out of the chair. "You know where I am if you want to apologize." She takes her bag and her hip flask and leaves the porch. The scarf around her head looks dirty, as if she's rubbed it into the dirt. I've never noticed before.

"I'll be right here." Uncle's voice is laughy and light. He takes the glass and drinks. When he puts it back down it's empty. "You can wait for an apology from me, Eleanor, but it won't come. Apologies are for normal people. Not us. You should know that."

He sits quiet and alone after she's gone. I sit quiet and alone too. I trace the inside of the counter with my fingers. Sometimes I get splinters when I do it, but not this time. With my eye to the peep hole, watching Uncle's unmoving form, I move my lips over the rough, uneven wood. *Hello, Head,* I mime. *Hello, Uncle.* I twist my mouth as if I was Head, imagining that I'm old and that I'll soon be dead and gone. I smile just like Uncle, baring my teeth.

* * *

When Svetlana arrives the next morning, Head has already driven off as she's done every day since she came here. I'm disappointed, because I wanted to have a look in her bag and see if maybe that photo she showed Uncle was still there. I stand on my stool behind the counter when Svetlana comes through the door. She heads straight for Uncle's office at the end of the hallway. Whenever she barges in there their voices turn loud and angry. It doesn't bother me, but she should learn to knock on doors. Even I know about knocking.

Sometimes when the telephone doesn't ring I play pretend and answer it anyway. I do it now to forget about Svetlana.

"You've reached the *Fading Sun*," I whisper, because I don't want Uncle to overhear. "How can I help?" The motel was called something else before. I like Uncle's name better. The other end of the line is silent, easy to fill with whatever words and voices I want.

Good morning, sweetheart, the silence says. It has a chipper voice that's both male and female, or neither. *I'd like a room for myself and my three children. We'll stay forever, me and my three boys around your age. They'll want to play with you every day.*

It could be just one boy, too. Maybe even a girl, as long as she's not too old. I put the receiver down and think about the games I could play with the three boys. Inside Uncle's office, Svetlana starts shouting.

"Hide-and-seek," I murmur to myself to drown out the office sounds, and because I sometimes forget what my voice sounds like. "And I'll be spying on them, and they'll never-never-never find me."

Uncle's office door opens with a bang, and I start as if I've had my knuckles rapped. Svetlana storms out, mascara and eyeliner running down her cheeks. Her eyes pin me down, pin me to the space between the counter and the wall.

"Your uncle is an asshole," she hisses, but her voice shifts at the last word, goes high-pitched and desperate.

"Don't you use that kind of language in front of him," Uncle calls from his office. He protects me, and it makes me glow inside.

"Fuck you!" Svetlana cries before rushing out to her car. With her thin legs and feet that sway this way and that in the high heels, she looks like the spiders that make Uncle twist his face in disgust before he crushes them under his boot.

He comes out of the office, leisurely, taking his time. I watch as he flattens his hair, then puts his hands into his pockets. There's not a crease in his jeans, there's never a crease in anything Uncle wears. "She asked for a raise, the greedy bitch," he says, smiling. Uncle's low voice is much nicer than Svetlana's. "We're better off without her. Isn't that right?"

I nod. For a second I think about Mother, but I shut that part of my brain down until it remembers. Remembers that we had no more use of Mother and that holding on to useless things is wrong.

"I think you're old enough," Uncle says, "to start cleaning."

* * *

The girls stay away this week. I wish they'd never come back. Uncle forgets about me when there are girls around and leaves me alone after the house has gone dark and the desert starts its night whispering. But now he is home, teaching me to play chess and to flay rats. Not for eating, only for practice.

"You've got to know how to do things," he tells me when the kitchen table is stained red and the matte grey fur has gone dark and sticky. "It's a bad world out there. That's why we stay here, you and me. But sometimes you've got to go into town whether you like or not."

"Will I be able to drive a car?" I ask. "Will I sit out on the porch just like you?"

"Yes." Uncle puts his bloody hand on my head. "You will do everything that I do."

* * *

That evening, Uncle takes his iced tea out to the porch and tells me to clean his office, before I've had time to slip into my hiding place under the counter. I don't mind.

"Just dusting, hoovering," Uncle says. "No touching any of my stuff, all right?"

I promise. Uncle nods and puts his glass down and the shades on, before he tells me to leave. His cowboy boots are the only part of him that's visible from inside the house. I go to the cleaning cupboard and take out what I need, a cloth and the old hoover. When I was small, Mother used to call it the Roaring Monster and chase me with it, both of us laughing. It doesn't look like a monster now.

Uncle's office is the coolest room in our house. The blinds are always closed in there. The office has shelves and folders and a desk with only his computer on it. On TV I've heard that other children play games on computers, but the one Uncle has is different. It's for work and I'm not allowed to touch it.

I wipe the dust off the shelves and desk first before I get on with the hoovering. The hoover is heavy to drag around, and the noise hurts my head, but it doesn't take long. When I'm done I stand on the other side of Uncle's desk, next to his swivel chair. I push the button on the hoover and it turns off, the house going quiet. I should put everything back in its place and return the hoover and cloth to the cupboard, but I've never seen Uncle's desk from this angle before. There are so many drawers, the slim one at the top and then three drawers on either side of where you should put your legs. The shelves are filled with folders and books, too, but not the kind of books you read for fun. I can tell just by looking at them.

What does Uncle keep in all his drawers? I guess that his gun is in one of them, because he doesn't have it on him most of the time. But that's only one drawer, and he's got seven.

From the porch comes voices. Head has returned from wherever she's been all day. I can't imagine Uncle has apologized to her like she asked him last time, because Uncle doesn't apologize. Head must have decided to forget about it, which is what Mother should have done.

"I'm not doing anything bad," I whisper to myself as I open the top left drawer to peek inside. "Uncle won't be angry because I'm not doing anything bad and I'd never-never-never take the gun."

The drawer is empty. So is the next one, and the bottom one, and the slim one at the top won't budge. Locked. It must be where the gun is, so I ignore it and move over to the drawers on the right instead. Empty. Empty. The final drawer looks empty at first, too, but then I notice something catching the light in there. Hair. Long strands of hair, blond and brown and black, tied together with ribbons in bright colors. One of them is braided, a thin colorless braid curled like a snake on a bed of human hair.

I close the drawer. It doesn't make a sound. The voices from the porch guide me out of the office, back into the real world. I put the hoover away. The Roaring Monster. I think of Mother in the tub and Uncle's strong hand on my neck. *She made it happen herself.* Uncle smelled of peaches and Mother of rot. *She didn't want to be with us so we had to let her go.*

"Where's the kid?" Head asks from the porch. "He doesn't go off on his own, does he?"

"He's cleaning," Uncle says, Uncle with his smiley voice and a drawer full of girl hair. Mother hair. "Should be done by now. Hey," he calls, and I know he's turned his head toward the doorway. "You finished yet?"

I step out on the porch. The sunlight blinds me, and I put my hand over my eyes. Uncle is like a river in his chair, all fluid and calm, long limbs dropping to the floor like water. He's removed his shades as if the sun can't get to him, as if nothing can get to him. Head holds her thermos to her chapped lips as she watches me. Her jeans are baggy on her. Everything she wears is coated with dust, as if she spends her days somewhere where the sand whirls up around her and the desert clings to her skin.

"Uncle," I say. He frowns, so I quickly add, "I'm done now."

"Good." Uncle doesn't ask any questions. He doesn't suspect anything. "You should sort out Eleanor's room tomorrow."

Head gives me a smile, or something like it. "Oh, you don't have to do that." Looking back to Uncle she says, "He's too young to work. You know as well as I do that he should be in school." Her voice is bitey. I'm surprised she dares to talk to Uncle this way. School—Mother used to talk about school. I would like to go there, because all the children on TV do, but Uncle says that if I went to school, bad people would take me and I could never see him again.

"He's being homeschooled." Uncle slurps up the last of his iced tea without looking at either of us. "End of goddamn story. You mind your own business, Eleanor, all right? We're living a good life here. He helps out and I teach him everything he needs to know." His voice is cool even when he's angry. I can sense his anger, I can see it in the way his jaw is set, but I can't hear it. "To be honest," he continues, "I'm surprised you're telling me how to raise a kid...you of all people. Bet Charlie would've had some complaints about you, if you'd let him live long enough."

Head jumps out of her chair and drops the thermos to the floor. There's nothing running out of it, no liquid, just the clang of metal crashing into the floorboards. "Don't you dare." Her face is drained of color. "You promised you'd never judge. You promised!"

Uncle shrugs. "Be nice to me, Eleanor, and I'll be nice to you. I'll let you stay for free while you're chasing your ghosts, and I won't ask for a thing in return. But cross me, and things can get pretty fucking unpleasant for you."

I watch them like I watch the news, eyes wide open. This is much better than spying from inside the counter. I hear and see everything.

"Yes," Head says, sinking back into her chair. Her arms fall to her sides. "I know that. It's why I'm here, isn't it? The real world has spit me out and I have to stay among...my kin." She starts fidgeting with the scarf around her head, rewrapping it, tucking her hair in. Her fingers look ashen, as if they were made out of clay. "Bill used to say that if I ever got into trouble, I should go see you. Well, he wasn't wrong, I guess." She stares into her lap.

"Good old Bill!" Uncle winks at me. "He sure wasn't wrong. I said you could stay here, and I don't go back on my word. I'm not a liar."

"All those girls," Head murmurs. "It's different. It's not like the things Bill did, and not like...like what I did."

I think about the drawer. The hair. I'd like to cover my ears now. I'd like to go inside the counter and be invisible.

"You did something unforgivable, Eleanor. Poor Bill. Poor Charlie."

Head sniffles. Tears and snot drip from her face.

"No one out there wants anything to do with us," Uncle continues. "We're cursed. Or blessed, rather, because we have our freedom." He claps his hands together and starts singing some song I don't recognize, which has no other lyrics in it but the word *freedom*. Uncle has a good voice, but I don't want him to sing now.

"You could stop." Head looks at him. Her eyes are raw, everything about her is raw as if her skull and bones are shining through her skin. "Stop what you're doing and I...I won't tell anyone. Ever."

Uncle puts his hands over his knees. His fingertips are tapping, drumming madly under the table. "Eleanor," he says. "That's the one thing I told you never to ask of me, and now you have. What a shame."

Head's sunken cheeks are wet. When she opens her mouth, snot runs from her nose and down between her lips, and I want Uncle to stop it. "No," she says. "You don't mean that. Please, you know I have to be close to—I have to be where Charlie—"

"You'll be leaving in the morning," Uncle says. "That's final." He stands and she does the same, shaking just like Mother did before she went into the tub.

"But I—" Head used to be interesting but now she bores me. "But I—"

Uncle takes his empty glass and hands it to me. It's damp and sticky and almost slips out of my grip. "But I," he mimics in a silly voice. "But I, but I, but I."

Head skulks away from the porch like a wild animal, a raccoon or stray dog. She presses her bag to her flat chest as if it was a child. As soon as she's entered Room 12 and closed the door, Uncle looks down at me. He smiles.

"Eleanor is old and sick," he says. "I really don't think she should be driving around anymore. It could be dangerous."

Uncle should know, because Uncle is good with cars. He can fix cars and he can break them, and then the girls can't get away from him.

"How old was Charlie?" I ask, thinking that there was another boy living in the desert, and he could have been my friend.

"Oh, I don't know. About your age." Uncle puts his shades back on. "Would have been all grown-up by now, though, if she hadn't done what she did."

I nod. Maybe Charlie is a ghost now, and he can be my friend anyway. Maybe next time I pretend there is a telephone call, Charlie will answer.

"All right, we should get to work." Uncle walks past me, through the hallway and into his office. When he comes back he's got the gun swaying in his hand. I think about Head's grey hair and wonder if he'll bother to put it in the drawer.

She'll cry, I think as we leave the porch. The sun shines in Uncle's hair and makes my cheeks burn. *She'll cry and beg just like Mother did.*

But Uncle knows how to stop the crying. And then it will be just me and him on the porch, and our mouths will taste like peaches.

In a Mother's Eyes

Andrew Punzo

Lieutenant Colonel R. Michael Strummond regarded his grim ghost staring back at him in the windshield, and beyond its reflection the dreary setting of the farmstead. The house, paneled in unfinished wooden clapboard and crowned with a tilted weathervane, sagged into the sparse, dusty ground it squatted on. He checked the address once more even though there were no neighbors for miles about. *Teatle, Robert. 1 Wollestone Road. Neary, Kansas.*

He exhaled and stepped out of the jeep. From the outside his reflection in the glass edged closer to material than ethereal. His face was steeled, bare, unlined, and disciplined, and his crewcut saw not a single gray hair out of measure. Above his thin lips and razor nose was the only feature perpendicular to his nature and career: eyes of a soft, cloudless blue.

He told Private Fontinello to keep the engine running, straightened his already straight tie, and walked towards the house with a pressed American flag folded beneath one arm.

The weathervane creaked in the cold, arid wind while sour-smelling dust whipped over his polished shoes. The chicken wire screen door looked like a muzzle over the mouth of a dog gone mean. It wobbled flimsily when he pulled it back, and as he rapped upon the flaking whitewashed wood a feeling of sinking unease that he had learned to conceal but never conquer enveloped his gut. He hated making the call.

Hollow footsteps replaced his rhythmic knocking. There was a pause where he felt himself being examined, then a layered clacking as locks were undone. The door opened, and Mrs. Aubrey Teatle stood before him.

"Good afternoon, Mrs. Teatle," he said. "My name is Lieutenant Colonel R. Michael Strummond, United States Army. Mrs. Teatle, the Secretary of the Army regrets to inform you that your son was killed in action yesterday just outside of Baghdad." He proffered the folded flag. "He fought honorably, in service of his country and God. Please accept this as a commemoration of his sacrifice from the President of the United States."

He kept his tone even, his appearance and movements respectful yet authoritative, and watched her face closely to anticipate what would happen next. There were those who were stricken by the news, made open-mouthed and dumb as gasping fish being dry-drowned. Others laughed at what they thought was a sick joke or flew into a rage. Once, a man looked at him square, took a long pull from a bottle of cheap bourbon, and then calmly asked how much the bitch was worth dead. Before he slammed the door, he told him to mail the check and to keep his fucking flag.

But Mrs. Aubrey Teatle just stared back at him. Her eyes, black as a beetle and boring into his own, were hard and alert. A gaunt woman, she was as worn a product as the farmstead around her, so much so that she seemed begotten from it. Perhaps nothing else could grow here, perhaps her presence had sucked forth the last drops of vitality from the land. In any case, this grey-haired, rawboned old woman with lines like a dry riverbed and wire-rimmed glasses perturbed him, deeply and totally.

"Robert . . ." she said, staring into his eyes as she reached for him. She caressed his wrist and then clamped down. Lieutenant Colonel Strummond yipped like an animal caught in a trap.

"Why did you go away from *me*?"

"Mrs. Teatle!" he shouted, his voice losing its measure and becoming high and frightened.

She flinched and her grip loosened. She blinked slowly. Once, then twice. "Oh . . . you're . . . I'm—"

"I'm sorry," he said, seeing her confusion and feeling once more in control. "I know this is horrific. Perhaps I can come in to explain as much as I can."

She nodded, dazed. "Yes . . . yes, come in. That would be good for you to be with me."

He turned to Private Fontinello, who sat watching from behind the wheel of the jeep, and flashed him all ten digits. Private Fontinello nodded. He followed Mrs. Teatle inside.

The narrow hall was as unfinished and bare as the outside of the house. Mrs. Teatle looked back at him queerly and turned left through a doorway before the laminate ugliness of the kitchen. He felt a stirring of sorrow for her. Living here all alone, now a mother without a son.

He entered a small parlor. Mrs. Teatle settled into a rocking chair and took up her knitting, needles clacking together in rhythmic concert as she began to rock back and forth. He understood. Comfort in consistency, like a child sucking its thumb long after being off the breast.

He surveyed the meager room as he sat in a lumpy leather armchair across from her. The only other furnishings were a loveseat colored a hideous green, an end table with a lamp, a coffee table made of raw wooden plats, and a television stand with a bricklike cathode ray tube relic atop it. Thin, white curtains provided gauze shrouds for the watery sunlight.

"Shouldn't have left me. Shouldn't have left me at all," said Mrs. Teatle.

"I can't begin to imagine your grief," Lieutenant Colonel Strummond said. He paused. "I'm afraid there's not much more I can tell you about the circumstances. Matters of national security. But he's being flown back here as we speak, and I have the paperwork to ensure you get every benefit you're owed. You needn't worry about your finances or the funeral costs." He reached into a manila folder and pushed the papers across the slatted coffee table. "For your review."

Mrs. Teatle stared at him. "Robert . . ." she said again. Her face twisted up in a tortured state somewhere between sobbing and screaming, but her eyes maintained their glittering acuity.

He forced a cough to break the silence and turned in his chair to break her gaze. Surrounding the base of the lamp on the end table were a number of framed pictures. From where he sat, he could see the forms of a baby, a boy, a teenager, and a young man in military formalwear, his portrait upon graduation.

He also saw another picture, tucked behind the rest and turned on its wire stand so that it faced away from where Mrs. Teatle sat. It wasn't framed, and was covered in a thin layer of dust as if forgotten. It showed a sullen boy who looked much like Robert, only younger, thinner, and fixing the camera with big blue eyes that conveyed the air of dog used to being kicked down stairs and sleeping in the cold.

He gestured at the photographs. "He was a handsome boy, Mrs. Teatle. And I see he had a brother."

"What brother?"

Lieutenant Colonel Strummond frowned and rifled through his papers. He was certain he had seen it. He pulled out a sheet and squinted at the small type.

"Lawrence. Corporal Lawrence Teatle. Making you the proud mother of two servicemen, I see."

She grunted something in response. Her chin was pressed against her collarbone and she was looking down at whipcord hands that tore at a bundle of cloth with a seam ripper.

"Pardon?" he said.

"Should've been him. Should've been him instead of my Robert."

The enormity of understanding that "What brother?" was not a question at all sunk deep and slow into his stomach.

"Do a lot of needlework?" he asked in too-quick, too-high voice.

Mrs. Teatle held up a crudely knitted doll, stretching it forth with one arm and squinting. Her eye darted between it and Lieutenant Colonel Strummond. She cast aside the downy blue button eyes that she had ripped from its face and with needle and thread began to sew on large, vacuous black buttons in their place. He looked into his lap and saw the picture of Robert Teatle in his folder, a duplicate of his graduation portrait across the room. He noticed for the first time that Robert had blue eyes reminiscent of his own.

In fact, he was struck, quite suddenly, by how much the young man resembled him.

"Why did the little boy run, run, run? And what was waiting for him in the desert?" said Mrs. Teatle.

Lieutenant Colonel Strummond's chest tightened in sympathy and a pang of something more preservative. He was certain she was mentally ill, or dealing with the grief in such a bizarre manner that it replicated mental illness. He wondered about Robert and his brother, and how life for the boys must have been; with such a mother, in such a place. He looked at the pictures on the end table.

The baby picture bore a trail of large, colored, gaily dancing letters along the top of the frame that pronounced *Baby's First Birthday*. Along the bottom, in similar legend, it read: *July 24, 1990.*

Something about that. He frowned. The clacking of the knitting needles started up again, sounding like a clock tick-tocking double-time. It interfered with whatever was trying to burst out of his subconscious. He turned past the picture of the smiling young man in his folder. The knitting clacked on. Mrs. Teatle began murmuring to herself.

Something about that.

He turned again and saw it on Robert's death papers. *Date of Birth: June 24, 1988.* His eyes flitted over the page. *Enlisted: June 25, 2006.* His brain paused . . . and then clicked. The day after he turned eighteen on paper, two years and twenty-nine days before his true eighteenth birthday, Robert Teatle had joined the Army. He had joined the Army and lied about his age to do it.

Why did the little boy run, run, run?

To get away, he realized. From this desolate home. From her. And that meant the little brother, Lawrence, the one whose own mother wished he were dead, couldn't have been more than fourteen when they ran. He suddenly felt dizzy.

And what was waiting for him in the desert?

The death papers told him that too. *Killed in Action: February 9, 2007.* But what was waiting for him here?

He looked back at the baby photograph, leaning out of his chair to better view it, and stopped breathing.

The baby's eyes were black. Hollow pits surrounded by white, ragged edges of torn picture paper that had been poked through. It was the same for all stages of his life: from the baby boy to the military man, eyeless evolutions of Robert Teatle stared back at him, as if what they had seen living here was too terrible to ever see again.

He didn't realize the clacking of the knitting needles had stopped until one was already through his eye, catching his lid mid-blink so that it was pinned half-shut. He spasmed and clutched at it, feeling an immense pain like boring fire and a goopy wetness run down the right side of his face. He began to scream for help, staggering to his feet and stumbling into the end table. The pictures fell and glass shattered.

Two small, hard hands pushed him from his blind side and he fell to the floor. He scrambled for his pistol and yelped when his knuckles crunched beneath a grinding heel. Lying on his back he saw Mrs. Teatle appear from over the top of his head, upside down and howling broken words of possession, hurt, loss, and love. She raised both hands, and as the impossibly long tip of the second needle zoomed towards his open eye, Lieutenant Colonel R. Michael Strummond saw himself, small, boyish, and dying, in a mother's eyes. And then he saw no more.

Private Fontinello was loath to leave the jeep, but when twenty minutes passed and the Lieutenant Colonel hadn't emerged—a man who was *never* late—he roused himself. He took off his aviator-style sunglasses and tucked them into his breast pocket as he approached the house, squinting at it with his mild blue eyes. The chicken wire screen banged open and shut in the wind. The door beyond it was agape. He didn't like it. It looked ready to swallow him.

He entered the hallway and saw the Lieutenant Colonel's polished shoes facing toes up. A dark puddle leached between them. He stepped forward and turned the corner, finding him on the floor of a sparse parlor. The knitting needles jammed into each of his eye sockets were still attached to lengths of black yarn, lengths that ran back to two balls sitting at the feet of the old woman in her rocking chair. Her glasses, face, bosom, and hands were spattered with rust-colored stains.

Private Fontinello thought those balls of yarn looked quite a bit like eyes, still connected by the optic nerve, that had been yanked out of the Lieutenant Colonel's head.

"Well look now, Robert," she said to the corpse as she raised the pistol. "It's your little brother, come back home from the desert."

Accessory
K. N. Johnson

It was a risk, meeting with her here, now. But she couldn't say no to her. Chrissy Gage never could. She liked to think this had been her grand mistake, loving Jenny Lane, but she knew better. That her biggest mistake was ever having been born.

Chrissy killed her mother. At least, that's how her father put it. And her older brothers, Caleb and Cole, liked to put it that way, too. Mr. Gage had expected his wife to birth a third boy, another son to round out their rowdy trinity. When Christopher didn't come forth, instead a rosy baby girl who required an intensive care unit to urge the first breath from her lungs, Mr. Gage slapped his wife and refused to consider another name for the birth certificate, simply stopped writing after the 's' as if she'd been half what he'd expected from a Christopher, the boy who wasn't born. His wife had jumped from her hospital room window as Mr. Gage and the boys dined on soggy turkey manhattan in the cafeteria.

Her father raised her as he had her brothers. While one could hope this would result in an independent young woman unaware of glass ceilings, it left Chris feeling like a mannequin. Her body wasn't her own. Mr. Gage cut her hair just as he cut his boys', bought her tee shirts and jeans from the same racks. And while he didn't encourage her brothers to rope her into their roughhousing, it happened on occasion, with a sprained wrist here and a broken ankle there.

Child Services visited once, but one look at Chris's uneven, chopped locks and baggy overalls and they wrote her injuries off as an accident, a tomboy trying to keep up with her older brothers. Though the pain inflicted hadn't been intentional–had it?–she couldn't shake the shadow of fear that followed her. She crept about the house, head cast down, ears alert, a rabbit among wolves. They tracked her, their eyes leering, some unmentionable threat hovering at the edge. She skulked, afraid the next tackle or tickle would cross a reprehensible line, brand her with the shame.

By the time Chris reached her teens, she'd convinced her teachers to call her Chrissy, and the nametag she wore on her uniform at a local diner proclaimed her Chrissy, too. This emboldened her to sneak lip gloss in her jean pockets, and, by high school, to devise a plan for moving out of the house. Her family didn't have the money for college–Mr. Gage had subsumed the boys into his modest family business–but Chrissy earned good grades and aimed for a college scholarship. Somewhere miles and miles away.

And then Jenny Lane had spied her. She'd strolled across the cafeteria from the senior section to Chrissy at the quiet end of a sophomore table. She'd flung her sheet of black satin hair over her shoulder, the movement sending a set of gold bracelets sliding up her arm with the sound of tiny bells. Chrissy knew of Jenny. Chrissy had cleared Jenny's dirty dishes from diner tables more than once. Hovering over the trash, she'd scooped Jenny's uneaten biscuits from the plate to her apron pocket, brushed her lips on Jenny's glass to sip the last of milkshakes like stolen kisses of vanilla, chocolate, strawberry.

But that day, in the school cafeteria, Jenny nodded at Chrissy, looked her in the eye. "Hey, diner girl. C'mon. You're sitting with us." Chrissy had obeyed, scuttled to the table everyone knew was reserved for Jenny and her current pets. Others watched them, not with admiration, but with the wary fascination of those witnessing a spider weaving the newest catch into her web.

Jenny walked in shoes that only Jenny would consider wearing to school. She wore a silky top unlike the other girls' tee-shirts and fitted black pants that stopped above her dainty ankles. Everyone supposed her mother sent these clothes from Europe as she'd left to join an artist colony when Jenny was young and hadn't returned since. Jenny and her father lived in that five-bedroom house with the iron gates. Sometimes, one of Mr. Lane's lady friends would move in for a few months, become the headline of town gossips, and then flit away leaving Jenny and her father alone again. Jenny and her real estate father whose face plastered several billboards, benches, and brick walls through town: *Live Large with Lane!*

Jenny's smile lifted only one corner of her lips while her eyes looked through you. As if at present, you proved to be a faceless bore and she could see an improved future you. Daring and interesting.

At Jenny's table, skinny Ashley Kemp had chewed her food with precision. Twenty-eight, twenty-nine, thirty. Swallow. Something about a diet, which made anyone who listened roll their eyes, especially anyone who'd heard her retching in the girls' bathroom after she ate. She'd kept herself tiny, she insisted, to guarantee her position at the top of the cheerleading pyramid.

When Jenny had introduced Chrissy to Ashley that day, Ashley had scrunched her mouth and slumped her shoulders. Jenny had pinched Ashley's arm until she squawked, hissed in her ear. "You look like a cow." Ashley's cheeks turned pink. Jenny smiled and turned to Chrissy. "We were just talking about the missing little girl. Did you hear about it?"

Chrissy nodded. Her father had read the story aloud from the newspaper as they sat for dinner earlier that week. He'd growled, "Bet she disobeyed her dad. That was the death of her, I bet." Chrissy hadn't corrected him, hadn't pointed out the girl was the daughter of Mr. Lane's current house guest and not his own. Chrissy's arm had been bruise-free for weeks and she wanted to keep it that way.

Jenny continued. "Ashley thinks I'm mean. Don't you, Ashley?" Ashley couldn't answer, her mouth still full, still chewing. "I know it's sad that little girl is missing, but she was a real brat. They forced me to babysit her once and guess how much her mom paid me?"

Ashley gulped and blurted, "Jack shit. She paid her jack shit."

Jenny sighed. "Don't use that word, Ash. I just wish they'd find her body, so we could have the stupid funeral and get over it already."

Ashley sucked on the straw stuck in her chocolate milk carton.

"How do you know she's dead?" Chrissy asked.

"Well, she's probably dead by now." Jenny spun the bracelets on her wrist. "Probably tangled with the wrong person. The little thief. She tried to steal my bracelets, you know." She tapped at the matching bracelets on Ashley's wrist. "Isn't that right, Ash?" Ashley's face turned pink as she sucked the last of the milk and her straw crackled. Jenny turned to Chrissy. "Someone who steals like that deserves what they get, don't you think?"

Chrissy stared, thought of the times her brothers punished her for leaving her laundry in the washing machine by tossing her damp bras on the driveway, the times they'd hidden her textbooks the nights before big exams. Siblings. Thieves. Chrissy nodded. "Yeah, someone like that deserves what they get."

Jenny beamed and, before Ashley could protest, slid one of the bracelets from Ashley's wrist. She then removed one of her own and handed the two bracelets to Chrissy. "There. Now we each have two. Every girl needs an accessory. And this makes you one of us."

Chrissy thought she'd found the sisters she'd never had.

One slumber party changed everything.

* * *

Mr. Lane kissed Jenny goodnight in his usual manner, a lingering on the lips that churned Chrissy's stomach, sent Ashley to fiddle with her bracelets. "I'll be in my room if you need me," he winked. Chrissy and Ashley had wondered why he didn't leave, why he locked himself up in his room when Jenny hosted their sleepovers. They never told Jenny, but it gave them the creeps. Something in Chrissy suspected that a familiar line had been crossed in this motherless house with its fancy iron gates.

The girls assembled in the lower level with a heap of blankets and pillows. They didn't call it a basement since they could step into the backyard through a set of glass sliding doors. Some nights, they'd roast marshmallows over a campfire while other nights, Jenny would toss the photos of classmates who'd wronged her into the flames, chanting foreign words and insisting they join her in circling the fire thirteen times. "Mother wrote to me," Jenny explained. "That's how gypsies curse their enemies." Chrissy read a lot and knew this wasn't true, but she'd learned not to question Jenny last time when they'd stripped her and locked her outside. "Beg, diner girl," Jenny had taunted through the glass. "Beg and I'll let you in before my daddy catches you naked out there."

That night, Jenny lit several candles and pulled a flat wooden board from under the sofa. "Robert's suddenly acting like I don't exist." She sneered at Ashley. "Know anything about that, Ash?"

"It's not like that." Ashley squeezed her pillow to her chest. "You weren't answering his texts, so he texted me."

Behind Jenny's back, Chrissy nudged Ashley. "Anyway, we all know he'd never go for Ash when he's got you."

"That's not what I've been hearing." Jenny placed a thin wooden heart on the board, her fingertips hovering. "Let's ask the spirits." Ashley scooted closer, ready to partner with her, but Jenny swatted her hands. "No. Chrissy's doing it this time." Ashley's chin quivered as Chrissy took her place.

Jenny closed her eyes and raised her voice as if the spirits had wandered upstairs to raid the refrigerator. "Hello? Is there anyone here who wishes to communicate with us?"

The girls stared at the board, its unique three lines of ornate letters, the bat wings and pentagrams along the bottom. Even Jenny's spirit board differed from the mass produced-look of everyone else's. "Mother sent this from Russia," Jenny had said once. Chrissy knew this was absurd. A Russian spirit board wouldn't use the English alphabet, but she'd bitten her tongue, swallowed the aftertaste of her last punishment.

Beneath their fingertips, the heart moved. It inched toward Chrissy and paused. Ashley gasped. The small round window in the planchette stopped over blank space.

Chrissy studied Jenny's fingers, her face. And while her knuckles didn't appear white from applying pressure and her face offered no clue of her trickery, Chrissy knew that Jenny controlled it all. The heart, the board, the message. Chrissy lifted her fingers just enough, so Jenny could continue, could direct the final outcome. The planchette slid across the surface of the board until the small round window landed on the word *Yes*.

"Oh, it never moved like that when I did it," Ashley wailed.

"Write down the answers, silly." Jenny nodded at the pencil and pad of paper and Ashley scribbled *Yes*. Jenny raised her voice again. "And who are we speaking to?" The planchette moved. From letter to letter, it spelled: R-O-B-S-G-R-A-N-D-P-A.

Ashley finished writing and read it aloud. "Shit. It says Rob's Grandpa. He died two weeks ago. That's what he was texting you about, Jen. Shit. He wanted you to go to the funeral, but you never answered." She grimaced. "So I went."

Jenny sighed. "Don't use that word, Ash."

The candles flickered. Jenny called out, "We acknowledge you, Rob's grandpa. And what is it you wish to tell us? What message do you have for us?" She glanced at Ashley. "For Ashley?"

Ashley bit the eraser end of the pencil and her eyes widened.

Jenny's deft touch pushed the planchette across the board with Chrissy's acquiescence. H-E-L-P-R-O-B.

Ashley tried to decipher the letters she'd written. "He'll prob? He'll probably what?"

Jenny rolled her eyes. "The first word is obviously *help*."

Ashley gulped. "Help Rob? Oh my god, he needs our help?"

"How? How can we help Rob?" Jenny asked the air, then hissed at Ashley, "Get a new sheet of paper." Jenny and Chrissy's fingers trailed with the planchette: M-E-E-T R-O-B. Ashley wrote as Jenny continued. "Where should we meet him?" This message spelled *willow*. Jenny asked, "When?" and the message spelled *tonight*.

Ashley rapped the pencil on the paper. "Where's willow? Does he mean Willow Point?"

"No," Jenny snapped. "And how would you know about Willow Point? Did you and Rob go parking up there?" She shoved the planchette and board back under the sofa. "He means Willow Drive." Jenny snatched the notes from Ashley, tucked them in her pocket. "That dead end with the old house." She handed them each a flashlight and threw her cell phone on the sofa. "Phones stay here."

Chrissy frowned, hesitantly adding her phone to the pile. Jenny nudged her. "My dad could track us." Chrissy tossed her phone on the sofa.

Jenny hadn't divulged her plan to Chrissy, but she could feel a quickening in her heart, a rushing desire to please Jenny's darkest whims.

* * *

They'd passed the last inhabited neighborhood. Jenny steered onto Willow Drive where the solid asphalt road dissolved into gravel and ancient trees encroached from both sides. She drove with a peculiar urgency, knuckles white on the wheel, hitting potholes that sent the car careening. The girls braced themselves as they lurched forward, winced as they smashed into their doors. From the backseat, Ashley yelped. They'd crossed a small creek when a copse of willow trees emerged on the left, the weeping branches obscuring a farmhouse deep in the thicket. Despite the darkness, Jenny located the crumbled drive without hesitation. Instead of filling Chrissy with confidence in their mission, Jenny's familiarity with the location filled her with unease.

"I don't see Rob's car." Ashley pressed her face against the car window as Jenny parked near the front porch.

"Did you hear that, Chrissy? Ash knows what his car looks like." Jenny mimicked Ashley's voice, repeated her denial from earlier, "It's not like that." Jenny harrumphed and exited the car with her flashlight. "It must be in the back." She hopped onto the porch and sent a beam of light across the overgrown grass, over the For Sale sign (*Live Large with Lane!*), into the trees, and then into her own car. "C'mon. He must be in the house."

The wooden front door was open, so Jenny pulled on the shredded screen door and slammed it behind her.

Ashley chewed on a fingernail, held her flashlight limp at her side. "The door was already open? I-I'm not going in."

Chrissy pushed past her, held the screen door open. "You don't want to stand out here alone, do you?" Ashley glanced at the dark trees and stepped inside.

The wood floor creaked beneath their feet. They ignored the narrow staircase and wandered the first floor. Ashley bumped into an armchair and squealed. Scuffling from the back of the house stopped them in their tracks.

Ashley called out, "Rob?"

Jenny tiptoed to the end of the hall and peered around the door frame. The girls crowded at her back, breathed heavy on her neck. She beamed her light across the dusty kitchen countertops, the cabinets, and then the farmhouse sink where a set of eyes glistened. A raccoon snarled, jumped to the floor, and scampered past them and through the shreds of the screen door.

"Did you hear that?" Jenny tilted her head. Hunched in the hall, they all listened. Distant crickets, the trickling creek, their shallow breaths. She moved past the doorway and into the kitchen, tilted her head again. "That? Did you hear that?"

Chrissy bit her lip. She wasn't sure if Jenny aimed for her affirmation, a resounding *yes* despite her lack of hearing a darned thing.

Ashley shuffled closer to Jenny, closer to an interior door in the heart of the kitchen. She tilted her head, too. Her eyes widened. "Is it Rob?" She reached for the knob but pulled her hand back. "This probably goes to the basement." She shook her head. "I hate basements. Can you go first?"

Jenny shrugged. "Sure." She yanked the door wide open.

Chrissy joined them, and the trio pointed their lights down to the cracked gray concrete floor of a basement.

Ashley called Rob's name and stepped back. "There's no...there's no stairs."

"What?" Jenny's voice sounded fake. She'd known. She'd known the basement stairs were gone. "But Rob's down there. He needs you Ash. The spirits said so."

Ashley shook her head and leaned back into the door.

Jenny snapped at Chrissy. "Grab her." Without a thought, Chrissy seized Ashley's arm and pulled her back to the edge of the basement. Jenny snatched Ashley's flashlight.

Ashley tried to wriggle free, screamed *no*, screamed, "What are you doing?" She flailed her other arm, clawed her nails into Chrissy's flesh.

Jenny smiled, kicked Ashley's ankles. Eight, nine, ten. She fell to the kitchen floor wailing, crying out for her mama. Chrissy released Ashley's arm and gripped the doorknob, trying to gain distance and convert her actions to mere observance. With her foot, Jenny pushed Ashley's head, and without anything to grab in the darkness, Ashley crashed to the basement floor below.

Jenny crawled, flashed her light across Ashley Kemp, her sprawled limbs, the pool of blood behind her golden hair. A cricket chirped as Jenny and Chrissy labored to catch their breaths. Jenny broke the rhythm with a flat laugh. "Rob won't think she looks so hot now." She retreated from the doorway and waved for Chrissy to close the door.

The hinge creaked. "You think she's dead?"

Jenny crossed her arms. "If she isn't, she will be. The well's gone dry, so no one will be looking to buy this place for a long time."

Chrissy closed the door.

Jenny strode to the front porch, flashed her light across the grass, the trees, then back into the house, into Chrissy's eyes. "C'mon. You're not gonna stand there all night, are you?" When Chrissy joined her on the porch, she patted her shoulder. "Let's stop at the diner on the way home. I promised Ash I would."

* * *

Chrissy kept her promise, too, pushing the event to a corner of her mind where unmentionables were stored. But Jenny struggled with such denial, enjoyed baiting her, bringing it up in the most cursory tone while Chrissy maintained her practiced air of innocence. Over the next four years, despite the eventual distance of university campuses between them, Jenny would poke at the memory, prod for a discovery of the body. This impatience nagged at Chrissy. It glowed like a hot coal beneath a stack of straw and crumpled papers, especially because of what Jenny did in the months after they'd left Ashley in the basement of the house on Willow Drive.

Chrissy had returned home from the sleepover with a fever. Even her father noted her face appeared spotted with scarlet; her neck and chest, too. At first, she worried her illness was a manifestation of the act she'd committed. She worried she'd willed her body into illness, so she could miss school, gather her wits about her, and consider the lengths Jenny would take to protect herself. But the doctor confirmed her illness authentic. Authentic and infectious. She prescribed weeks of rest and plenty of fluids. The diagnosis kept her brothers away and her father stacking apples and water bottles at her door.

If it weren't for her homework, she'd have sworn it was a vacation.

Her diagnosis didn't keep the police away. They arrived within a week. Yes, she'd been at the sleepover. Yes, Ashley was there. But. The sleepover was her cover. Ashley snuck out to meet up with her new boyfriend. Rob. No, we haven't heard from her. Chrissy coughed after each answer, sipped her water.

The police nodded and left, continued their search for the missing cheerleader. She was certain her answers matched Jenny's. They'd practiced that night at the diner, shared a chocolate milkshake. Promised not to text or talk about it on the phone.

They'd shared a milkshake. Chrissy distinctly remembered Jenny pushing the glass to Chrissy. "You finish it. I'm stuffed." Chrissy hadn't thought twice about it then, but now that she was sick in bed, she wondered. She wondered if Jenny had tried to get rid of her, too.

* * *

Chrissy finally returned to school. Her bubble of giddiness grew as she looked forward to seeing Jenny and sitting at their round table again. She bounced into the building, her bracelets jingling through the busy lobby, past lockers. But Ashley kept poking holes in her happy bubble. Ashley's face hounded her from posters plastered on wall after wall. *Missing. If you have any information...* Classmates peered at her over their shoulders, some turning away, some offering a wave, their mouths drooped with sadness. She hadn't sensed it right away, but the air was heavy with questions, thick with mistrust. Chrissy wiped the grin from her face, slumped her shoulders for the remainder of her morning classes. After all, she'd been a friend of the missing girl.

In the cafeteria, Chrissy stopped in her tracks. Jenny sat in her usual spot at the round table. Her black hair shimmered under the glaring lights. She stretched her long legs, crossed her ankles, a pair of cosmopolitan wedge heels on her feet. She reached her hand out, patted the arm of a girl sitting next to Ashley's empty seat. A cheerleader. She'd been close friends with Ashley before Jenny had reeled her into her circle.

"Chrissy," Jenny called to her, and in a series of effortless movements, fluttered Chrissy into a light embrace then into her seat at the table. "Chrissy, you know Erica, right?" Jenny lifted Chrissy's hair from her shoulder. "It's longer. It looks good on you."

Chrissy tried to smile.

Erica misread Chrissy's face and reached across the table with a tissue. "Don't worry. We're going to find her soon."

Chrissy stared at the bracelets on Erica's wrist. Bracelets that matched hers and Jenny's. She dabbed at her eyes.

Jenny slid her own lunch tray in front of Chrissy. "Here. The pasta's your favorite." Chrissy pushed the food with a fork but didn't eat. Jenny continued. "Erica's organizing a search. The cops haven't found a thing, so a bunch of students are going to look for her. And while we're at it, we're going to look for that missing little girl, too."

Chrissy dropped the fork.

* * *

The gymnasium filled with students and parents volunteering for the search. It was the weekend before Thanksgiving break and Chrissy supposed the season triggered people's humanitarian side, a drive to help or at least revel in their position of safety, unscathed by injustice or tragedy. Jenny made sure they were assigned the search of Willow Drive. "It's my dad's listing. It only makes sense."

Mr. Lane drove the girls in his SUV. The rugged tires skimmed over the potholes as if the vehicle was an extension of the Lane family: immune to life's difficulties, impervious to pain. Ahead, the weathered house peeked through the dead branches of the willow grove. Jenny nibbled on a croissant and sipped her strawberry milkshake.

Erica tapped on her phone then poked her head between the front seats. "Trina says they're checking the park. She says this house is haunted. Is it haunted?"

Mr. Lane laughed. "It's not haunted. But I will tell you, it *is* cursed." Chrissy held her breath, looked in the rearview mirror to discover Mr. Lane studying her. He smiled and launched into a story. "Yeah, the family left years ago. First, the main well went dry. Then they dug another. That one went dry in a week. Then they had one of those dowsing rod guys come up here. He walked around with those two sticks. Swore he'd find a spring. Said the willow trees guaranteed it. Finally, those sticks pointed to a spot and they dug and dug. Nothing."

Erica scrunched her face. "But we just drove over a little creek."

"Doesn't matter. You can have a creek, doesn't mean you'll have groundwater." Mr. Lane parked near the front porch.

Chrissy wiped her sweaty palms on the thighs of her blue jeans. Her mind raced, considered the possibility that Jenny had told her father everything, that he knew, that he was just like her.

Mr. Lane zipped his jacket. "I'll search out here. You girls check the house. But listen," he pointed at them, looking each girl in the eye, "do not open the basement door. The stairs rotted out and haven't been replaced." When no one responded, he asked, "Got me? I'm serious. You'll break your neck." They all nodded, so he walked away from the vehicle, ambled toward the willow grove, calling out the names of the dead. "Rose? Ashley?"

Jenny carried her croissant and coffee into the house. She took a bite then nudged Chrissy and counted each chew, "One, two, three…" Chrissy didn't laugh and instead pushed her shoulder and followed Erica.

Erica stood in the kitchen with her hand cupped over her nose and mouth. "It smells disgusting in here." With her other hand, she reached for the basement door. "Is this the basement?"

Before she turned the knob, Chrissy smacked her hand. "Didn't you hear, Mr. Lane?"

"I wasn't going down there." She rubbed her hand. "I was just going to look." Erica walked to the green refrigerator in the corner. "This place is a death trap."

Jenny and Chrissy glanced at each other.

Erica wrenched at the refrigerator door but couldn't open it. "Haven't you heard about little kids climbing into old 'fridges and dying? The doors seal shut, and they suffocate to death." Erica yanked at the door handle, but it didn't budge.

Jenny pushed her aside. "You seriously think we should check in here?"

Erica nodded and protected her nose and mouth from the stench again.

Chrissy joined Jenny and together they tugged on the refrigerator handle. They grunted and pulled, rocking the unit from back to front until it lurched, tilted forward so far it fell towards them. Erica screamed as the girls jumped clear and the refrigerator crashed to the floor. They choked on billowing dust and fled for the front porch where they shook dust from their hair, brushed it from their sleeves and jeans.

Mr. Lane approached. "Nothing here."

Jenny coughed, spat dust onto the yellowed grass as ladylike as she could have mustered. "Nothing in here either. Let's stop at the diner again. I promised we would."

Chrissy took a deep breath of the crisp fall air, tried to clear her nostrils of what could only be the scent of death.

* * *

Jenny didn't seem to grasp the meaning of keeping a secret. Keeping. The keeping of a secret as an ongoing act of suppressing information in its every possible form of escape: body language, word choice, vocal tone. It's an action that requires energy and strength. It wasn't an art, a pretty performance of beguilement. It was work. Something Jenny knew nothing about.

Through the winter months, fresh posters of the missing girls appeared taped on school halls, stapled to utility poles, pinned to the corkboard in the local grocery store. Chrissy passed their faces on the diner window as she tied on her apron for her weeknight shifts. Each time, she heard Ashley cry for her mama. One night, Jenny sat in Chrissy's section, ordered a mint milkshake in honor of St. Patrick's Day and whispered, "I'm going to the cops."

Chrissy froze for a moment, bent over the table to wipe it with a damp rag and turned to face her. Jenny smelled of roses and, this close, her skin remained flawless, her lashes long and teasing as she blinked. Her lip gloss shimmered under the diner lights. "Don't look at me like that, Chrissy. I just wish they'd find her body, so we could have the stupid funeral and get over it already."

Though Jenny didn't waltz into the police station, her behavior at the candlelight vigil steamed Chrissy enough that she wondered if their small town could handle a third missing girl in less than a year.

That evening, the local park freckled with points of light as people held tiny candles, read scriptures, recited prayers. When someone rallied the crowd into a hymn, Jenny wept. Tears trickled down her cheeks. But to think these tears were real would be to not know Jenny. Pleased with her production and not wanting to waste the spectacle, Jenny strode to the police officer. Chrissy tried to grab her but trailed behind, only reaching them as Jenny pulled a folded piece of paper from her pocket and handed it to him.

He unfolded it, stretched it between his stubby thumb and two fingers. The note from the night they played the spirit board with Ashley. Ash's uneven letters: *Meet Rob. Willow. Tonight.*

The officer raised his eyebrows. "She was only using your sleepover as a cover, huh? Sneaking out to meet with her boyfriend, I see." He refolded the note and tucked it in his breast pocket. "Thanks for bringing it forward. We'll look into it." He nodded and retreated to his squad car parked at the curb.

Jenny glowed when she heard the police called Rob in for questioning but seethed when it resulted in nothing more but another search of Willow Point. "They're as dumb as Ash."

With graduation looming, Jenny insisted Chrissy sleep over one last time. She lit candles and Chrissy shook her head. "Uh, no. You're not pulling that spirit board shit on me."

Jenny laughed. "Don't use that word, Chrissy." She blew out the match and sulfur clouded the space between them. "We're making a blood oath. A promise to keep our secret." Jenny held a small knife in the candlelight, turned the blade so the metal flashed. "Mother bought it from a witch."

Jenny. Thinking a secret could be kept with a magic trick, with droplets of blood. Chrissy didn't point out they'd already shed blood together. A pool of it.

Jenny pricked their fingers and they pressed them together as she chanted, "With this blood, we bind our secret. At risk of death that we must keep it."

Something inside Chrissy shattered. Like the glass bird she'd stolen from a local shop as a child. It had enchanted her. The delicate crystal beak, the creases in its feathered tail. In her backyard, she'd spun in circles, holding it high to catch sunbeams, imagining herself nestled on its back, flying to places unknown. The bird was perfect. It was beautiful. She believed. Believed so much that she climbed from her bedroom window to the roof of their front porch to watch the bird fly. But the chunk of glass dropped like a rock to the pavement below, burst into bits of jagged light.

Jenny wasn't sophisticated. She was silly. And silly girls don't keep secrets. At least not for long.

* * *

In the years after Jenny's departure, Chrissy kept busy. She left the diner when Mr. Lane hired her to work in his real estate office. "Jenny won't be coming home for summer break," he'd said each summer since Jenny had left. Chrissy saved enough to buy an old car, earned the scholarship to the out-of-state school and left baggy overalled-Chrissy far behind.

But Jenny's silence made her nervous. If she wasn't talking to Chrissy, who was she talking to? The police never found Ashley's body and they'd likely never find her bones. Willow Drive was dead to their old town. A corpse because of the dry wells. Something everyone hoped to God wouldn't happen to them; something they trusted that if they ignored it, it would keep the curse away. Demolition seemed to be the next step. Would Jenny let that happen without a hitch?

And then Chrissy got the call. Jenny wanted to meet up, talk about old times. The request played a familiar note in Chrissy, something made her want to sing, but she remained calm, invited Jenny to meet here, now.

Chrissy rearranged the salt and pepper, the sugar dispenser, the hot sauce, and catsup bottles. The parking lot remained empty. She looked up the street, past the abandoned factory, the junkyard, the lots of gravel and crabgrass, and forced herself to sit back down on the cracked vinyl seat. A closed metal panel blocked the pass-through between the diner's kitchen and counter, but the steady rattle of silverware and cookware clanged, an exhaust fan hummed.

Jenny arrived. The bell rang on the door and she sauntered to Chrissy's table, her heels clicking on the worn linoleum floor. "Well, this place is dead, isn't it?"

Chrissy hopped up and two bracelets, her first gift from Jenny, jingled. Her heart raced, and her tongue tied.

Jenny dropped her purse on the booth seat. She shook her arm in the air. She, too, still wore the bracelets. Her long black hair swept over Chrissy's shoulder as she wrapped her in a hug. "Not like the diner back home. Are they even open?"

Jenny slid next to her purse, but Chrissy remained standing, fighting to find her voice. "The owner said this is their slow day. The server didn't even show up for work." Chrissy pulled an apron from her seat and tied it around her waist. "He was going to close up, but said he'd stay open just for us if I fetched our food."

"Aren't you bright-eyed and bushy-tailed?"

Chrissy grimaced at the cliché, Jenny's lack of original thought. Her lack of noticing Chrissy's extra effort to style her hair and make-up. Just a crystal bird, she told herself. Just a crystal bird. She pretended to write on an invisible notepad. "Your usual?"

Jenny laughed. "What, a milkshake? No, no. I'll take a coffee. Plenty of cream, slightly warmed."

Chrissy nodded, disappeared behind a swinging door with a small round window, and emerged balancing a brimming cup of coffee on a saucer in one hand and a stainless-steel carafe of creamer in the other.

"So, this is close to your campus?" Jenny blew across the top of her coffee and reached for the bowl of sugar substitute packets.

"No. I mean, it's not too far. This was a good halfway spot."

Jenny stirred the warm cream into her coffee with a spoon. She raised one eyebrow. "Aren't you having anything?"

Chrissy retreated to the kitchen and returned with another cup of coffee. She trembled as she poured sugar into her cup, scattering white granules across the table. With the side of her hand, she swept them over the edge and onto the floor.

Silverware clattered in the kitchen. "Did you order something? He's making a lot of noise for no cooking."

Chrissy blinked her eyes and pressed her fingers on the table. "Yes. Yes, I ordered an omelet. Would you like one, too?"

Jenny shook her head, sipped her coffee. "You know why I wanted to meet, right? Memory lane is fun, but we need to talk about Willow Drive."

"We made a blood oath."

Jenny tilted her head, narrowed her eyes. "If the house is demolished, they'll never find her bones. They'll never blame Rob."

A steady hum accompanied the rhythmic clatter in the kitchen. Spoons and forks, the knock of a pot, a dish. Chrissy tapped her cup, the pads of her fingers drumming without sound.

Jenny raised her chin. "They think she ran away. She wasn't smart enough to know how to run away." She rolled her eyes. "They need to know it was someone. Someone else who saw her for what she was. A cheat. A thief. And that someone did what needed to be done."

"It was our secret."

Jenny reached across the table and squeezed Chrissy's hand. Chrissy pulled her hand loose and sighed. Something crashed in the kitchen. "It's an omelet. What the heck is he doing in there?" Jenny stood up and clicked her heels across the floor to the swinging door. Chrissy rushed behind her.

"Hello? Hello?" Jenny strode past a blender, a small coffeemaker, a microwave. A timer beeped and Jenny opened the microwave door. An omelet steamed on a plate.

Jenny frowned, ran her hand along the edge of the dusty countertop. She stepped across the mud-streaked floor, stepped over a cardboard box stocked with a syrup bottle, a box of pancake mix, pouches of milkshake powder. Vanilla, strawberry, chocolate. Over a large steel sink and across a cobwebbed window, a string stretched from cabinet to cabinet with silverware, coffee cups and a small pan dangling from knots like laundry hung to dry. To her right, a small fan whirled, sending the pieces clanking, knocking. Jenny's eyes widened, and outside the window, the engine of a generator grumbled.

Glass shattered into Jenny's skull, pieces matted in her hair, trickled into the sink. She screamed, stumbled and turned.

Chrissy gripped the handle of a broken coffee carafe. Jenny didn't look through her as if she was a faceless bore. Her eyes glistened, seeing Chrissy for the Chrissy she'd always been.

Chrissy tossed the carafe aside and dragged Jenny to a door. She flung it open, sweat on her upper lip as her plan climaxed. She'd driven past this diner for months, remembering her first job, the first time she served Jenny. Abandoned. Left to rot because the factory had closed, the workers moved on. Borrowing the generator from her father had been easy. She just didn't ask. Cleaning the dining room had only taken a day but dismantling the basement steps had taken an entire week. Splinters still ached her hands from shoving the pieces out the small basement window, bruises still blue from climbing out, removing her ladder through that same window. And now it waited, dark and gaping, to receive what had been promised.

Blood dripped through Jenny's hair, down her face. She wobbled in her shoes as Chrissy wrenched her to the door's threshold. Jenny patted her own head, scowled at the blood in her hand and grabbed the door frame. Her voice rasped. "Chrissy? What are you doing?" She twisted in Chrissy's grip.

Chrissy smiled, kicked Jenny's ankles. One, two. Jenny's back collapsed on the ledge and, with a scream, she plummeted to the basement floor below.

Chrissy peered into the dim light where Jenny Lane's body lay face down, a pool of blood growing beneath her head of raven black hair. Chrissy slid the bracelets from her arm, gave them a jingle, and tossed them onto Jenny.

Chrissy caught her breath and straightened her back. She untied the apron and held it in the air. Not a drop of blood. Clean and fresh as damp laundry strewn across a sidewalk because her brothers wanted the washing machine. She wadded it into a ball and shoved it in the box of supplies.

"Why are your clothes out here?"

Chrissy had recognized the little girl. Knew she lived with Jenny Lane. And while she wasn't Jenny's sister, surely the loss of Rose would break her heart? Jenny would cry over a milkshake in the diner, seek Chrissy's company. Jenny would need her, want her.

Chrissy had squeezed the damp bundle of clothes in her arms. Her father, her brothers weren't home. They'd be gone for hours. "Do you like ice cream, little girl?"

The girl's face lit up. "Oh, yes, I love ice cream."

And she'd followed Chrissy into the house. Just like that.

Chrissy looked around the diner kitchen, gazed at all of her careful preparations. No, she decided. This had been nothing like killing that little girl.

The Wolf Gang
Barrie Darke

Sending out for pizzas didn't help them much. All that grease slicking up their bellies couldn't stop the momentous loss of Zen when word came from the Portsmouth office that the branding still wasn't quite "present." The hour was closer to eleven than it was ten, but they hunched over their devices once more.

Greg was flailing the hardest of all; he knew this was plain to everyone, knew he was scant minutes away from being muttered about now and reported about tomorrow. His performance was normally somewhere above average, he had reason to believe, but this crisis had coincided with long-arranged renovations to his house, and he hadn't slept worth a damn for the last three nights. It wasn't the boxed uproar—bad as that was—it was the dust in the air. It altered the atmosphere for sleeping in subtle but charged ways. He would say this to anyone prepared to listen.

At one o'clock, everyone having given up and taken to staring out at the mournful lights of the city, it was decided they could go home. This team had winged twenty percent of their pitch with satisfactory results before this, and if they had to do it again, so be it.

Greg sat back in his chair while the others stretched and slipped on their jackets. Some frowned at him.

"I might as well stay here," he said. "It's the dust at home, it's murder."

Most grunted and carried on collecting their things, but Al wasn't sure. "The air in here isn't exactly blowing through a Swiss mountain range," he said. "And the cleaners'll be in soon."

"I…yeah." Greg hadn't reckoned with the cleaners. He put his head back and shook it at the same time.

"It's fine. You could stay at mine," Al said.

Greg squinted at him blearily.

"It's no problem. I'm closest. And our couch turns into the plushest sofa bed you've ever encountered. It's impossible—*impossible*— not to succumb to a deep, replenishing sleep on that thing."

Greg knew he was in no position to turn this down. Within minutes he was ducking into Al's car and forgetting to fasten his seatbelt till something beeped.

"It'll be good, actually," Al said. "You'll get to meet the family properly."

"That'll be great," Greg said. Al was known to talk in detail about his family, though he was by no means the worst offender when it came to that. Greg had seen his wife, with the funny name, at some social evening or other. A Nordic type to look at, though she was from Scotland originally. She had been friendly enough with him, in a brisk way. There was also a young son.

"We call ourselves the Wolf Gang," Al said.

"Right, yeah." Greg had heard this before. He supposed he hated it a little, but it wasn't that important.

"It's a play on Mozart, I think."

"Ah, yeah, I get it, I get it."

"Minty's a fan. If classical music has fans, as such. Sounds wrong, doesn't it? *I'm a big Beethoven fan.*"

"Yep. Does."

Inside, Al switched on a single lamp and offered Greg a nightcap. Greg could've done without it, but Al was already uncapping a bottle of whisky, so yeah, why not.

It was while Al was pouring them that Greg saw something a bit off. Or thought he did—the light from the lamp was soft, and there wasn't time for sufficient scrutiny before Al was turning and handing him his glass.

They collapsed in the deep armchairs, ties unloosened, top shirt buttons undone. They talked through the arbitrary, indeed punitive, nature of the Portsmouth office and the fallibilities of others in their team. Greg made an effort to keep up, but he really wanted to have a look at what he thought he'd seen, and not being able to was proving a whole other distraction. On the other hand, it left him more alert than he'd felt in over fifty hours.

Al finished his drink at last, tapping the glass against his lip while he contemplated another. Greg silently willed him not to, and Al, in the end, didn't. He stood, put his hands on his hips, and contemplated the couch. It obviously could be opened with a single flick of something, if only he could remember how.

Greg went to the bathroom, where there was nothing wayward to be seen, he made sure. He rubbed his eyes so they were definitely functioning correctly.

Back downstairs, Al had stretched out a bedsheet and was shaking a quilt. When he said goodnight and left the room, Greg sat still for a couple of minutes. It was possible Al had forgotten something and would come back for it. When it didn't look like he would, Greg eased himself up slowly.

It was the pictures—the framed photos around the place, on the mantelpiece and bookshelves. He went to the one he had spotted first, and it was as he had thought. Minty, screaming at the camera, and not in delight. She looked furious, transported with rage. She even had that heat flush some people got on their necks at the height of upset emotion. In another she was crying, her long blonde hair a tangled mess and a tissue pressed to her nose. This was a very well-composed black and white portrait, her cheekbones showing up dramatically beneath the puffy eyes looking sullenly into the lens. On the windowsill, there was one of her looking dazed and queasy, leaning against the wall outside near the front door, eyes half shut, mouth open as if she was trying to draw in enough air so as not to be sick on the path.

The shots of Al were of equal interest to him. In the first Greg came across, he had his back turned to the camera and was making a "wanker" gesture over his shoulder. There was a huge sweat patch down his shirt. On the far-left side of the mantelpiece there was one of him mid-spit, spraying and scowling like a footballer with the decision against him. That had been taken in the kitchen. In a third, he was scrunching his face while sticking his little finger in his ear, bedeviled with itchy wax.

On the bookcase, before an exemplary row of modern American novels, there was a display of Al and Minty arguing. She had reached out and pincered his face around the mouth, as if to stop his asinine yap. He was leaning back to get away from her, his hands raised but in a placating manner, as if to say, *I'm not going to use force back on you.* This was in their flower-sprung garden on a bright day.

Their young son, Phil, perhaps six or seven, did not go unrepresented. Here he was, wearing a t-shirt with *AWW GO FUCK A DUCK* printed on the front in a crescent above a cartoon duck flicking the v's. Phil was laughing hard at something and pulling the t-shirt down so it could be read easily. In another, he was kicking a cat, its body twisted and its mouth open; Al had never mentioned a cat or any pets as far as Greg knew. Pride of place in the middle of the mantelpiece, there was an image of Phil smiling with bloodied teeth.

Greg slowly went back to the first one, good old Minty screaming, and looked at them all in turn again. He was scratching at the back of his head. He thought about taking one—Al spitting jumped out the most, for whatever Rorschach-y reason—and calling a cab for home, thinking he could now very happily endure a spot of dust. He got so far as taking out his phone before telling himself not to be so stupid. It was a little after two. He could have about five hours of sleep, as long as he blotted everything out of his mind. The pitch was the important thing. This was just…something they did as a family. All families had their moments.

He slid under the quilt, but after a minute slid out again. He turned all the pictures so they were facing the other way.

Even then, sleep wouldn't come. Every creak in the house was Al slinking down with his phone, or perhaps a real camera around his neck. Perhaps there were hidden night eyes recording him in the hope he would wake up bellowing from a bad dream. The thought of the pictures they didn't have on display, of those they had in their bedroom, under the bed, filled his mind with terrors for twenty minutes.

Eventually he dozed, and it didn't seem long before doors opening and taps gushing upstairs woke him. It was minutes before seven. He wasn't sure he felt any better, and wasn't sure the bed had lived up to its billing, but soon there was a hand on the door handle. "You decent in there?" Al called.

"I am," he replied.

He had a shower. Soaping his armpits, he wondered how the photos would look in the natural light of morning, and in so wondering he remembered he'd forgotten to turn them round again. His arms dropped. He considered making it such a long shower that they would have to head immediately for the office when he went down, but the hot water woke him up, brought him back to himself a little. It was done now, and leaving straight away would be the coward's way out.

The whole Wolf Gang was there. Minty gave him a sparkling hello, and the boy Phil even waved, following a slight prompt from Al. Greg waved back. Minty, her hair tied back, wrapped in the softest-looking dressing gown Greg had ever seen, bustled about, giving Al orders concerning the breakfast. It was as good as ready.

The pictures were facing the right way once more. Greg sat opposite Phil, who was playing with a superhero action figure. It was Thor. When Minty told him to put it down, he did so without too much demur.

They ate a breakfast of oatmeal followed by eggs followed by yogurt, with many refills of orange juice and coffee. Not the sort of thing Greg would have bothered with himself, but he enjoyed it, he couldn't say otherwise. Minty made polite-but-rote inquiries about the testing day ahead of them, no doubt having heard about it endlessly already, and Greg said as much as he thought her interest could bear. His thoughts were much on cowardice again.

Towards the end of his yogurt he said, "So, I noticed your pictures. Wow. I mean, they're quite something."

Minty was sipping from her mug of coffee when he said this. She put it down slowly, her eyes steady on him.

"Very original approach, very," Greg went on. "Whose idea were they?"

He felt a mild impact on his knee and Phil laughed. He presumed the boy had kicked him under the table.

Minty held her stare. He could swear the blue of her eyes was icing over.

"I hope we've got our act together today," Al said. "I'd quite like to not—"

"Who took that one of you both arguing? Was it you, Phil?"

Phil laughed with his head back and kicked him again. That was the only answer he received.

"Are you still taking them that way?" he tried. "Any ideas for new ones in the works?"

Minty slowly turned her cup this way and that. Al picked up the remote and turned on the TV.

"I might get some of my own done like that. Punching a window through, that would be a good one."

The TV came on to a news channel, people talking about an election in Canada.

"Having a bad acid trip as well, if it would show up so people knew what it was."

Al put his finger on the volume button and held it down.

"Cutting off a TOE, MAYBE," Greg said, his voice raising but still drowned out.

He finished the rest of his yogurt and drained his coffee while the TV roared and distorted; he didn't ask for anything else. Phil didn't kick him again, but Minty was still watching, and carried on watching until he stood up and started pulling on his suit jacket. Then she began to clear the table, while Al switched off the TV and Phil retrieved Thor.

Neither Minty nor Phil replied when Greg said goodbye. He thought about cupping his hands around his mouth and shrieking it as loud as he could, but by then Al was at the door. "We ready?" he asked.

"We are," Greg said.

Al was perfectly normal with him in the car, talking over their approach for the day all the way into the office. But after the pitch—which was diabolical and swiftly led to the break-up of their team—he never spoke to Greg again.

His Death Brings No Respite
Thomas Kearnes

Bishop Medical resembles a big beige cereal box. Sunlight hits the building at a slant. The main entrance, its row of moving glass doors, buzzes in shadow. Would-be patients rush inside on two feet, but the discharged creep out in wheelchairs. Some won't survive. That's the nature of a hospital: no one can guarantee escape. I'm reasonably sure, myself, entering, I will be lucky. Bishop Medical will not claim me today.

I drove two hundred miles to see him. Two hundred miles to watch him wither. Two hundred miles to bid him good night. Stomach cancer. Terminal.

He's not dead yet.

There is time. There is this afternoon. There is the matter dangling from the tiny canister on my keychain. There is the box cutter snug and secure in my pocket.

He told me his room number when I called from the interstate. *I look really different*, he warned. I kept tabs on his Facebook page. It's how I knew he was in the hospital. We aren't friends, but he agreed to a visit. I was halfway to Dallas before I called. I was stunned to learn that he must have, at some point, unblocked me.

I approach the help desk. *Caden Quaid*, I tell the lady. I tell her I'm visiting. I'm an old friend.

It's been a while since I've stepped inside a hospital. Dell didn't need a hospital. When the ambulance ferried him away, the driver didn't engage his siren. No need for flashing lights. It was too late for Dell O'Dowd.

Getting that apartment in Houston suddenly seemed deeply naïve.

The oblivious old woman behind the desk gives me the information I already possess. I never have problems accessing the forbidden. I appear meek and pleasant. Strangers often strike up conversations. No one considers me a threat. No one bothers to speculate the damage I might do.

I don't expect Caden to be alone. In almost all the Facebook photos of his quickly dwindling frame, his best friend poses beside him. Ken is balls-out queer, one of those middle-aged gym rats so common in gay circles: the two-day scruff, biceps showcased beneath short sleeves, shirttail tucked to leave no doubt his waist is trim. I'd let Ken fuck me on one condition: photographic evidence for Caden. I'd savor his reaction to me pissing on his favorite hydrant.

The elevator deposits me on the fifth floor. Going up, an old man, scabs covering his bald head, attempts conversation. When I make no reply, the chunky woman behind me volunteers. I am not being cruel, simply too focused on the box cutter tucked in my jeans. My timing has to be precise. Walking the fifth floor, browsing room numbers until I spy 534, I rehearse in my mind the moment I'll press the blade against Caden's throat.

"Knock, knock."

My Converses squeak as I enter the room. It's bigger than I expected, private: the walls and linoleum floor are each the same soothing gray. The stiff cream-colored curtain is drawn back, but the sun nears the opposite horizon. Caden must enjoy the dawn each day. At rehab, he was always up before sunrise, crossing the courtyard while I had my nightcap cigarette.

"I knew you'd come." There's a slight tremor to his voice, but it brims still with mischief. "I told Ken—I said, *Don't worry, Avery will absolutely be here.*"

"And on time, too." I smile.

The clock's minute hand stands a few ticks shy of twelve.

Caden laughs. The sound dies in his throat. "Actually, a little early."

He's a neglected prune, the last in the box. Were we not acquainted, I'd peg his age at sixty, maybe even sixty-five. In truth, he hovers well within his mid-forties. His face, once round and plump, has collapsed. Sunken cheeks and eyes, his hair now gray and perilously thin. Stringy tendons articulate themselves down his neck. I make a point of landscaping that throat. He was once overweight—not much, and the extra pounds perched agreeably atop his hips. Now he might top out at 130 pounds, that sparse mass stretched over his six-foot frame. His arms and legs shed all their meat—they're sticks, twigs, the brittle kindling used to nurse a new flame.

He's not dead yet.

The box cutter, still in pocket, presses against my thigh. I carried my keys loose while searching for his room. It's an old habit. I like the dull jingle. But I don't want him to make note of the tiny canister dangling from the keyring. At rehab, I once mentioned it's where I kept my tweak. It was a precaution, jamming my keys into my other pocket just before I entered his room.

Ken glares at me. I respect his frank disapproval. I'll soon confirm his worst suspicions.

"When did you finally get clean?"

"Caden says you're in recovery yourself."

"And gratefully so. How long, Avery?"

He's a tenacious muscle mutt. During that exchange, Caden has eased himself from bed into his wheelchair. An IV pole stands at the ready, but no tube connects the hanging bag of solution to his arm. Will he soon be released? No one wants to die in a hospital, though that's often the point. Had I waited just one day more, I might've missed him. Caden groans as he settles into the chair.

Ken rests his elbows atop the bed's metal rail, arms folded. He can foil my little plan, insist I conduct my visit under his eye. Caden is in no position to protest—assuming he would.

"About eight months," I make sure Ken knows it means nothing to me. "Give or take."

"You don't know your sober date?"

"Careful there, Caden. You can't be king without a throne." I cross the room. He smiles and weakly raises an open hand. I reach for his shoulder, but my hand retreats to my side. I'll need to do more than touch him, soon, but not this moment. "What does it matter if I stayed clean last summer?" I counter. "I stayed clean today."

Caden's friend grunts. "He said you were a pragmatist."

I laugh. "Caden doesn't know that word."

Stricken, Ken's eyes pop.

Caden bats my hip, laughing himself. "Still a snob, aren't you, asswipe?"

"Still a philistine, huh, Prom King?"

Back at rehab, Dell and I liked to peer over the balcony as Caden sauntered across the courtyard. So confident, so satisfied with himself. His steps fell upon the grass like kisses, he blessed with a smile all who passed. *He's scrumptious*, I muttered. *I wanna suck his dick*, Dell replied. It always came down to sex for him, that dear man. I smirked. All hail the Prom King, I proclaimed. The birds sang of love. The mosquitoes hunted flesh.

Caden and I laugh. I push his wheelchair toward the doorway. Visitors and nurses skitter up and down the hall. Over the loudspeaker, a doctor named Killingsworth receives marching orders: *Trauma Room Three, STAT.*

"I'm gonna jump in the shower after this show ends," Ken declares. Glancing over my shoulder, I catch him reclining upon Caden's unmade bed. The intimacy of this transition both sickens and stirs me. "Back in thirty?"

Caden gives the affirmative. Thirty minutes, I think. Should be enough time. I imagine the click as the box cutter's blade snaps into place. The hall teems with fated life. It will soon be Thanksgiving. I know this because turkeys and pilgrims cut from construction paper loiter upon the corridor walls. I'm waiting for Caden to resume the conversation.

His wheels on his chair smack upon the sticky linoleum, sounding like a hungry child's lips. My Converses squeak. We exist, Caden Quaid and I. Our tired, mundane noises fill this tired, mundane world. It doesn't register with me that I've slipped my keys from my pocket, not 'til I hear their jangle. That tiny metal canister complicates the melody.

"I wanted to wait until…" His breath leaves him. He hasn't craned his neck to look back. His bony shoulders hitch as he inhales. "Ken doesn't need to hear this."

"It's just us now, Caden. Prom King and the Geek."

"I'm serious, Avery."

We've lost velocity. I'm looking for an empty room. A room-number placard denied cut-out Turkey Day tokens. An agreeable male nurse passes us, scrubs a bit too snug, haircut a bit too precise. This time, Caden does turn his head. At least until it snaps back, accompanied by a wince.

I smirk. "He's far too young for us. For *you.*" I don't break stride. I don't turn to linger on the twitch of his ass as he hurries past. Dell has been gone eight months. I've toured a few bedrooms since his broken heart ceased its beat, but these trysts soothe nothing, solve nothing. I fuck men for the same reason dogs bark—and have just as little to show for it.

The box cutter lies in wait. I've never before threatened a man's life.

"I meant to call you. After you…after *we* lost Dell. I meant to, I swear." He gasps. I'm not sure how to interpret this candor. "I unblocked your number. I don't know what stopped me." He turns back, twists his face toward mine. His hazel eyes have lost none of their salesman shimmer. "Why didn't you call me?"

Because I imagined every explanation you might offer, and each only nursed my rage. It did not abate. I did not acquit you. I say none of these things.

"You blocked me after our last fight," I remind him. "Right before his overdose. I had to message Ken on fucking Facebook."

"You never tried me."

"You wouldn't have liked what I said."

Caden chuckles. I can't see his expression, but hear the weak, low sound. "I would've listened. I needed to talk, too."

Room 517! No Thanksgiving kitsch! No placard stamped with a patient's name! Waning afternoon sun fills the room. I swivel Caden's chair a neat ninety degrees. So excited to spring my trap! I lost all hope of an afterlife after turning five, but I can't help—almost forty years later—indulging juvenile fantasies of Dell. He might spy me from the heavens, overjoyed to know vengeance may travel slowly, but it does make the station. I nudge the door shut with my foot.

"If you wanted somewhere private…" He takes a breath, loses it before it can fill his lungs. He takes another. "There's a solarium on the first floor."

"I dare you to define that word." I've stopped pretending we're friends, and so has my voice.

He turns back. Fear pulses across his gaze. "What do you want, Avery?" I wish he'd *yield* to me: hands held aloft to protect his face, a quaking voice, maybe even a startled cry. I must proceed. No doubt Ken counts the minutes.

He's not dead yet.

I maneuver myself before him. I've rehearsed this moment for months. I've never liked speaking in a formal setting. It requires charisma and poise. Dell enjoyed an abundance of both. When he confessed his heart to Caden, he didn't stammer once. I know because I listened, unseen, from the doorway. One day, a man might speak to me so plainly. Dell might have been that man, had heartbreak not hobbled his spirit. I left the doorway before they finished.

"I don't feel good, Avery. I need to—"

"You remember Dell had a sister, don't you?"

I drop to my knees before his chair, my hands folded atop his knobby knees. I shudder to imagine his bare legs. "Imagine calling Eden to say her baby brother has died. Imagine telling her he *wanted* to die."

Caden flinches. He hiccups for air. I watch him struggle. I should've started filming the moment I shut the door. "Avery, I'm sorry. I knew how you felt about Dell. I knew—"

"You *knew* how he felt about *you.*"

Beads of sweat flee his forehead.

"And you erased him. From your phone, from Facebook. You erased *me* when I asked why."

His tone sharpens. "I let you keep tabs on me. I'm sure you kept Dell informed."

"I told him you were terminal."

Caden grunts. His eyes brim with tears. I need him to reclaim his composure before I start recording. If Eden pities him, I'll have no one to indulge my forest-blaze rage. It will devour me, like Caden's cancer devours him. "That's why he overdosed..." His face clenches with indignation. "Why did you fucking tell him that, Avery?"

Dell and I spent our first month in rehab, before his arrival, constructing a universe made for two. Brick by brick, confidence by confidence, the bond refusing to sever no matter how brazenly Dell later consumed Caden's each step across the courtyard. We knew each other over three years, and I never lied to him, not once.

"You and your fucking rehab romance," he spits.

I've explained enough. Ken awaits our return. I whip out my iPhone. I will record him confessing his guilt to Eden. His refusal to love Dell cast him into an abyss so deep, he might never—even in death—reach its stone-strewn bottom. No one else will see it. At least his sister will know I loved him enough to obtain his killer's confession.

"Fuck you, Avery." He swivels his chair toward the door. "I'll wheel myself back."

I stride across the room. My keys and the canister jangle still. Somehow, as I advance toward him, the box cutter finds itself in my grip. I make note of the emerging blade's click. I force the blade against Caden's withered throat. He doesn't scream or call for help. I'm not sure how to interpret this toneless moment—the threat of violence shouldn't seem so banal.

"This won't bring Dell back."

"I'm more deeply aware of this than you can fathom."

"I'm so goddamn sorry. I don't—"

"Ready to party, Prom King?"

With my thumb, I flip open the lid of my keyring canister. I instruct him to wheel himself into the bathroom. I follow, box cutter blade wavering at the stretch of shoulder left bare by his gown.

The mirror, a dour rectangle bolted above a gleaming sink, is positioned too high to reflect the seated Caden. But I find myself, trapped inside smudged glass, all too visible. I've filled out since rehab. I think of myself as slender, but my belly flattens only with effort. I'm shorter than the men I pursue, taller than the ones I dismiss. My eyeglasses came cheap, the dark frames defiantly thick and graceless. With my coal-black eyes, cheekbones set at too high a slant and pointed jaw, I am no one's idea of handsome. I used to fret about keeping a lover. I made him laugh, Dell liked to tell me. I found this reassuring, sometimes.

I dump the canister's contents on the counter. Three clear shards, all of modest size—enough for a thick, healthy line once crushed and scraped for snorting. I, however, don't plan to partake.

"You crazy son of a bitch…" His jaw hangs open, he looks at me like he *knows* me. It's an expression I've never seen. For a passing moment, guilt blips on my radar. I congratulate myself: there it is, proof that grief and rage have not eroded my humanity in full.

I return the box cutter to his throat. A single drop of blood hugs its lethal edge. I could hurt him. I could end both his suffering, and mine, with a clean cut.

He looks ashen. "There are tumors in my stomach, Avery." His voice breaks, he brushes his knuckles against his eyes. I hadn't expected him to cry. The Prom King has no reason to weep. "Snorting that shit might kill me."

I crush the shards beneath my bathhouse membership card. "You're terminal, Caden." The card scrapes the counter as a dazzling white line of speed takes shape. "You have a choice: you can die or you can die happy."

"What the fuck will this prove?"

I crouch down, my head level with his. I whisper, like a lullaby for a child already asleep, "If you tattle, I'll demand the doctor test your piss. What would Ken think?" I rise to my feet. "Now finish your dessert like a good faggot. We have to start filming soon."

"Not here, man. Take me to the solarium."

Again with the wheels smacking the sticky corridor floor. Again with the abstractionist pilgrims convened around the placards outside each patient's room. Everyone fleet of foot, so many places to reach, so little time to reach them. There's no plausible way to keep the box cutter at his neck. An orderly or nurse might glimpse the weapon. Getting him spun was my only way to assure his cooperation. It tickles me, though, my lover's killer must endure an unwanted high—and all the urges no doubt ignited in its wake.

Caden pants as I push. He twists and fidgets. He complains of cramps. He's afraid he might die. I hiss one warning after another: can the theatrics. We have less than twenty minutes, and the solarium is five floors below.

He refused to confess in Room 517. He's convinced I'll slash his throat once we're done. Caden assures me the outdoor deck adjoining the solarium boasts privacy and adequate light. Patients, visitors, and staff, however, will be within shouting distance. I suppose I could've forced the issue—after all, I have the box cutter. Parading down the hall, knowing he is the Prom King, and this is my coup…well, why not enjoy every one of the thirty minutes afforded me?

As we travel, a trim Latina nurse approaches. Pausing, she tilts slightly forward, her face brightening. I stop pushing. Whether Caden is clever enough to signal her, or anyone we encounter, I'll soon know. She places her hand, tender and graceful, on his shoulder. He won't meet her gaze. He clutches his armrests to tame his tremors. I do not wish him to know kindness.

"Hey there, handsome. Heard you discharge tomorrow."

His torso spasms, head jerking in response. They are now face to face. Still, he does not reply. She rises to full height, perhaps eager to address me. I bend forward and kiss Caden's temple. Whispering, but loud enough to assure she hears, I promise him a few minutes in the cool breeze while we watch the sun surrender to the horizon. He grunts.

He's not dead yet.

"Will you stay with him?" she asks.

"For however long he needs me."

Caden's breathing has grown labored but he finds the fortitude to dazzle her, that same smile beneath which my Dell capsized. She waves and continues down the corridor.

I roll him the opposite direction. One more turn, another corridor, and we'll reach the elevators.

"I used to hate hearing I was handsome."

I refuse to engage. The tweak has made him chatty. He requires a witness. Unless another man watches as you bare your soul, it hardly seems worth the toil. The wheels shriek in protest as we take the corner.

"I was other things, too. Besides handsome."

Perhaps fortune will smile upon me, and our car will carry others, strangers. Surely, Caden won't insist they rubber-stamp his humanity as he hopes I might. I punch the down button, and we wait. He won't stop squirming. He moans as if pained.

"Suck it up, Prom King."

"Please, I need…I need to find a bathroom."

"No, sir. The elevator will be here any second."

He chuckles, but it's a bitter sound. "Don't worry, we'll make your fucking movie."

After the ding, the elevator doors slide open. To my delight, we're at no loss for companions. A black, overweight orderly stands at the front of the car, facing the corner. A frazzled woman in her thirties wearing too much eye shadow holds two grade-school girls, one by each hand. The girls' rude stares trouble no one. Finally, an older woman wrapped in an ankle-length corduroy coat stands beside me. I feel her gaze. She wishes to speak. The doors slide shut. She has mere moments to overcome her trepidation.

"Is it cancer?" Her smile flickers. "I'm about to see my husband. Should be done with the chemo by now."

Caden moans. I press a firm hand upon his shoulder.

"My husband's been sick over a year." This answer surprises me, too. I stretch my back, shoulders rotating with affected fatigue. "Whatever time we have left, I want to spend it together."

Her lips part, but she does not speak. Caden's head and shoulders jitter. Why claim Caden as my own? Perhaps it's humiliation. Perhaps it's to force-feed him the toxic tableau of a life spent sharing one bed. He was so unwilling to grant that wish to Dell but now has no choice—he must indulge my perversion of it.

Clutching his abdomen, Caden moans, a deep and primal eruption, then doubles over. This time, everyone reacts: the orderly, the frazzled woman, those impudent girls. Even in sickness, the Prom King has no trouble drawing a crowd.

"Stop the elevator," he pleads. "I need to—" I shush him, crouch down to whisper whatever threat seems plausible. Before I begin, however, he butts his head against mine. "Now, Avery!" My ears ring, and it takes a few moments to remember that I'm a kidnapper, but my hostage refuses to obey.

The older woman reaches for the panel of lighted number beside the sliding doors. She promises Caden that "we" would find him a bathroom. *No!* That simple directive blots out all other thoughts. I'm running out of time. Desperate, I reach out to grab her hand, but the *ding* distracts her. She refrains and, like the rest of us, waits.

The doors slide open. We're on the third floor.

Caden calls out for someone to hold the door. An elderly couple shuffles forward, perplexed, perhaps sensing a discord clumsily tamed for their benefit. They step aside, the husband extending his delicate, spotted hand over the groove into which one of the sliding doors retreated.

We have to go, Caden and I. Delays, delays, delays. Surely less than fifteen minutes now. Still, I've yet to give his wheelchair that bon-voyage push, the force needed to turn the wheels. It's those wheels that Caden, himself, vainly tries to turn, but I clutch the handgrips with brute force. We can't leave this elevator without a plan.

"Sir, your partner's in great pain, it seems." The older woman must have problems with the word *husband*. "Do you need some help?"

The elderly man outside the passenger car flops his open hand against the sliding door each time it tries to emerge. Ignoring the older woman, I push Caden into the lobby. There are six elevators surrounding us. The third floor looks just like the fifth. Even the brazen aroma of antiseptic has been replicated to perfection. Two parallel corridors sandwich the bank of elevators.

Caden whines and curses. "It doesn't matter which way. Just keep going till we find…" He gasps, head thrown back with such force, he lifts from his seat for a moment. "An empty room." He stabs his pointed finger at the left corridor. "Find me an empty room."

Nurses, visitors, they risk leery glances at our two-man revue.

"Fine, Caden. But let's make the potty pitstop a quick one."

We're already in motion.

"You'll get your fucking video, Geek."

Down the corridor, football helmets cut from construction paper festoon the placards bearing patients' names. I wonder who decided the themes for each floor. Helmets seem a mite bland compared to the rosy-cheeked pilgrims two floors above.

Caden's breath turns shallow and harsh, as if he were in labor. The sheen of perspiration coating his face reflects the corridor lights. His hair is drenched. Eyelids clenched shut, he trusts me to find an untaken toilet.

More visitors, more nurses. Orderlies. Even a few doctors. We've passed at least twenty rooms, both sides of the corridor considered. The corridor, itself, opens not far ahead. A nurses' station, probably. If even one indulges her curiosity, filming might be (again) delayed, or worse. Ken won't hesitate to unleash the hounds if I fail to return Caden unharmed. I will not disappoint Dell, however, no matter how formidable the forces against me. I never did our three years together, and his death brings no respite.

"Avery, turn left! Right here! Room 323!"

I instruct him to deep-six the high decibels. If no one looked before, they damn sure might look now. Once we've entered the empty room, I hope, we'll fortunately be forgotten.

Caden sobs, insisting the pain intensifies with each breath. The bathroom door catches against the wheelchair's footrest. I strain my shoulder jerking back the chair, allowing the door to swing wide and admit him. He rolls to a stop beside the toilet, and I dare entertain relief. He's too weak, he cries, to lift himself from the chair to the commode. Hurry, he begs. My belly is about to explode! Just then, a wretched odor fills the bathroom. Caden's bowels, it seems, believe Room 323 needs a fragrance both fecal and fierce. I'm holding his skeletal form upright, by its armpits. I try shifting him to the toilet, but his wheelchair stymies my every move. I refuse to panic. I knew Caden was sick before I hit the road, and sick people have volatile relationships with toilets. Just ten more seconds, and I'll recover my wits— just ten seconds!

Caden Quaid doesn't have ten seconds to spare.

His unplanned bowel movement announces itself with a fanfare loud, wet and lingering. Fortunately, Caden wears gray Nike athletic shorts beneath his papery gown, but the good news stops there. He neglected to slip on briefs beneath those shorts. The runny fecal follies stream down his bony legs and pool upon the linoleum. Moments later, a smattering of foul-smelling chunks, too unformed and moist to bear the label of *turd*, form dainty little heaps upon that same linoleum. The stench is so pervasive, so intense, I wouldn't blame anyone who might doubt one man alone could spawn such epic nasty.

It's humiliating and no shilling of shame could meet the expense. I still hold Caden upright, my hands cupped beneath his armpits. I look him dead in the eyes. I don't offer compassion. Did he show any compassion to my sweet Dell? How will the Prom King handle shitting himself while tweaked and trapped with a man ready to mock his misfortune? If filming must wait, only a distraction this delectable will satisfy. Caden simply stares ahead, blankly, through me, as if this bathroom were measured in acres, not inches.

"No one's calling you handsome now."

"I'm fine with that. Actually, I prefer they call me Caden."

I'm stumped at his refusal to trot no matter which carrot I dangle before him. Whatever abdominal pain he was suffering seems vanquished, but he's no doubt still tweaking. I may have trouble keeping his bitch mouth shut.

He's not dead yet.

"You can put me down, Avery." I drop him abruptly, but his balance does not deny him. "I need a shower. You're not rolling me down the hall while I simmer in my own shit."

I can't argue with his logic. Reeking of turds would draw first the noses, then the nosiness of all who crossed our path. Still, at most, ten minutes remain before Caden's chair reverts back into a pumpkin. I instruct him to hurry. He asks me to excuse myself to the main room. Forget it, I reply. The bathroom door locks from the inside, and fuck him for thinking I haven't noticed. Irritated, he slips off his paper gown and steps into the shower. He hasn't the strength to stand for the entire ordeal, but a wide-topped stool awaits in the stall. I watch as the spray wets his desiccated form. I'm thankful Dell never has to witness his dream lover's decay. He wouldn't allow himself the perspective necessary to enjoy it.

"That tweak you forced up my nose was bunk, by the way." The bathroom is so small and the spray so weak, Caden's voice carries. I'm in no mood for banter so let the remark sink beneath the silence. "Bet you saved the good shit for yourself, huh?" Tweak makes Caden bitchy. He doesn't bother to look my way. "I bet you're spun right now. This very fucking moment."

For the record, I've been sober since Dell's suicide. Eight months—I was telling that pissant Ken the truth. I know tweaking will spur illusory multi-hour conversations with him. Such seductive fantasies, and most would forgive me if I succumbed—but there are boys quite alive who need me more. I work overnights for a gay hotline in Houston. I field everything from coming-out trauma to suicide threats. I stay sober. Indeed, after I record Caden's confession, I must make haste down the interstate, Dallas receding in my rearview. The hotline expects me at midnight.

"Fine," I say, my voice toneless. "I did a couple of bumps in the parking lot. Vindicated?"

Caden shuts off the water. "I'm not judging you. I should, but I won't." He dons his paper gown, perhaps not noticing the dried shit spattered along its hem, then drops into his wheelchair. Its creaks and rattles bemoan the blunt impact of his bones. Clearly, he's exhausted.

"Forget the solarium," he says. "Let's get this fucker over with right here and now."

"What convinced you I won't slash your throat?"

"All those assholes we traumatized in the elevator—they're my witnesses, Geek."

Besides, he adds, his Nike shorts are ruined so he's totally nude beneath his paper gown. While we're outside at the solarium, there might be a gust of wind. If not that, the gowns themselves are more than a little transparent, particularly under harsh fluorescents, hard to avoid at Bishop Medical. *Please*, he says, *I've played along with this. I could've stopped this farce at any time.*

Caden has a point. But I have a box cutter, and he's high on crystal meth.

"The solarium seems a reachable goal. We still have time. But we have to scoot."

As we return to the elevators, the squeaks and smacks of the wheelchair form a sort of tune, one played on crude instruments. Caden takes deliberate breaths, his chest and head rippling, adding a kinesthetic component to the wheels' meager music. He hadn't bothered to articulate his disappointment, in expression or with words, when I insisted our adventure end with the solarium. Slumped upon his throne, he muttered capitulation, ready for me to push.

At the elevators, the waiting nurses and suited gentlemen pay us no mind. We lumber into the open car. When the doors open to the ground floor, I allow myself to sample the ripe satisfaction promised me the moment Caden's confession ends. I must discipline myself. He silently lifts a leaden hand, pointing this way or that. We're approaching the lobby. Those sliding glass doors shift left to right, right to left. A half-hour earlier, they admitted me—with my box cutter and bit of crystal. I should recall the scratched twang that calls out from what I only now recognize as the help desk. When I glance her way, though, nothing stirs my memory.

"Yoo-hoo! Over here, handsome." She laughs. "You didn't come flirt with me today."

Caden smiles, lifts an open hand with more vigor than I would expect, signaling me to stop. We're down to mere minutes, and my only advantage beyond Ken's deadline is that the gym rat has no idea where we are. Our potty break, however, resulted in witnesses, as Caden took pains to mention. As he flirts with the help desk hussy, I speculate whether further booby traps await.

A harried husband barges his way to the help desk. His wife was brought here. *Reba Blakely?* I wheel Caden away, grateful for the distraction. Moments later, he announces our arrival.

I expect a solarium to be more heavily beset by plant life. Instead, palm leaves and intimidating ferns line three of the walls, rubber-cushioned sofas and chairs positioned before them. It feels like the waiting room at a clinic in a bedroom community, one where several doctors split the steep rent. The only things missing are back issues of *People* and *US Weekly*. Caden slaps my chest with the back of his hand. There, he mutters, that door takes us outside.

Despite the aggressive greenery obscuring the glass walls, I glimpse enough of the sky for my skin to prickle: such maroons and deep oranges appear only at dusk. I extend my arm to push open the hydraulic door, allowing Caden the latitude to wheel himself outside.

"Gentlemen, the observation deck closes at sunset."

Caden pauses upon the threshold. We turn our heads to greet the latest in a ceaseless series of roadblocks. She's a stout woman, her middle years soon ending. Too much foundation showcases instead of conceals her jowls. A badge offering her name and mugshot rests above her left breast.

"Please, ma'am." I smile and furrow my brow to simulate sincerity. "It's the first time in weeks my husband's felt well enough to leave his room." Caden places a loose hand atop mine, and I stutter. I don't want a partner in crime, I want justice for Dell. "After the sun sets—we'll come back, I swear."

The stout woman fingers a strand of pearls not there. "Your *husband*, is that right?"

Caden smiles, and it occurs to me, like a bulb's dying flash: he has an agenda, too, and maybe I've been foolish. Still, Dell is counting on me. Caden thanks our hostess and urges me, in an affable tone the tweak seemed to silence, to wheel him outside.

The deck is comprised of shapeless slabs of burgundy stone, bits of sprouting grass, twigs and acorns shed by the massive oaks, their drooping lank limbs. A squat brick wall, hardly high enough to meet the knee, lines the perimeter. The air has chilled. Errant gusts flirt beneath Caden's gown, its hem ballooning one moment, dropping the next. *You see*, he snipes, *fucking wind.* He insists I wheel him to one of several patio tables stationed in front of the solarium's windowed wall. You can sit across from me, he adds.

"You don't have to pretend we're married anymore," I snap. He keeps forgetting who has the box cutter. Across from him, I tap and slide until my iPhone is ready to record.

"Give me another rundown. I'm not confessing more than once."

It's simple, I remind him. Tell my lover's sister your name, how you met Dell, how you learned of his love and how you dismissed it. I glance over my shoulder. That molten orange orb will kiss the horizon in mere moments. If only we'd found an empty room sooner, if only Caden respected the dynamic I forged between us. I double-check the viewfinder. I tell him we're recording.

"Hello, Eden. I'm Caden Quaid. I'm forty-four years old and live in Dallas. I met your brother three years ago at a rehab in Houston." He pauses, gulps air. "As I'm sure you know, Avery was there, too. He's making this little motion picture. You deserve to know what happened to your brother. So do you, Avery."

My shoulders tense. I worry Caden may have fallen from the frame. But we're running out of light and Ken must surely be worried by now. Still, why address me? More disconcerting, I detect no remorse or shame. He speaks like a suburban dad as he delivers punishment to his toddler. He whips through our history as a threesome: Dell, Caden and Avery—the Three Faggoteers. This may interest Eden, but I'm waiting to hear his misdeeds after we left, after Dell and I found a shitty apartment in a shitty neighborhood, and he returned to Dallas. What precisely did he say to Dell that night over the phone, inducing such anguish I could listen no more?

"We were on the phone. I told him I had cancer. He started crying. He said he loved me too much to lose me. I didn't return your brother's feelings. He knew that. He didn't care."

Dell O'Dowd needed *me*. Dell O'Dowd loved *me*. Dell O'Dowd chose *me*.

"He volunteered to drop everything and move to Dallas. He said he'd nurse me through, no matter how long it took." His eyes dim, and he appears unnerved. "I asked about Avery. What would he think if your brother left him in the dust? All that bastard could manage was some lame-ass promise that Avery would find a way." His breathing becomes labored once more, but it's the anger, nothing else. A vitality besieges him. The Prom King never wastes the spotlight. "I told him I was about to hang up. He and I? We were strangers now. Any man who would shit on some dude so devoted to him had bigger problems than dope. We never spoke again."

I'm looking elsewhere. I'm looking anywhere. Over my shoulder, I glimpse the last of the sun slip behind the horizon. It's good he's nearing the end. Eden needs to see his face. Wait, why is it quiet? Just crickets and white noise from the nearby interstate. I must've zoned out. I can't remember what Caden last said. My eyes dart to my iPhone, wrist resting on the table. No way Caden remains in the frame.

Caden snatches the device from my hand and slams it on the table. His eyes burn with a fury that's my due, not his. He holds my gaze. His breath slows. That stout woman who believes we're married must wonder why we broke our promise.

"Fuck his sister. I'm talking to you. The day I heard Dell died, I had one thought: what will Avery do with his freedom?" He gasps for air. The adrenaline must be wearing off. Dell will be so disappointed in me. "Loyalty should be earned, Avery. You see what Ken and I have? You deserve that, too." He must need what little stamina remains, after our half-hour adventure, to deliver this pep talk. "I'd be happy to cash in my chips, but I stay alive. My best friend needs me."

I can accept failure. I can accept defeat. I'm the Geek. Our tribe rarely ascends the winners' podium. I leave Caden as he hunches over the tabletop, too desperate for oxygen to notice that I'm almost to the solarium door. He calls my name. He whines that he's too weak to roll himself back to his room. The Prom King needs me.

"I hope your death is both painful and pitiful." I don't wait for his reaction.

The stout woman asks what happened to my husband. She needs to close and lock that door, it's security protocol. I don't break my stride. She's too much of a creampuff to accost me. Back in the corridor, I pause. Which way to the lobby? I must go to work. I'm welcome there.

Except, I dart off in the opposite direction, deeper into the hospital. Except, I find the elevators. Except, I wait patiently, my head bereft of thoughts, as I ascend five stories. Except, I hustle down the corridor until I see Caden's name and that perky pilgrim. The door to Room 534 stands ajar.

That night, after Caden hung up on Dell, he flopped onto the bed we shared and sobbed. Did he need to talk? He didn't tell me, not then, that Caden had discarded him. Instead, his small, timid voice insisted he didn't deserve me. Life is chaos, I told him. Be thankful someone wants to hold your hand while the world burns. I don't deserve you, he repeated. Later, dozing, he slung his arm over me. One day, I was certain, he'd open his eyes and truly *see* me for the first time.

Someone, presumably Ken, is taking a shower. It seems he isn't as vigilant as I feared. I slip into the bathroom. I close the door, wince as the lock clicks after giving it a twist. He's nude, of course. Rather impressive rear end. He hasn't noticed me. No one bothers to speculate the damage I might do. The box cutter finds its way into my grip. The blade emerges with a quick nudge from my thumb.

I'm standing close enough to touch him. Instead, I slash his bare back.

I stay alive. My best friend needs me.

He gasps and whips around, stumbling, to find me brandishing my box cutter. He was right about me. He demands to know what I did with Caden. I answer by slashing his face, the gash running from ear to chin. I've prepared for bloodshed. *Please*, he begs, *Caden needs me.* I nod. At last, we agree on something.

He struggles, at first, but won't scream. He begs me to stop, but I cannot. He's not dead yet.

My Father's Home
Jeremy Billingsley

I stand in front of my father's house on Evers Street, staring at the boards over the front windows like duct tape over the mouth so no one can hear it scream. The street is empty this time of night. Always has been. That's what he loved about this neighborhood: they always rolled up the sidewalks at the same time every night.

If anyone were to see me, they might think I walk aimlessly. My head down, hands tucked in my coat pockets. No one would recognize me. It's been years and I've changed my name, anyways. If I showed them a picture of me when I was thirteen or if I told them my real name, they'd remember. In a heartbeat, they'd remember. No one in this city will ever forget. They'd know who I was and who my father was and they'd fear me, more than likely, imagining that the sins of the father are passed to the son.

A couple jog past me as I cross a neighborhood park. It's cool and the man and woman are dressed in neon spandex that accentuates each muscular curve. I watch her closely much as I imagine my father might have. I feel sick watching her with his eyes and force myself to look away as I walk on. Luckily, they move at a fast pace and are out of view quickly.

The park leads to a pedestrian bridge that rises over an expressway that is still busy enough with cars this time of evening, probably mostly people coming home from work to their families. This was usually when my father would leave the neighborhood to start his other job. Not the one at the electric company, reading meters. The other one. The one that they got him on. He'd have come to this park regularly. There were a few female joggers who weren't as lucky as the one I saw tonight. She gets to go home. She gets to pretend that she's safe, next to her man, and that monsters no longer exist. Still, if she knows anything about this city, she might wonder if the monster still lurks in the shadows. If somehow it weren't slayed. Or maybe it reproduced.

I cross the pedestrian bridge and see the downtown and *smell* downtown and it is the first time I really admonish myself for returning to this city. I shouldn't even go to the job interview tomorrow. I should just go home and tell my wife I didn't get it, and we'll stay far away, and everything will be okay. Though as I think these things, I still cross the bridge and enter the tenements of downtown. I smell the sewer and the disease. Downtown is busier. The sidewalks are still alive, but the alleyways are just as dark. Every manner of humanity exists at all times here. My father wouldn't have seen them as humans. He would have seen them as something else. Something less.

The first time we went to stay with him at his new place after the divorce, I remember asking him about this spot on the wall. It was reddish brown. Just a little spot. He said he'd killed a fly there. He'd been in the home only a few weeks at that point, but the spot still looked fresh. Turns out, he'd "killed that fly" only two days before we arrived. That's how he saw them: as insects.

A dirty man in a ragged dun coat buzzes around me, shoving a flyer in my face. I wave him away and keep walking, head down. I see a beat cop on the other corner talking to a couple of women in fishnets and tight bodices. He eyes me for a second, so I avert my gaze, sure he recognizes me. I wonder if my father did the same thing even as I'm sure the policeman, also thinking about my father, is warning these women against being on the streets. My father proved time and again streets weren't safe.

The building on the corner of Main and 5th looks as though it should be condemned. It's dirty and stained with all manner of filth. I buzz the number (I have memorized the address after so many years of staring at it) and when the voice asks who it is, I proclaim the words I'd prepared so carefully.

"John Silver," I say, a close but not accurate pseudonym for my real name, invoking my born middle name and mother's maiden name. "We had an appointment." I feel a jolt up my spine, tingling and buzzing me, from using a pseudonym that could potentially tie me back to my real identity and, therefore, to my father, and I wonder if he felt the same when he played with the police.

The door unlatches and I pull it open before she can change her mind, then take the stairs to the second floor and find her apartment easily. She stands in front of the door, her hand behind her and on the knob, I think, as I top the last riser, hoping I'm sure to get a good look at me.

She eyes me suspiciously, her left eye squinting from old injuries from which she's never fully recovered. She's impossibly skinny with blotchy skin, her tee stained various shades of dark and her sweatpants baggy, her pale feet bony and flat. I force my eyes up. My father was a foot man. Her cheeks are sunken, her hair stringy and unkempt. There is a greasy quality to her, like she's a silverfish that's been plucked from a mud puddle.

My phone rings as I reach out to shake her hand. I glance to see the number is local and know it's probably one of two people who might call me. She spies my hand and offers it a quick, limp shake before pulling it away and casting her door open for me to enter.

Her apartment is small and smells of old cigarettes and booze. A sulfurous tint hangs over the entirety of the apartment. I find it ironic that having survived my father, she's been reduced to the very thing he saw her as in the first place. Is that survival?

She offers me some coffee and I abstain. I have to sleep, I say.

"So you're writing a book? Why in God's name?"

"The story needs to be told. Your story needs to be told. Of course, I've worked it out with my publisher that you'll get some of the royalties. You deserve it, after all."

This is a lie. There is no book. At least, not from me. Not my line of work. Not even a hobby of mine. But they are the best way to reach such people. Survivors. Stroke the ego.

"What about the families of the other victims?"

"Some didn't have families," I say. "But the ones they found, sure."

She sits across from me and takes a pull at a bottle of Jim Beam that she'd already been working on, as the bottle's half empty. At this range, in this light, I can see her age around her eyes and mouth and in the strands of hair that are no longer as dark as the rest.

"You look familiar," she says, and for a minute I catch my breath as she lets her eyes roam over me.

"I guess I have one of those faces," I say as she takes a drag off her cigarette and raises the bottle to her lips.

"So, what do you want to know?"

"Well, the story really is about you and who you were then and who you are now. I have a lot of research on him, but only what they released about you publicly during the trial."

She shrugs. "My mother was a prostitute and I was her only little girl. I was trying to rise above, you know. I'd just enrolled in the community college. He caught me getting off the train one night."

I nod. This was all in the court transcripts. "That's fine, but I want to humanize you," I say. "I want to know who it was that was able to beat him. How did you do it? What did you feel?"

She shook her head and looked away. I saw her eyes well up, and with the cigarette in her hand, she pointed toward her door.

"Turn around," she says, and I do, and I see a series of locks up the side of the door, like something out of a cartoon. She has deadbolts and chain locks and latch locks and reinforced hinges hidden from the outside. I look to the windows visible from where I sit and see that they've been nailed shut. She follows my gaze for a second before looking at me and nodding.

"Even the one at the fire escape?" I ask, and when she nods and takes a draw on her cigarette, I quip, "Isn't that a safety hazard?" but the joke doesn't go over.

"Does it look like I beat him?" she asks. "People tell me how strong I am. How I won. I beat the monster, but this don't feel like winning. I didn't finish college. I live off my disability that he gave me. I lived because I was scared. I was scared of him, of dying. And secretly, you know, I wanted to die. I wanted it to end right there, but I was scared too of being seen like a failure."

As she speaks, her tears are falling and her voice gets louder and louder like a screeching beetle and I feel the beginnings of a headache coming on, and I remember going to see my dad after he was sentenced and he looked so much different. Like the face I'd known as my father was a mask and this was the real face. There was nothing in his eyes but a dull matte blackness, and his voice was monotone. It was the one and only time I saw him in prison.

"You know you found the right one," he said, "because they sound like razors. Their voices cut into your brain so much it hurts and there is only one way to stop it."

"You alright?" she asks. I look up and nod. Since planning on coming back to this city, this has been happening more and more.

"Have you sought help in the years since—"

"Yes," she says matter-of-factly. "Three therapists over the past ten years. They all try to remind me that I survived. That I beat him. That I accomplished something."

As a response to this, she takes another pull from the bottle and another drag from the smoke before tapping the ash in the glass tray on the table by her chair.

"You sure I can't get you something?" she asks and uncrosses then crosses her legs. I see the bruises on her shins and know those aren't from my father and I realize then how she's subsidized her income over these years. Returned to the family trade.

"I'm fine, really." I say and choke down revulsion like it was the greasy burger I'd eaten earlier at the diner just a mile from my old house.

I get up to leave, turn to face the door and stop, then turn around to see her sitting there, her insect legs rubbing together like she could get them to chirp like a cricket. Her fly-like eyes bulging out of her pale, thin face. Like I can see her skull. A blue vein throbs in her forehead.

"Can I visit you again? Maybe in a few weeks? Like I said, this is your story and I want to get it right. What happened then. How it started. How you beat him. And the ending."

She nods and says sure and rises but I wave her away, open the door and shut it behind me, feeling sick and my head pounding, I make my way to the stairs even as I hear the locks all latch. I know she'll unlatch them when I return.

As I return across the bridge and return through the park, my head clears. I know it would be best not to return those two phone calls, to fly back home and tell my wife I didn't get the job, but still I check my voicemail even as I walk back to my father's house and open the door.

Two messages.

"This is Captain Ross. I'm afraid we need to move your appointment tomorrow to two, if that's alright. I know you flew into town for this, and I apologize. Please rest assured that we are very interested in a cop with your credentials joining our Detective Division, and we are looking forward to meeting with you. Still, if this conflicts with your departure flight, let me know and we'll work something out. Looking forward to speaking with you."

"Hi, Detective Black. This is Andrea at Midtown Realtors. Yes, the house on Evers Street is available, and with your loan approval you should have more than enough for renovations after purchase price. I still think we can get them down some. Let me know if you're still interested."

I stare up at the house, mentally retracing my steps through all the rooms. I know it's too late to call my wife. I call the captain's number and get a voicemail and say that two o'clock will work fine. I also get the voicemail of the realtor and tell her to see if they'll come down ten thousand, and I imagine all the things I could do with this house once it's mine. I can get this job and move my family here and once we are back in my house, then I can revisit the one woman who survived and, at some point perhaps, see how many others are out there that my father missed.

Itch
Louis Stephenson

Hayley hadn't meant to be so careless that morning. She was tired from binge-watching shows with her boyfriend the night before, so it slipped her mind. But she knew better than to walk into the bathroom without shoes or slippers on. And yet there she was, hunched over the end of her bed in her dressing gown, scrubbing away at the bottoms of her feet in utter disgust.

Her soles were peppered in flakes of her older brother's dead and discarded flesh. Seb left it everywhere he went. On chairs, on the carpet, anything and everything he touched was befouled by his forever moulting skin. He couldn't help it, of course, because of the severity of his condition. Still, that didn't make day to day life any less unpleasant.

Within mere seconds her poor left foot began to pink up under the abrasiveness of her manic scouring. She stopped cold when she feared the worst. It had finally happened. Little pieces of pale skin, belonging to her, not her brother, were peeling away from her heel. Hayley's open mouth became bone dry and her eyes wetted with tears. She slowly plucked one from the bunch and held it up, her stare boring into it.

Frightened, the girl failed to fight off the images that flooded her brain as she recalled the morning she had caught Seb looking himself over in the mirror, after hunching himself into the bathroom like an invalid. From her viewpoint, she couldn't make out even an inch of his morbidly obese body that wasn't affected by those sickening white scales. He wasn't human. He was a disease, a walking scab.

"Calm down." Her boyfriend tried his best not to sound amused. "You've been rubbing your skin too hard. That's all."

Mark stood by the curtains holding a mug of coffee with both hands. He set it down on the windowsill and made his way over to Hayley. Taking her free hand, he gently caressed the back of it with his thumb as he relieved her of the dripping wet towel in the other.

It was an easy mistake to make. Sometimes her brother's skin came off in specks, hundreds of them. Maybe even thousands. Small enough and light enough to float through the air like snowflakes or particles of dust. The thought that she may have breathed them in just once shook young and beautiful Hayley to her core.

She was indeed the youngest in the family, and the most beautiful. She loved her makeup. She loved her hair. She loved her boyfriend who worshipped the ground she walked on. With cheap rent and a job at the local salon, she lived a cushy life at home with a hard-working father, and a dedicated stay-at-home mother. At least, it was cushy until her brother came home.

"God, we need to get out of here," Hayley whined. "It's taking us forever to save up enough money."

Tossing the wet towel into the corner, it landed a few inches short of their hamper as Mark ran his fingers down the length of Hayley's ponytail.

"Are you going to wear your hair like that?" He asked with creased eyebrows and pursed lips. "You know your face looks slimmer when you wear it down."

"Babe." Hayley put a hand to her cheek before she pulled her hair free. "I always put it up so I can wash all of my face properly."

She draped her locks down either side of her face, hiding herself behind them.

Then, as if Mark had read her mind, he dropped the towel into the hamper where it belonged, returned to his girlfriend and gave her a soft, warm kiss on the forehead.

"That's much better." He smiled as he kissed her again. "You look stunning."

She hid her tears with a silent yawn and returned his smile.

Mark hummed contently as he went back to his mug of coffee. And each time he turned away Hayley snuck another look at her foot.

"Breakfast!" Her mother's voice rang from downstairs.

Hayley sat across from her brother at the kitchen table, trying not to gawk at him as he munched miserably at his cereal like a scolded child. As big as Seb was, somehow he had managed to find an ugly, army-green coat that could hide the entirety of his hideous figure. And it smelled, too. It was mostly body odors that offended her nose, but she could also sense a tinge of copper. Dried blood stained the insides of the nasty thing. Plenty of the stuff dripped free whenever his needlessly long fingernails dug too deep. And he was scratching again right then. It never seemed to stop.

It made a sound like the grinding of a butter knife on cold, dried toast, scraping and scraping away.

She shuddered, letting a breath of revulsion escape. She froze and looked up to make sure that he hadn't noticed her reaction. The coast was clear, and he was still going at it.

Clutching her side of the kitchen table she quietly leaned over to one side as she glanced underneath. Flecks of her brother's skin floated down to the hardwood floor as if she were looking into some filthy, old snow globe. Except that these didn't look like glitter or coconut shavings.

Sitting upright, Hayley spent the rest of their morning meal scowling across the table in disbelief.

Mark was sitting through in the living room with his feet up on the large, wooden coffee table. He sprinkled some sugar onto the strawberry-topped pancake that was balancing on his lap as his eyes were transfixed on the football game playing on the huge flat-screen.

Hayley entered the room slowly as she carefully ferried two cups of steaming hot tea. She planted one in her boyfriend's hand along with a brief but noisy kiss on the lips and the other next to her laptop, which sat open on the computer desk in the far corner.

The machine chimed out a friendly welcome as she took her place in the swivel chair in front of it. She opened her social media pages. She responded to her private messages, commented on comments and updated the world on how she was feeling and what she would be up to later that day.

Despite the volume of the TV, she heard the rattle of Mark's fork as it fell to his plate.

"Mmm! Not enough sugar." He muttered, grabbing the shaker from the table.

Hayley watched soundly as the grains of sugar started to fall. It all looked a little too familiar, as if Seb had somehow snuck flakes of his scaly flesh into the shaker. She winced as she returned to her laptop.

She opened a search engine, but her fingers hesitated warily. After a moment's thought she continued typing.

List of contagious skin diseases

Taking a breath, she punched the ENTER key.

MRSA

Impetigo

Scabies

Hayley slammed her laptop shut. She couldn't read anymore. Her next breath was longer and shaky. *Scabies.* She didn't know quite what it was, but just the sound of that word in her head made her squirm.

Something irritated her arms. She could feel it from her shoulders all the way down to the backs of her hands. They began to get hot and itchy. Her fingers twitched as she became increasingly restless. She had to look, so she ripped up each sleeve. But there was nothing to see. Not even a single sign of discoloration. Her skin did feel better uncovered though.

"Babe, what are you doing?" Mark asked, only half-interested. "Did you forget to moisturize this morning?"

Pulling down her sleeves, Hayley turned in her chair as she narrowed her eyes at her boyfriend. "I always moisturize…"

"If you say so." He responded lazily, failing to return her gaze.

"But I do…" She said soundly to herself as she sadly lowered her head.

Hayley lightened up with a smile as she noticed the family cat by the radiator.

"Molly," she beckoned soothingly. "Molly—"

The furry creature was trying to eat something off the floor and having no luck at it. Every time she took it up in her jaws, it would just fall back out onto the hardwood.

"What's that you got there, huh?" She curled her fingers loosely around its tail.

"Leave it." Mark grunted. "You know you hate it when you get cat hairs on your clothes."

Hayley rolled her eyes at him. "I'm barely touching her."

"Just saying…"

She shook her head and leaned in further to get a closer look at the tiny dark lump that kept falling from Molly's mouth. Whatever it was, it was gray in color and resembled a considerably smaller breed of caterpillar. "What is that?"

Drawing her phone from her pants pocket, she took a picture of the insect and quickly made her way back through to the kitchen. "Mom!"

She found her mother at the other end, wearing a colorful cotton sweater and dark, form-fitting jeans. She whistled as she loaded everyone's washing into the dryer.

"Mom?" Hayley approached her with the phone held out in front.

"Yes, darling?"

"What is this?" Her daughter demanded. "Have you seen this?"

Her mother squinted at the little blob. "Oh yes, those are carpet bugs."

"Carpet bugs?" Hayley already felt the urge to itch again. "We have carpet bugs."

"No, honey, your brother has carpet bugs." Her mother explained as she carried on with her chores. "He had an infestation of them in his apartment before he moved back in with your father and me."

"An infestation?" Hayley whimpered.

"Now don't get yourself into a state just yet." Her mother sighed. "We're hoping that maybe a handful came over with him. We just need to put this special powder stuff on the floor here and there. Keep his room clean. Hopefully that'll be that."

Still unconvinced, Hayley decided to delete the picture from her phone. If she couldn't erase the thoughts from her brain, she could at least erase the images from her sight. She was about to leave when she stopped and turned back to her mother.

"Mark and I were thinking pizza tonight." She informed her. "You want in?"

"No, no, no, I'm fine." Her mother replied. "But make sure to get something for your father. That man is supposed to be watching what he eats, but you know he gets pissed when everyone's having junk food for dinner and he can't have any. It'll just be healthier for everyone that way."

* * *

Driving through the night, driving through the darkness was the one thing that could calm Hayley completely. As a passenger, she surrendered. There was nothing to see, nothing to be, nothing to think about. Moments of blackness. Moments of bright lights. White, yellow, red and blue. Colors of the night. Colors of peace. Colors of death. But at the same time, not death. More of a respite from existence, and all the pains and desires that come with it. But on that drive, as they made their way back from the restaurant, the night cracked.

Hayley slipped away into the hum of the road as it roared beneath her like rushing water. In the void of seemingly infinite space behind her eyelids, she saw that the windshield of her boyfriend's car had fogged over like a Coke bottle filled with cigarette smoke.

There was no sound as this heavy mist illuminated with brilliant red light. An odd little shadow, no larger than a baseball appeared on Hayley's side of the glass. It began to grow. Not only was the shape growing, but it was getting darker…closer?

Suddenly, a shimmer of glitter and glass as a shatter pattern akin to a widow's web appeared on the screen only inches away from Hayley's face. A ripple of impact seemed to liquify the solidity of the car around her. Glistening shards suspended in mid-air like raindrops dipped in sunlight and frozen in time.

The windshield gave way as something pierced the glass. It was a pulverized human face. The blood that ran down the screen appeared black against the blazing beams of red. The surviving eye quivered open.

It was Seb.

Hayley recognized him immediately. Even if she hadn't noticed the scar on the far end of his left eyebrow, she knew that sad, but kind, stare.

Before she could speak, before she could even move, that one soft eye rolled back as Seb shook in agony. His flesh stretched like cooking dough until his face tore in two opposite directions as his skull split open.

Out rolled a wriggling ball of carpet bugs that flew apart as it landed on Hayley's lap. The creeping, crawling creatures swarmed up her belly, past her chest, and toward her mouth as it was locked open in a scream.

"Hayley!" Mark's voice snapped her back to thinking, feeling, being.

"What?" She moaned drowsily, stretching and palming at her face.

"We're home." Mark frowned in his concern. "Are you okay, baby? Looked like you were having a bad dream."

"I don't remember." She lied, avoiding his eyes.

"Well, you were kind of scratching yourself in your sleep."

Hayley's spine straightened up. "I was?"

"Yup." Mark nodded. "I would've stopped you, but I thought— you know—I better not risk it."

Hayley was about to respond when she first heard it. A single, loud popping sound came from somewhere outside the car. She couldn't be certain, but it sounded like—

Mark's head jerked around away from her. The car shook a little. "Hey, did you hear that?"

"Yes!"

"That sounded like—"

"Like a gunshot." Hayley finished his sentence as each of them met one another with a worried gaze. "Let's just get inside the house."

The young couple quickly vacated the car at the same time.

"Don't leave me behind!" Hayley pleaded as the gravel crunched uncomfortably beneath her feet.

"Get the food!" Mark ordered, ignoring her.

They each pulled a 14-inch pizza box out of either side of the backseat, shut and locked up the car, and began heading towards the house.

The sound came again, startling them both to a standstill. This pop was not sharp at all. It echoed up and down that dark street, which dead-ended only a couple of houses away.

"Shit!" Mark's body jolted so hard with fright that it hurt the bones of his toes as they curled up tight inside his sneakers.

"It wasn't that loud before," Hayley whispered as her arms started to get hot.

Mark peered down the street. "It's getting closer."

"Do you see anything?"

"Not yet." Mark squinted hard at the shadows. "What's up with the security light? There could be someone running right at us and we wouldn't know until the last second."

"Don't say that!" Hayley hissed quietly.

But he was right. For whatever reason, their presence failed to activate the security light above the front door. Hayley couldn't wave so she gave it one good jump. Nothing. "It's not working."

BANG!!!

"Get in the house...now!" Mark nudged her ahead of him as they both ran for the door.

His girlfriend made it in first, as intended. He slowed to a halt as he got inside and inspected the light switches on the wall by the entrance to the house. It didn't take long for him to work out the problem. He snickered to himself.

"Hey!" He called out as he set the pizza box on the sideboard usually reserved for mail. "The light is working."

Hayley returned from the kitchen. "What is it?"

"The light is working," Mark repeated as he put a finger on the switch and leaned through the open front doorway. "We just forgot to turn it on!"

He flicked the switch. The light came on. And there it was.

"Jesus—" Mark carefully stepped outside. His gaze never left the ground.

"What do you see?" Hayley pressed impatiently as she marched towards the front door. "Is someone out there?"

"Hayley...babe, I don't think you want to see this." Mark warned her shakily. His legs trembled as his eyes welled up with tears.

Hayley hesitated for a moment. But only for a moment. She had to know. She had to look. So, she looked. And then she knew.

It was Molly.

She lay beneath the orange glow of the welcome lantern. She could have been sleeping. But Hayley knew. Her chest didn't rise and fall. Her ears didn't flicker. Her tiny snores had silenced. Molly was gone.

"Oh, Molly." Hayley sobbed as Mark put his arms around her, holding her tight.

"It looks like she went peacefully," he said softly before she burst into tears.

As sorrow clouded her vision, the moments that followed passed like a blur of sadness in Hayley's mind. She wept in her mother's arms as Mark buried the family pet between the bushes in their backyard. It was a shallow grave in which Molly would spend her final rest wrapped up in her favorite dishtowel. They didn't know if it was the color, the smell, or the texture, but she loved to claw and chew at it every morning.

Hayley rested her head upon Mark's shoulder as he held her in the shower. Between his warm, soft body and the hot stream beating down on them, for a moment she felt truly enveloped in the relief of unconditional, unselfish love.

Until the floorboards in the hallway began to creak as something large and heavy moved slowly behind the bathroom door. Her brother.

"Guess who's home," Mark quipped with a giggle.

But Hayley didn't laugh. Instead she looked into her boyfriend's eyes and said, "I think he did it." She said the words calmly and for the first time since finding Molly, without any tears.

"You can't be serious." Mark took his arms from her.

"And why not?" She demanded. "You heard those sounds, too."

"I just think you're way off on this one, babe."

Hayley couldn't stand to look at him. So she stared at the floor of their walk-in shower instead. The tiles were flooded. "Aw, dammit!"

"Shit!" Mark exclaimed as he realized. He pointed across the room. "Babe, can you pass me the plunger? Please? It's on the floor, just next to the sink."

Mark crouched down into the gathering pool and unscrewed the shower's drain lid before taking the plunger from Hayley, who leaned over him as he went to work.

SQUELCH, SQUELCH, SQULECH! GARGLE!
SQUELCH, SQUELCH, SQUELCH! GARGLE!

"I think I got it!" Mark strained against the suction as he gave it one last try.

SQUELCH, SQUELCH, SQUELCH! GARGLE!

The shower drain choked open as a roaring torrent of bubbles puked a huge dollop of soggy, dead skin across Hayley's stomach. She froze there in disgust and horror as the gunk plastered her belly like old porridge. She screamed as she tumbled backwards.

Mark caught her by the arm. "I got you. I got you!" He forced the showerhead from its hold and aimed the stream at the slimy, graying flesh.

"Get it off! Get it off! Get it off!" Hayley shrieked.

She fell silent as she heard the creaking again.

Someone was listening.

* * *

It was a bright and beautiful morning when Hayley climbed out of the bed she shared with Mark. He was still sound asleep, so she decided not to wake him. Instead, she just smiled and kissed him softly on the cheek.

Slipping on her baby blue dressing gown, she tip-toed out into the hallway and across to the bathroom. Running her fingers through her hair, she looked herself over in the mirror and sighed. "Okay. Let's have a look, shall we?"

She spread open her gown and gasped with excitement.

A large, pale scab had formed in a perfect circle over her belly. It was all lumpy and shiny like uneven bubble-wrap.

Humming in her satisfaction, Hayley reached down with both hands and dug her nails into the bottom of the circle and began to slowly peel the crusty flesh away from her body. Once it had detached, she held it out like a wet face towel, rolled it up like a scroll and placed it neatly next to the sink.

"That's much better." She said, resting her hands proudly on her hips as she admired herself.

There was only a transparent, film-like layer between her glistening intestines and the outside world. They made a squishing sound as the center seemed to move on its own.

Hayley clasped a hand over her mouth as she cried with joy.

A kitten's head had emerged from the middle of her guts. She could hear its faint meows as its face pressed up against the goopy, translucent membrane. This wasn't just any kitten. It was Molly reincarnated.

As she reached in to pet the new Molly through the thin tissue, somehow her touch opened a small pathway for the precious animal to crawl out onto her palm. She giggled as she held her returned loved one to her cheek.

When she turned her gaze back to the mirror so that she might capture this wonderful moment in her mind, she saw Seb behind her. His presence appeared like a dark scar as he stood in the far corner of that perfect, white bathroom. He held a double-barreled shotgun proudly across his chest. His mangled face squelched as it split open. But instead of insects, there was shadow. And from that shadow came a chorus of laughter.

Hayley awoke with a gasp, startling her mother on the other side of the living room. She soon found Mark sitting next to her, sound asleep with crossed arms. The three of them had sat down to watch reruns of one of their favorite sitcoms. Unfortunately, the laugh track was all too familiar.

"Sorry," Hayley yawned. "Is Dad still at work?"

"Oh yes." Her mother rolled her eyes before letting out her own little yawn. "Your father's just got to be there to hold up the ceiling."

Hayley chuckled. "And where's Seb?"

"Sebastian should be enjoying a deep sleep by now, God willing," her mother sighed. "Today has been absolute hell for him. I don't know how your brother does it. He's been so strong."

It was Hayley's turn to roll her eyes.

Turning, she gently nudged Mark awake with her elbow.

"What?" he grunted.

"Come with me," she said quietly.

"What are we doing?"

"Just come with me," Hayley repeated through clenched teeth as she turned to her mother. "Mark and I are just going to get some late supper. Do you want anything?"

"No, no." Her mother shook her head. "But hurry back, or you'll miss the next episode. It's going to be a good one."

"We'll be right back." Mark smiled at her before following his girlfriend out into the hallway. He found her just outside the living room door, standing at the bottom of the stairs. "What is it?"

"You're going to be my lookout," Hayley whispered as she explained. "I'm going to go into his room, and I'm going to look for that gun."

"Hayley, no." Mark took hold of her wrists. "Listen to me. This is crazy. Your brother did not kill your cat."

She shook free as she glared down from her step. "Prove it."

"What?"

"I said, *Prove it.*" Hayley did not blink as she pointed over her shoulder to the top of the stairs. "You think he's innocent? You go up there and you prove to me he didn't do it."

Whatever flaws Mark may have, he always knew when there was no point in arguing with her. With a scowl, he motioned her out of his way and jogged up to the landing as soundly as he could.

Hayley followed closely behind. She perched herself down on the top step, peering out from behind the bannister like a child playing hide-and-seek.

Seb's room was right next to theirs and the closest to the bathroom. She noticed his trail of breadcrumbs leading from his door to the other.

Mark turned the handle. It squealed. He hesitated.

"Go!" Hayley yelled under her breath.

Mark waited just one extra moment to curse at her in his head. Then he took a breath. He opened the door. He stepped inside. He seemed to vanish into the wall of darkness that was waiting for him.

As Hayley's eyes were fixed on that dark doorway, she became wholly unaware that her fingers were pressing hard into her arm. Beads of blood appeared where fingertips met flesh. Her nails dug deeper as they slowly began to rake up her skin. Her eyes finally fell down upon the sight. But before she could register—

"JESUS!" Mark's cry rocked Hayley to her feet.

A light snapped on, and with it came horrid retching sounds.

"Help! Help!" Mark cried on, prompting Hayley to race into the room to his side.

"Oh, God!"

Seb's limbs thrashed wildly as his body rolled and twisted in that bloodstained bed. They were hot and raw and wet. Most of his wounds wept rather than bled. But as bad as his arms and legs were, the worst was his mouth. He had unravelled an entire roll of his bandaging and stuffed it down his throat. And now he was choking to death.

"No!" His sister scolded as she drove both fists into his chest, pushing him down against the mattress. She looked to Mark. "Hold him!"

He did as he was told as Hayley grabbed hold of the soft white material piled inside her brother's mouth and started to pull.

Seb's eyes bulged as he tried to fight them off, but Mark held him still.

"I heard shouting," their mother's voice came from the hall. "You kids better not be fighting again, or I swear—" She peered into the room. "Oh, my God!" She ran to her son's side. "What have you done?" She grabbed the bandaging as it streamed from her son's bluing lips. "Hayley, please, you're not doing it fast enough! Give it!" Her daughter surrendered as she patted Mark on the back. "You keep holding him down!"

Hayley backed away and watched them all helplessly from the bottom of the bed. She trembled as she cried for her brother. She cried for her guilt. She cried for Molly. And all the things she had lost and could lose. But she stopped at the realization that she was tearing at her arms again.

For the first time since she had stepped into that room, she discovered that several carpet bugs had found their way into her brother's bed. On further inspection she found that some of them had become stuck to the gooey fluid oozing from his steaming, weeping wounds.

Her stomach began to turn.

"Hayley!" Mark tried and failed to catch her as she puked up her own stomach acid and fell to the ground.

She was still clawing at herself, even when she lost consciousness.

* * *

Hayley sat at the family dining table. Legs of iron and a top made of clear glass. Molly leapt up onto the placemat in front of her. She was exactly the way she had been.

"Put her down," her mother said. "You know she's not allowed up here with us."

"Oh, Mom, she's just playing." Hayley dismissed her as she reached out to stroke Molly's fur.

A raspy breath that filled the room sent the poor feline running for cover. The sound shredded through the air like a rusty saw.

Hayley reluctantly turned her eye on her brother, who sat at the head of the table.

From what she could see, he wore no clothes as he placed both hands on either side of his placemat. The hair from his head, eyelids, and eyebrows was gone. He inhaled deeply. The flesh all over his body seemed to vibrate in lumps. And then he exhaled. Again came that unnerving raspy breath. And with it, countless flaps of dried skin opened on Seb's body and stood on end. With every move or sound that he made, they flickered and fluttered like moth wings.

Hayley looked to her mother for help.

Her mother opened her mouth to speak, but instead of her voice, a pale dust spilled out of it onto the table like sand through an hourglass.

The kitchen door flew open as Mark graced everyone with his presence. He was draped in a quilt-sized form of the dishtowel Molly was buried in. His eyes were lifeless below a single bullet wound in the center of his forehead.

"Dinner's here!" He announced heartily as his body levitated towards the table, carrying one large pizza box.

He set it down in front of his girlfriend and smiled warmly as he gave her a kiss on the forehead. "Did you forget to moisturize this morning, babe?"

Before she could give an answer, Mark's body drifted towards the patio doors as they opened themselves for him.

"I always moisturize." She finally replied as she turned to watch her boyfriend hover out into the backyard and across the grass to the center where a life-sized shallow grave was waiting.

The quilt fell in first. And then Mark's corpse.

There sounded a familiar *POP!* of a gunshot as the pizza box blew wide open behind her. A river as gray as the gravestone rushed out of the torn cardboard. Thousands upon thousands of hungry carpet bugs.

"No!" Hayley cried as she jumped out of her seat and threw herself through the patio doors.

She laid down beside her beloved in his grave. If this was how the world was going to end, she wanted to die next to him. And even as the ravenous carpet bugs found her and began flooding in all around her, she was still grateful to have that choice.

In her last moments, Mark's eyes opened as his body reanimated. He smiled and whispered, "Hey babe."

With those words, the world was suddenly filled with blazing bright light. The muddy walls of their grave were gone. And in their place, a hospital curtain.

"Mark?" Hayley croaked. She felt groggy, like a bowling ball was inside her skull, weighing her down to the pillow.

"We're in the ER." Mark explained. "You really scared us. You scratched yourself raw when you were out of it, so we took you here to get fixed up."

What he said made sense as she could feel the warm pressure of the bandages and tape used to dress the wounds on her arms. Then she remembered. "And Seb?"

"He's fine. He's fine." Mark assured her. "He's got a room in another wing. Looks like he's in for some serious counseling, but your mom's with him."

"That's good."

"I have some great news, babe," Mark went on.

"What is it?" Hayley could only bear to whisper with her aching throat.

"I know you've been worried about things because of your brother."

"Uh-huh?"

"Well, the doctors took a look at you and did some tests and stuff while you were sleeping."

"What did they say?"

"They said what you've been feeling is totally normal."

Hayley scoffed at him and rolled her eyes.

"No, seriously!" Mark insisted. "They said you've got a condition called P.U.P.P.P."

"What is that?"

"It's a rash that shows up in pregnant women during their 3rd trimester, but in your case, it's very rare because you're still in the first trimester."

Hayley eyes widened as she suddenly felt a little more alert. "Pregnant women?"

"That's right." Mark couldn't hold back his tears. "We're going to have a baby."

Hayley joined him as she put a hand on his wet cheek. "We're having a baby."

"So, you see?" Mark caressed her hair. "You've been worried about nothing."

"Yes," Hayley sighed with relief until her eyes narrowed at her boyfriend. "How did you remember all that stuff about trimesters?"

"Yeah, I had to write it down!" He confessed, holding up a crumpled piece of paper.

The two of them laughed together, sharing in an embrace and a kiss.

* * *

Almost a year had passed since that morning at the hospital. In that time, Hayley's father had taken early retirement, her brother's condition began to improve, and she and Mark decided to do the adult thing and get their own place where they would raise their new baby boy, Brady. But they visited their old home as much as they possibly could so that Brady could get to know both of his grandparents well. Still, it would be a while before Hayley could stand to be there for more than a few hours at a time after everything that had happened.

Nevertheless, it was on one of these many visits that a concerned Hayley had a particular question for Brady's grandmother.

She pointed at his head as he bounced away in his bouncer on the kitchen floor. "Mom, do you know what this is?"

Her mother raised a hesitant eyebrow at her before leaning down to inspect her grandson. He took no notice of her as she gently moved the silky locks of his golden hair from side to side. She noticed the orange, crusty lumps on his scalp and rolled her eyes with a huff. "Silly girl, it's just cradle cap. It'll clear up on its own eventually."

"Cradle cap," Hayley repeated softly as she gazed down at her baby's head.

Her fingers twitched. They curled into claws. They began scratching at thin air. Scratching dead and dry flesh that wasn't there.

Heart Skull Heart

Bryan Miller

IMPORTANT: Read this before you open the door.

DO NOT OPEN THE DOOR.

It's hard to explain the physical sensation of hearing your daughter spoken about the way people spoke about Zoe. *Killer. Witch. Psychopath. The girl who killed that boy with just her telephone. Monster.*

These words trigger a physiological reaction for a father: bile burning the stomach, blood vessels contracting in the brain, the vertiginous droop of equilibrium as the world around you bends in all the wrong directions. These words have a physical effect.

Yes, I appreciate the irony.

The words people use don't match my Zoe at all. They're a description of some other girl, a dark, twisted, inexplicable person I would never hope to meet. My Zoe is the four-year-old who kept hobbled butterflies in shoeboxes to help them convalesce; at night, Caroline and I would sneak into her room to empty the size-ten cardboard coffins of their dead monarchs so we could tell her in the morning that they must have gotten all better and flown away. My Zoe is the one who buried her face in my shoulder while I fast-forwarded through the scary parts of *The Lion King*. The eight-year-old who insisted Caroline and I drive her around town to bury acorns in all the city parks after she learned about Arbor Day. Who sang "You Are My Sunshine" to her comatose grandmother in those final, grim days of hospice care.

Of course, there is more to the story.

I know what she did to Josh Mason. The police told me. The lawyers described it in great detail. Zoe confessed it to me herself, crying across a metal table that was bolted to the floor while she curled herself into a ball of baggy orange jailhouse jumpsuit. That one was the worst. She told me herself, in the same voice she used to sing to my dying mother, how Josh was just so sad, how he said he would never feel better until he killed himself and she believed him, she just wanted him to feel better, was that so wrong?

I pictured a shoebox emptied of all those butterflies she thought flew away, restored.

Yes, what Zoe did was wrong. But does it outweigh everything else, all those triaged butterflies and sapling oaks and the "You Are My Sunshine" that sits in my heart with the density of moon rocks?

* * *

What you probably remember about Zoe is the beautiful blonde girl with the wide, expressionless green eyes sitting between two dark-suited defense attorneys.

When you think of her, you likely remember one of the two most famous photos of her.

In the first, a snapshot from the *New York Times*, Zoe stands before the judge in a red-and-white checkered short-sleeved dress Caroline picked out for her. So much got made of that dress, how high it stopped over her knees, the snug fit of the waist and bosom. Just another cruel joke the public couldn't appreciate—that the gawky teenage girl with the spindly legs and braces and chipmunk cheeks flowered into womanhood just in time to be cast as a seductress who sang Josh Mason toward the jagged rocks with her siren text messages.

Also, in that same photo, the one where she stands with her hips cocked sideways, as though she's posing for a glamour shot—some people say it looks like she's rolling her eyes at the victim's family.

What to make, then, of the other photo? The one from the day of her arrest when the police couldn't cajole her into letting go of her stuffed green alligator, which she held onto as though it was the only thing keeping her from floating right up into the empty sky? They let her ride to the station that way. The press was on hand to photograph her arrival. A photographer captured her through the tinted back window, red-faced and teary eyed, curled around that stuffed animal.

People don't know that stuffie's name was Gary Gator, that I bought it for Zoe when she was six, hospitalized with an inflamed appendix. Caroline and I were more scared than she was. We couldn't conceive that someone would slice into our tiny, soft, seamless little girl to scoop part of her out. I bought one of every stuffed animal in the overpriced hospital gift shop downstairs so that Zoe would awaken from the anesthesia to find herself packed in fuzzy animals. She loved fat-bellied Gary Gator above all of them. He became her constant bedtime companion, for so long that it became a little inside joke when she would bring him to sleepaway camp or to my office for Take Your Daughter to Work Day, where she dazzled all the other programmers with her precocious computer skills. Gary Gator was even in the photo of Zoe I kept there on my desk. The police returned him to us after they brought her into station, just before they fingerprinted her and took her to her cell.

So which girl is Zoe, the one who looks like barely a teenager as she presses her burning face against Gary Gator's worn fabric? Or the almost-grown woman who knows to stand with her hips cocked just so?

Can't it be both, or neither? How you answer this question probably speaks to your reaction to the verdict.

* * *

I'll admit, the methodology of Josh Mason's death is difficult to reconcile. Undeniably, that was Zoe's idea.

Josh's phone recorded the entire exchange. His teenagery speculations that the world would be better off without him. Her replies. Chilling replies, yes. I'd never heard my daughter speak that way before.

> just fucken do it already get a rope or a hose for ur car
> dont ur parents have pills in the house?
> at least when ur dead u wont be a pussy anymore

In court, I could see that the jury was swayed by the texts in which she gave him specific instructions.

> *are ur parents home?*
> *get the drano and duct tape you bought. be fast. this way you wont bitch out like you did with the rope*

Josh followed Zoe's instructions to the letter. He sat down on the Masons' kitchen floor. He tore off one long, silver strip of duct tape. He opened the white plastic jug of Drano. He ignored all the warnings. He tipped it back and took one stinging chug. He dropped the bottle of Drano, which leaked out and ate through the linoleum tile down into the sub-flooring. As quickly as possible, quick enough, he wound the strip of duct tape around his head, over his lips, sealing his mouth shut. Seconds later when his stomach rejected the drain-cleaning sludge, it had nowhere to go.

Technically, the cause of death was asphyxiation. Drowning, if it's possible to drown in your own melting lungs.

Both the prosecutors and the defense considered her final texts to be the most potentially damning.

> *ur gonna do it now right?*
> *dont wait i luv u*
> *but first put your phone in your room somewhere ur   parents wont find it*
> *[Inside my old hockey skates? he replies]*
> *perfect. turn off the phone finder app first. now do it.*
> Heart emoji. Skull emoji. Heart emoji.

* * *

If we're going to talk about culpability, what about Josh Mason?

Poor Josh. A sweet kid to be sure. Maybe too sweet for his own good. We first met him as a wary-looking kindergartener in Zoe's class, tentatively hovering around the periphery at birthday parties, holiday pageants, chaperoned field trips. Rather than toughen up as he hit puberty, he wilted inward. A tall, good-looking kid who walked around appearing fragile as crystal stemware. Other parents claim they didn't notice that, but they did.

Zoe and Josh spent so much time together as kids, a rare pair of boy-girl pals, that Caroline and I didn't know how to refer to as they grew into teenagerdom. They called and texted one another constantly but never kissed or held hands in our presence. Were they boyfriend and girlfriend? Did kids even use such terms these days?

It didn't seem strange, then, when two days after Josh's death Zoe appeared on the Masons' doorstep in tears, asking could she come in to see Josh's room and get some things she left there to remember him by. Rhonda Mason would later testify that she hugged Zoe—she said "hugged" with a voice full of acid—and told her to take her time. Zoe emerged a few minutes later with a book and a strip of black-and-white pictures of her and Josh making goofy faces in a carnival photo booth.

What Rhonda didn't see then was that, in her back pocket, Zoe had Josh's cell phone, which she'd found deep in the back of his closet, jammed down toward the toe of one of his smelly hockey skates.

This is the detail that goddamn ghoul Nancy Grace focused on when she made money every night talking about Zoe on cable TV. The so-called proof of intent.

Zoe knew the phone was evidence. She convinced Josh to hide it. "The murder weapon," Nancy sneered. Then Zoe had come to his house to collect it.

Our lawyers, from the outlandishly expensive firm of Milliwae and Seachord, argued: Zoe didn't consider the phone evidence because she never thought she committed a crime. She knew she might get in trouble if people ever found the phone and saw how she was helping Josh. All she wanted was to help, she just didn't want to jeopardize her own future to do it.

What Zoe neglected to take into account was that the police didn't need the actual, physical phone to retrieve the call logs from the cellular network provider. They seized Zoe's phone, too, and her computer. This all happened on that chaotic day when the police showed up at our front door with warrants and evidence bags and took our daughter away.

The cops were frustrated to discover almost all of Zoe's online records completely scrubbed. Email messages, Facetime conversations, Snapchat, search history, even phone calls she'd made through an app on her computer. She'd conducted most of her business online through a Tor browser she'd installed. Dark web stuff. I remembered my co-workers cooing over her facility with code, even at age eight. A chip off the old block, Daddy's girl. The prosecutors argued that essential evidence from Zoe's end of the conversation was missing, recordings that would have further implicated her. But it was in the ether, as lost as Josh Mason.

* * *

Innocent.

So decreed the jury.

The courtroom erupted. Outside, news cameras hummed to life. Somewhere Nancy Grace was screaming into a pillow, hopefully.

I couldn't process the full implications of the word. I knew Caroline and Zoe and I would have to do a lot of work before we could think that way. It did mean that Zoe would finally be coming home. We could start trying to understand. We would likely have to move, perhaps even change our names. We would deal with that eventually. First we had to get Zoe out of that cell and back into her room where Gary Gator and the rest of her stuffie pals waited patiently.

We didn't talk about it at first. Zoe didn't speak much at all. She stayed in her room, in her pajamas. Caroline and I brought her soup, paperback books, glasses of water to swallow her new pills. We could feel the outside world desperate to look in through our windows. Caroline and I took turns running the diminishing media gauntlet on the front lawn when we needed groceries.

She was off on one of those grocery runs, late night when the store is mostly empty and nobody is paying attention, when I went to check on Zoe. She had dozed off, sprawled in a crooked tangle of pink comforter that took up every inch of her bed. I had to lean in at an awkward angle to plant a kiss on her forehead. My hand wobbled on something uneven beneath the covers—Gary Gator and his fat, fuzzy belly. And in that second, as I steadied myself, I felt something strange through the cotton and fabric.

Zoe barely stirred when I extracted Gary from her sleepy grasp. I carried the stuffed animal down the hallway to the dining room table to conduct my examination. Looking close at Gary, who was a little worn and worse for the wear, I could instantly remember that desperate falling sensation in my chest when I stood in line at the hospital gift shop, holding him in the crook of my arm while I passed my credit card over to a disinterested cashier.

I squeezed Gary between both hands. Inside I could feel something hard and out of place, like a tumor. That was accompanied by a muted crackling sound.

I flipped Gary over. Hidden beneath the crease of his tail was a two-inch-long slit sealed shut with five stitches of thread in perfect matching Gary green.

I popped the stitches open one by one between my pinched fingertips.

Gary's cotton bowels spilled out onto the tabletop, along with a little cache of hidden treasures. Several folded-up sheets of paper, a plastic miniature of the Statue of Liberty, and a red key ring with *"Guys & Dolls* cast member, MHS 2019!"

I glanced back down the dark hallway at Zoe's closed bedroom door.

I unfolded the paper.

The first sheet was a black-and-white printout of a photo, a boy I'd never seen before. He had close-cropped bleached hair. The bags under his eyes belied his baby face. His jaw was clenched solemnly. In his right hand, he held aloft a noose.

The second sheet was screenshot printout of an online message conversation conducted on a private, secure site.

> *make sure the bathwater is warm. itll feel like nothing at all.*
> *Nothing sounds good. :(*
> *it will be so much better now i promise. just get in the tub and do it like i said. do it right now.*
> *You're the only person who loves me.*
> *& i always will* Heart emoji. Skull emoji. Heart emoji.

The third sheet of paper was a handwritten note, on lined paper in number-two pencil like a homework assignment. I only managed to read the first sentence.

Dearest Zoe, my love, that you so much for giving me the courage to do what I could not otherwise...

I threw up in the kitchen sink for awhile. When my stomach was empty, I emptied the soggy bits out of the drain plug and scrubbed the whole stainless-steel basin with dish soap. By then my hands were steady enough to use my phone.

I googled *MHS Guys and Dolls teenager suicide.*

A photo of a bright-eyed African-American girl appeared on screen. She grinned broadly showing too-big teeth in her uncomfortable looking marching band jacket and hat. The obituary beneath the photo filled in all of the tragic details.

Well, almost all the details.

Headlights swept through the living room window. Quick as I could, I stuffed all the wadded cotton and dark souvenirs back up inside Gary Gator. I used a stapler to re-seal the slit beneath his tail. You could barely tell the difference. I padded down the hall to Zoe's room and left Gary laying on the pillow next to Zoe. I got back into the living room just in time to see Caroline come through the front door.

I waited. Two days. I convinced Caroline to take an evening for herself. Get a drink, see a movie, just drive around, whatever she wanted. Before she left she kissed me harder than she had in a long time.

I walked down the hall to Zoe's room. She sat cross-legged on her mattress in a Taylor Swift t-shirt and baggy *Adventure Time* pajama pants.

She looked like the girl in both photos.

I reached past her to snag Gary Gator. Zoe smiled at me quizzically, unsure what I was up to until I tore Gary in half. He spilled his guts onto the bed. The both of us looked down at the papers, the keychain, the little Statue of Liberty. I dropped Gary's head to the floor.

I asked Zoe if she could explain this.

Her expression flattened.

I asked her, how many times have you done this?

"According to the jury I didn't *do* anything, Daddy."

That expression never wavered.

I let it all go. I told Zoe she would never understand the terrible, icy feeling of raising a child who did something so monstrous. Like it was your own left arm committing sins while you were forced to watch. How it was worse for her mother than me, because those texts, those poison ideas, they had physically come out of her body. How I could never once look Rhonda or David Mason in the eye during the trial, because I couldn't handle the spark of recognition that would pass between us that our clueless parenting led to such tragedy. At least they got to be sad. They got to mourn. We weren't allowed to be happy or to be unhappy. One was gloating, the other ungrateful. We had to be brave, be somber, be contrite. Be supportive. We had to bring this *thing* home with us, and live with it.

Zoe didn't break down or cry. She wouldn't give me that much.

I told her to look me in the eye.

I told her, you know what you have to do next.

This is the only way to fix all the problems.

The world will be better off without you.

Don't wait. Now is the time.

Those dark little worry lines Zoe got on her face when she fretted vanished.

She said, "You know what you have to do too, Daddy."

I told her, yes. Right after her.

I'm sorry. I'm sorry to everyone. Most of all you, Caroline. I could never have stopped being sorry. To whoever is reading this, call the police. Don't open the bedroom door. Especially if it's you, Caroline. Leave the house now.

DO NOT OPEN THE DOOR.

Love,
Daddy

Cuckoo
Liam Hogan

I never really got along with Elsie. Call it first child syndrome if you will, but what my parents took to be the cruel taunts of an older brother—fingers plunged into pudgy flesh, nose firmly pinched, a casual shove as wobbly legs struggled to support her first steps—these were acts of curiosity, not malevolence.

I wanted to hear her cry.

According to my father, my first memories came from after this, around the time of my fifth birthday. A day of sun and water, cake and joy. The only happy day I can remember, before the tragedy that meant I'd never celebrate anything again.

He refused to discuss earlier recollections, two whole years prior to that halcyon garden party. All the way back, in fits and starts, to a night of jagged lightning, of wind, and rain, and hail. A night of blood, and screams, and tears.

The night my sister was born.

He refused to believe that a child who had only just begun to speak could remember overhearing the ashen-faced midwife telling him the screaming child wouldn't last the night and that was surely for the best. That his wife was heavily sedated. That she was torn up inside and would never conceive again.

Words I did not yet know the meaning of, so how could three-year-old me possibly remember?

How could I forget?

Despite my best—or worst—efforts, Elsie never cried. Never echoed the piteous mewling from that terrible night. A happy, gurgling baby, Elsie. Healthy, everyone agreed.

About as unlike me as you could possibly get.

I waited to see when—*if*—her hair would turn from spun gold to mousy brown, as mine had done. In the half-filled family photo-album, there's a picture caught of the in-between; salt and pepper strands mimicking my father's aged hair in color if not in length. In the next snap, I was a silvery brown and from then onwards it's sometimes hard to tell my hair wasn't black.

But Elsie's hair never changed. It stayed yellow, even to the end. Screaming the truth.

The midwife had been gone fifteen minutes when the doorbell rang. Hardly audible over the hail rattling the windows, over the gut-wrenching wails from the cot in the corner, over the suffocating silence from above. My father ignored it, slumped over the kitchen table, an unwashed tumbler awash with something the color of un-milked tea. It came again, punctuated by a solid thud, and his hollowed eyes followed mine to the darkened hallway.

The child in the basket left on the doorstep was well-wrapped and sleeping peacefully, even when she was carried into the kitchen, lowered incredulously onto the cluttered surface.

There was a note; I'm sure I remember it dangling over the side of the ridiculously old-fashioned wicker basket. A tag, bound by parcel string to one of the handles. I remember Dad's lips moving to the unspoken words.

And then he put me to bed. Tucked me in, kissed me once on the forehead, his touch cold, the fumes foreign and disquieting.

I lay awake, listening to the soft sobbing from the room next to mine. Lay awake until I felt the breath of cold air as the front door opened; the sharp *snick!* as it closed.

In the morning, it was as if nothing had happened at all.

* * *

I couldn't forgive my father; not for that and not for what followed later. He'd been warned: my mother's fragile womb; but he went and got her pregnant again anyway. Shortly before my sixth birthday, in a blur of flashing blue ambulance lights and after Elsie and I had been thrust into the arms of a neighbor we'd never met, mother and the unborn third child died, tearing our family apart and leaving an unbridgeable chasm between my father and me.

It did not help that even in the midst of such a tragedy he so obviously doted on the fair haired, easy-going interloper. Favored her superficial similarity to a dearly departed wife over his own flesh and blood. It did not help that his misplaced love for Elsie crowded out any feelings for me. My father was unable or unwilling to meet my childhood gaze; his guilty secret shared, but never acknowledged.

Over time I began to doubt my memories, to ponder the logistics of this dark and improbable fairytale of changelings, of orphans abandoned on doorsteps. I stopped talking about it, to the relief of my father. But I didn't forget. I smothered my resentment and let it fester, treated both my dad and my fake sister with cold disdain.

Four and a half decades after her dramatic entrance, Elsie's perfect life was over.

It was nothing as clichéd as cancer, and nothing as abrupt as a traffic accident. Class A streptococcus and severe sepsis. Three short days from infection to the critical care unit of the local A&E, from flu-like symptoms to a rash, to abdominal pains, to organ failure. A mere twelve hours from diagnosis and induced coma to death, her blood pressure plunging to zero while medical staff flooded her puffed up body with fluids and antibiotics.

I missed all that. Missed saying goodbye to her by a little over an hour. The first time we would have spoken—albeit one-sidedly—in five years, since the wedding I almost didn't attend.

Maybe I shouldn't have waited until morning. Maybe I should have driven through the night, after the awkward call from my father, the slow difficult conversation, strangled by pauses. But who was to know it was *that* serious, that sudden? And what difference would it have made anyway? To her? To me?

Dad wrapped me up in an uncharacteristic hug as Elsie's husband, Tim, looked on, shell-shocked. I was astonished at how frail my father had become. Astonished at how different Tim looked out of his wedding gear. Beneath the harsh hospital fluorescents, both of them were haggard and I felt briefly guilty for the night's sleep I'd stolen before the drive north.

We sat silent in the condolences room. The one room in the hospital still allowed flowers, though they turned out to be plastic. Nursed cold half cups of insipid tea for interminable hours until I stood and patted my pocket. "Right. Well, I guess I need something to eat. And then I'd better book a hotel for the night—"

"Don't be bloody daft," my father said. "You'll stay with me. But you're right enough about the food. Tim?"

Tim shook his head. "I'm going to stay," he said. "Until..."

I wasn't sure what the *until* was. I'm not sure he knew either.

My father nodded, wrapped a scrawny arm around Tim's shoulder, and handed him a set of car keys. "When you're ready," he said, voice soft and gentle.

Then, perfunctorily to me: "Drive me home, son."

I'd not set foot in that house since I left for college. It was exactly as I remembered, the same ghastly paisley wallpaper, the same cluttered bookshelves with the same tattered paperbacks. There was a single nod to progress, to the intervening decades: a flat screen TV bigger than the Formica coffee table I used to play my solitary board games on.

I wondered what my father watched on it.

Dad settled in the kitchen as I traipsed upstairs to the avocado green bathroom, ducking a head into my old room as I went. Nothing but cardboard boxes, stacked floor to ceiling, buckling at the base. No sign of a bed. I didn't check Elsie's room. Bed or no, I wasn't sleeping there.

As I was about to return downstairs to make my excuses, to work out where the nearest cheap hotel was, I hovered in the door of my father's bedroom. I'd thought to drag out the family photo album. Thought that, painful though it would be, this was the time for it.

Assuming it wasn't in one of those stacked cardboard boxes.

I dragged the suitcase out from under the bed. Flicked the metal latches, the sound familiar though it'd been over thirty years since I'd last heard it and never while my father had been in the house.

I didn't get to the faux-leather album, with its faded portraits coming loose along with their ivory photo corners. Because there, lying on top, was a yellowed, hand-cut parcel tag, string still attached.

The writing was neat but tiny, crowding to the edges. I had to put my glasses on before I could read it.

"Out of despair, comes hope. If you would take this child to be your own, to nurture and raise and love and cherish, in short: to do all the things the mother cannot, then leave your child on the doorstep in its place. I shall return within the hour. Yours, a friend."

Fingers burning, I left it where it fell, flipped over to reveal the roughly trimmed picture of a local church. Left the case full of old photos, letters, odds and ends from a shared lifetime cut short. I left it open, stranded in the middle of my father's bedroom floor, evidence of my trespass.

Downstairs I could hear the whistle of an almost boiling kettle. I couldn't enter the kitchen, couldn't confront him, so I pushed through the back door and into the garden. Sat on a once white plastic chair as dusk's blacks and blues draped themselves around me. Sat in the lee of the potting shed as the lights in the house flickered on one at a time, hearing the muffled call of my name.

I sat and tried to reconstruct sunlight filled memories from the darkness. The old apple tree *here*, the paddling pool must have been *there*, a table crowded with party food, a sun awning protecting Elsie over by the French windows. Mum...

I scrubbed the thoughts from my head. Sat, and waited.

And waited.

Cold, wet leaves soaked through my slacks. Pink ebbed from the sky and a cuckoo mocked the occasion.

When my father finally emerged, he had the card clutched in his bony fingers. I rose from my seat to tower over him.

"So it's true, then," I spat, angry, hurt. "All the things you lied about as I grew up."

He hung his head in shame, displaying his thinning crown.

"All the things I remember--"

"You *don't* remember," he said, repeating the old refrain.

"I do," I insisted, bitter and sullen. "The midwife... mum. The knock on the door. The baby on the doorstep. You changed my sister for a stranger!"

There was silence. In the distance, a radio blared a snatch of some popular song, before being dialed down to a less audible level. Then he spoke, his voice flat. "It's not Elsie that was changed. Did you...?" my father tentatively asked. "Did you look at the other side? The church?"

He held out the tag, but I refused to take it, already scalded, wary of being damaged further.

"No religion would excuse what you did."

"St Mary's Centenary," he read, though it must have been too dark to see. "1869-1969."

"So?" I scowled. "It's an old card."

Dad shook his head. "Elsie was born in '72. We never... we never expected her to happen. Had given up trying. Our little miracle."

"Some miracle," I laughed, the sound harsh and alien.

"No, son. She was... perfect. And the pregnancy, the pregnancy was trouble free. We didn't realize we were playing Russian roulette."

"Perfect? So perfect you swapped her for another?"

"That's what I've been trying to tell you. You couldn't remember. *Can't*. Because it was you in that basket. *You* were the baby on the doorstep. The one who replaced our poor, crippled first born."

In the gloom, I couldn't see his eyes. The hazel eyes I shared, one of his few gifts to me. At least, that is what I'd always thought, always assumed. I turned to go, my shoulder brushing his, forcing him aside.

"Please..." he begged from the darkness at my back.

I paused, hand on the garden gate, waiting for one final lie to remember him by. I had my cars keys in my pocket and everything and everyone else could go hang.

"Please... forgive me?"

Lemonade
Paul Stansfield

"Have you ever seen so much shit in one house?" said Bart, as he pulled out yet another heavy cardboard box from his great uncle's bedroom closet.

"Language, Barton. You're not at work, or hanging around with your friends," said his mother, who was sitting on the floor, going through the contents of a lower dresser drawer. His dad was in the corner, rummaging through a giant desk.

Bart sighed. "Fine, have you ever seen so much crap in one house, then?"

"No, I haven't. I thought my parents' place was bad, but Uncle Thomas leaves them in the dust. It's weird, too—when he was younger, he was a bit of a neat freak. I guess he got lazy in his old age, or was slipping mentally or something." She sneezed. "Lord, this dust. I need to get a tissue." She stood up and walked out of the room.

"Hey Dad," Bart said, in a lower voice. "Speaking of crap, did you ever hear about Crazy Eddie from Philly?" His dad shook his head. "I heard about him on Stern years ago. He was this bizarre millionaire pervert who collected human feces. He'd pay guys—only guys, too, he was gay—to do it in pizza boxes, and he saved them. Apparently, he had a whole warehouse full of them."

"I'm so glad you're spending good money to hear such scintillating, intellectual news." His dad shut a drawer sharply, and returned to sorting.

"Well, just saying, it could be worse." Bart got back to work as well, just as his mother returned, tissues in hand. The current box, he saw, held appliances. As he pulled each one out, it was obvious that each was broken. The toaster's one side was gone, and half the innards were poking out. The blender had a long, wide crack in its mixing bowl section. And here was yet another toaster, also clearly damaged. "Broken appliances now. Why didn't he throw anything out?" His father and mother both looked at him and chuckled.

"That's weird," said his dad, "But this is even more absurd." He held out a handful of strips of paper. "He kept old receipts. Look, one from Rite Aid for cough drops and Band-

Aids, from March of 1986. One for his Betamax VCR, which, oddly he actually did get rid of and replace with a VHS. And a handwritten one from Pucchino's, in 1969. He got a medium pizza with pepperoni and a Coke." They all laughed.

"Look at this," crowed his mother. They did, and saw she was now wearing a sombrero with *South of the Border* printed on its ridiculously wide brim in orange letters.

Bart chuckled, and he stood up and hoisted the box onto the bed. There were two categories of items on it—the Throw Out side and the Save side. The former held about ten times the number of things. The springs squealed as he put down the box. The bed was ancient too, at least thirty years old. Probably they'd find the bill of sale for that soon, too.

"Promise me when you guys get old, and feel yourselves slipping and all, that you'll start giving away or throwing out all the shi—stuff you don't want before you die."

"Don't worry," said his mother, "We've learned our lesson." His dad added a nod.

Bart went back into the closet, and saw he was down to the last box. Great. Finally he could see the end of this task. It was their fourth day here, and after the bedroom, all that was left was the kitchen. Like he wanted to waste his precious summer vacation cooped up in his strange old great uncle's house. And Aunt Ginny and Uncle Ray weren't doing squat to help. He hoped his folks ignored the will and kept more than 50% of the money after they sold all of Uncle Thomas' crap, and his house.

He flipped the lid off the box and saw it contained books. Well, that was something. His friend had made him paranoid, talking about what he called "The Fuck Box," a guy's porn stash. Gene had gone through his grandfather's things a year ago and had found out some alarming things about his Pop-Pop's sexual tastes. "If you find an unmarked videotape in the bedroom," Gene had said, "throw it out immediately. Whatever you do, don't play it!! Not unless you want to spend the rest of your life with nightmares, or in therapy!" Gene had also said that he'd read in Maxim or somewhere that it was the trend these days for guys to have a specially appointed friend who would go into your bedroom and remove your porn if you died unexpectedly, so your siblings or folks didn't find it. Well, apparently Uncle Thomas had a similar arrangement, or he'd thrown it out before he'd died, because they'd found nothing more erotic than old *Sports Illustrated* swimsuit issues (mixed with every other, regular issue of *Sports Illustrated*, from the past fifty years. God forbid you'd not have access to the article about the 1961 World Series in 2009).

The books were a mix of paperbacks and hardcover, nothing of interest to Bart. Mostly westerns and mysteries, along with some *Reader's Digest* condensed books. Bart had never understood the point of condensed books—to him that would be like watching an hour version of an hour and a half long movie. Either experience the whole thing, or don't read it at all. At the bottom of the box, though, he found something different.

There were three books, all with weird covers. Bart picked them up, one by one. *Malleus Maleficarum* by Heinrich Kramer and Jakob Sprenger, *Fanny Hill* by John Cleland, and *The Wizard of Oz* by Lyman Frank Baum. Their surfaces were some sort of strange leather, very rough and pebbly, like a basketball, only more extreme. He opened *Oz* and saw, to his surprise, that the book was handwritten—small but very legible brown script, with a large fancy capital letter on the first word of each chapter. The other two books were the same. Bart put all of the books back into the old Ortlieb's box, with the three odd ones on top, and lugged it out by the bed.

"Hey," he said to his parents, "check these out." He pulled out the handwritten books, and his mom and dad looked them over briefly. "The rest of the books are regular, cheap mysteries and Zane Grays, but these might be worth something. My friend Jim is a collector, he might be able to help us out."

"Guess it wouldn't hurt," said his mom. "This Jim wouldn't lie to us, rip us off, would he?"

Bart laughed. "Not a chance. He's a complete Boy Scout. Literally, and figuratively. He's the type of guy who gives the cashier back the extra cash if they give him the wrong change in his favor."

"Okay, fine," said his mother. She turned back to the drawers. His dad just grinned and nodded.

A moment later his father burst out, "One from Grant's department store. The store hasn't even been in business since the mid-70s. Jesus!"

* * *

The car ahead of him was a Ford Explorer. Bart laughed out loud. That was a good one. A friend of his had told him of a fun game involving vehicle names. You put the word "anal" in front of each name. Some of them were really funny, like the Explorer, the Expedition, the Legacy, the Intrigue, the Liberty, the Commander, the Focus, the Mirage, and of course, the one that probably started the entire game, the Probe.

There it was—Canal Street. Bart signaled, and then turned right. Canal Street was actually in the shopping district, so traffic here was heavier. After another two blocks, he saw the store on the right side. He started to look for a parking spot, and just as he did, a car pulled out, leaving him a good one only two stores down from his destination. Bart parallel parked his Honda Civic (sadly, the game didn't work well on all cars), got out, and locked up with his remote key.

The window read *Antiques, Collectables, and Ephemera*, printed in gold paint that was just starting to flake off in places. The large shelf facing the street looked like the results of an attic's attack of bad nausea. Old sports equipment was against one wall—baseball bats, gloves, some bowling balls, and a couple of wooden tennis rackets, still in their presses. Taxidermied animals manned the near wall—a raccoon, a squirrel, a possum, a disembodied deer head, and a ratty looking raven. Between these were toys and archaeological objects. Soldiers staged a mini-battle next to Smurfs, and next to these were Civil War guns and bayonets, boxes of Minié ball bullets, and flint arrowheads. As Bart reached for the doorknob he had a brief moment of panic—what was this guy's name again? Then he saw, on the window in smaller letters, *Paul Johnson, owner and proprietor*, and he signed in relief.

The shelves inside were slightly more neater and organized. The back half or so of the establishment was nearly all books, stacked floor to ceiling. A sliding ladder was against the left wall. A man was at the top, scanning some titles on the top row. He looked down at Bart as he approached.

"May I help you?" the man said.

"Yeah, I'm looking for Paul Johnson. A friend of mine, Jim Shapiro, left some of my great uncle's books here for him to evaluate. I'm Bart Duckett."

The man climbed down the steps quickly, and held out a hand. "Right! I'm Paul Johnson. Call me Paul." Johnson broke the grip and stepped behind the counter. Seconds later the three books were in view. Bart noticed, to his mild surprise, that the guy wasn't some old fossil. He was maybe late 30s, early 40s, tall and thin, with significant hair loss. "I was waiting for you. Those books you brought in were quite fascinating, Mr. Duckett. Fascinating, and disturbing."

Disturbing? thought Bart. *What did that mean?* "So are they worth anything?"

Johnson laughed. "They're worth quite a bit. A ton, actually." Bart stared hard at the books. Johnson produced a cardboard box, placed the books inside, and handed it over to Bart. "I'd love to buy them from you, but I don't have the money. I would, however, like to find a buyer for you, in return for a small percentage. Doing this would get you a much higher price than from a dealer. I have connections, you see, relationships with rich collectors. But of course, that's up to you."

Bart sighed. This was reminding him of *Antiques Roadshow*. Why didn't Johnson just tell him what they were worth? Why the song and dance? "So how much are we talking about?"

Johnson smiled and indicated an overstuffed easy chair behind Bart. "I would take a seat if I were you."

Bart sniffed in irritation, hesitated, started to say something, and then finally he backed up and did sit.

"I can't say exactly, because of course I don't know for sure how anxious collectors will be, but I'd say about a million dollars for each. Two-point-five million for the trio at a bare minimum."

Bart stared down at the books, and went silent. Finally, he put the box gently on the floor, and started to pace.

"You're shitting me, right? Jim got you to play a little joke on me, huh?" He looked around the store dramatically. "This being filmed for some pranks show or something?"

Johnson laughed. "I know it's unbelievable, but it's true. But don't hesitate to get other opinions. You should, actually.

Although I would like a chance, as I mentioned before, to find a buyer for you. But hold on. I'm not finished. There's bad news, too. I would take a seat again."

Bart stared at Johnson, tearing his thoughts away from his mom being able to retire, new cars for each of them, no more student loans. Hell, he'd be able to attend Syracuse now, if he wanted. He hesitated again, and then found himself back in the comfortable chair.

"No doubt you noticed the strange feel of the leather covers of the books. There's a good reason for that." Johnson paused and looked away, and then refocused his gaze on Bart. "They're bound in human skin."

Bart looked down at the books sitting right by his feet, and stared. After a moment, he turned back to Johnson. "Again, very funny. Is this a joke, then? Are both these revelation jokes? C'mon, be straight with me."

"Once again, I'm telling you the truth. About their value, and what they're made from. I had a book binding chemist take a look, and he confirmed it. Check with other book sellers—they'll tell you the same thing. Please, get more opinions. But yeah, it's real skin. Which is extremely rare, but not unique. Brown University has three books bound in human skin in its library—one of them is an anatomy textbook. Harvard has one too, a lawyer's practice manual dating to 1605, using the skin of a guy named Wright who was killed in Africa. The Philadelphia Mütter Museum, which houses medical oddities, has some, and the Cleveland Public Library has a Qur'an bound in a previous owner's skin. There's more in Europe, too—often court proceedings of executed criminals, using their hides. But my favorite is the one held by the Boston Athenaeum. It's the 1837 memoir of James Allen, who was a highway robber under the alias of George Walton. He requested that it be bound in his own skin, and then he donated it to a would-be robbery victim who fought back bravely. Rumors tell of a thirteenth century human skin bound Bible, but the first reliable examples are from the 16th and 17th centuries. There's even a name for it: *anthropodermic bibliopegy.*" Johnson grinned slightly. "Sorry, I didn't mean to lecture—it's just that rare books are a passion of mine." His smile faded. "But there's more disturbing information."

"Jesus, what next?! Really!" Bart uncrossed his legs with a quiet bang on the floor. His left leg rested against the box of books. He moved it away with a jerk.

"Well, most of the other human skin bound books I mentioned were of volunteers, or at least somewhat justifiable, because the people committed serious, capital crimes. But these weren't. There was a particularly nasty devil worshipping group in Europe during the late 18th to early 20th centuries. Real Satanists, not like the hedonistic, relatively harmless Hellfire Clubs and such. These books were made with innocent, murdered victims. Of children. Specifically, using the genital skin. The group called them the "Books of Pain.""

Bart gasped, and then hiccupped a couple of times. Johnson sprang up and ran around the counter. He handed Bart the trash can, and it was put into position just as a torrent of vomit cascaded into it. After three episodes Bart pulled his head up slowly, breathing heavily, his heart booming in his ears. He took the offered tissues and wiped his mouth and nose with disgust. After his body stopped trembling, he stood up. "If this is a joke it's in terrible taste. And if it's not it's worse. Jesus... I'm out of here, you sick fuck!" He stumbled out of the store, slamming the door behind him.

Johnson picked up the trash can and went behind the counter, down a hallway, and into a small bathroom. It had a toilet and large utility sink. He dumped out the trash can, then washed it out thoroughly in the sink. Then he picked it up and walked out to the counter again. The day's *Wall Street Journal* was off to the side of the counter next to innumerable books. Johnson sat on his high chair and started to read. He'd gone through a couple of pages when he glanced up at the clock. 4:51. Just then, the door to his store opened up again and Bart entered. He sat down in the chair again with a grunt.

"Sorry, I shouldn't have yelled and...cursed at you," said Bart. "I know you're just the messenger. It's just—" he stole a look down at the box of books—"that's quite a disgusting thing to hear."

"Don't sweat it. As I mentioned, it is disgusting, and obscene."

"That wasn't a valuable old trash can, was it?"

Johnson chuckled. "Nope. It's like ten or fifteen years old, plastic, worth like a buck. But it has its uses."

"Okay, let's get this over with. Finish the story. Unless that was it?"

"Afraid not. You want all the details?"

"Not really, in a way. Just say it. I don't think I have anything left to puke up."

"Fine. It wasn't just the covers. The pages themselves are like vellum, which means calf skin, in this case, newborn babies' skin. The ink was from girls' first menstrual blood, and from boys' rectums after they raped and killed them. The string used to stitch the whole thing together was from human guts. You know, like tennis rackets are from animal guts—not literally cat, though: that's a myth. All the skin was tanned using the victims' brains. And the covers are boys' foreskins and girls' labia. That's why the surfaces are so rough."

Bart gulped and peered at the books, and then looked away quickly. "Foreskins and… labias? They're so tiny. That must have taken, what, dozens?"

"At least. But aside from that, what made the books so blasphemous, and therefore perversely valuable, was who did this to the kids, and where. The torturers and rapists were all ex-nuns and priests. Some weren't even exes, but active, still serving their posts, and did this secretly. And one was a saint, and another, a Pope even. And these evil rites were always done on sacred grounds, on the altars of cathedrals and churches. But anyway, about twenty of these books were made, and almost all of them were destroyed. Usually along with the killers, if they could be located.

The Group, as far as anyone knows, died out between 1915 and 1920. Your uncle's copies are mostly the later ones: *Malleus Maleficarum*, originally published in 1487, was made in 1827; *Fanny Hill* was first published in 1749 and this copy in 1761, and *The Wizard of Oz*, originally written in 1900, was made in 1903. The last two, incidentally, in addition to all their other crimes, were breaking the copyrights."

"Wait, that's another thing I don't understand. I looked it up: *Malleus* is a witch hunter's handbook, *Fanny Hill* is an erotic novel, and *Wizard* is a children's book. That makes no sense.

Wouldn't Satanists' books be…Satanic spells and stuff, you know, pro-witchcraft?"

"Yeah, most of them were. But part of the point was also to kill the kids for nothing, for a colossal waste of time. They had sick senses of humor. *Malleus Maleficarum* was done to be ironic, *Fanny Hill* was just because they liked the first, somewhat socially acceptable, dirty novel, and *The Wizard of Oz* was funny to them because they killed kids to make a book that the kids probably loved."

"So, what's my great uncle doing with them?"

"I was going to ask you that. A man named Luke Sebastian had several, including these, as late as 1930, but no one knows what happened after that. After he was executed, the trail went cold. Until now."

"Shit. I only met my uncle a couple of times—he was antisocial, a real recluse. Never said too much. Knowing what I do now about his book collection, maybe that was for the best." Bart stood up and stared at the box on the floor. "I have to talk to my folks about these, and about my uncle. Thanks for telling me about this, though…I guess."

"Sure. Hey, you want a pair of gloves for carrying that?" Bart nodded, and Johnson reached under the counter, and produced a packet of dishwashing gloves. He opened the package and handed them to Bart.

"I know this is fucked up, but I hope you think things over, talk to your family, before you do anything. Bear in mind, there's no legal issues here, if that helps a little. The victims, and the killers, are both long dead. And you know how to get in touch with me."

Bart snapped the second glove on and picked up the box. "Yeah, okay. Goodnight."

The ride home seemed to take forever. A couple of times cars beeped at him as his speed went below the posted limit, or when he was slow responding to a green light. Bart's mind kept returning to the obscene books locked in his trunk. Oh God, he'd touched them! They'd sat in his room, he hadn't washed his hands after handling them; his whole house was contaminated. Little kids, babies even! He felt his stomach turn over again.

As it turned out, his conversation with his parents was long and frustrating. Even though he only gave them a bare bones version of what the books were, they were similarly repulsed as Bart was. His mom didn't have any relevant new info on Uncle Thomas, either. Apparently, he'd been quiet and secretive all of his life. At first, she angrily denied that he could have been a Satanist, but after a while she claimed she didn't think he was.

When they heard about the books' values, a new hubbub arose. Bart was a little surprised by the outcome. He'd figured his mom would be more emotional, and his dad more practical. But it was just the opposite. His mother kept talking about the mortgage, and being able to retire, while his dad agreed with Bart that they should torch them. Then his mother started to cry, and Bart and his dad felt bad for accusing her. Eventually they decided on an uneasy truce and to sleep on it.

* * *

The score in the set was 4-5, and within the game, it was ad out. Bart served, and it was a decent one, right in the corner with a decent pace. Jim, though, returned it well down the line on Bart's forehand side. Bart scrambled to reach it, but when he did, he lasered it down the line on Jim's backhand side. Jim's return was weak and shallow, and his effort to return back to the middle of the court was late. Bart charged in and took the ball in the air, aiming for the empty forehand side on his opponent's side. His shot was low, hard, and at least six inches wide.

"Goddammit," said Bart, albeit in a conversational tone. He struggled mightily with his temper during sports and games, and this was a compromise of sorts. His hand ached to send his offending racket into the net, but he resisted, and the urge waned. Bart growled softly and joined Jim on the side of the court, up by the net, where they'd put their tennis ball cans, towels, and water bottles. Bart took a long swig from his bottle, whose faded letters read, *Bal m r Or le*, and slumped against the chain link fence that surrounded the courts. Jim sat down heavily on the court and ripped his baseball hat off. His dirty blonde hair was lank with sweat.

"You had me worried," said Jim, after a moment, and long pulls off his water bottle. "I thought I was headed for an easy win when I was up 5-0, but then you stormed back."

Bart stared at his friend briefly before responding. Jim's compliments of opponents were notoriously stingy, but at the same time Bart found his words to be a little condescending. Or was he being too paranoid? "Yeah, I thought I had a chance too. At first, I was just trying desperately not to be bageled, but then I thought I'd settled down and was playing well. Just not enough."

Jim started to say something, but he was interrupted by a tinny version of Newcleus's "Jam on It" coming from Bart's cell phone. Bart went over and picked it up and flipped it open. Jim took another long swig instead.

"Hey Mom, what's up?" There was a long pause as she replied. "Yeah," he continued, "Johnson said two-point-five million minimum, three more likely." Another wait as she answered. "I'll be home in about an hour or so, probably. I'll talk to you later. Yeah, love you too, bye." He flipped his phone closed with a grunt, and then peered at his friend. "Just got a third opinion on the books. Apparently, your guy was being honest."

"Yeah, he has a good reputation, and I've never been treated unfairly. I mean, he's a businessman, he's trying to make a living, but he's straight with you." Jim toed Bart's old, chipped paint Prince racket. "Guess you'll be playing with a $200 racket soon, a Babolat or something, huh?"

"Doubtful. We're doing a straight vote, and my dad and I are against Mom. Most likely those books'll end up in the fireplace, or in the trash can."

Jim choked a little on his last gulp of Smart Water, and shifted around so he was facing Bart. "Are you serious?!" Bart nodded. "I know they're sick and disgusting and all that, but why can't you and your folks benefit? I know that money would come in handy. Hell, it would for any family, save the Gates or the Trumps."

"Sure, we could benefit. Wouldn't that be great, my parents in a new McMansion, me going to Syracuse with no student loans or a part-time job, all paid for by the literal skin, blood, brains, and guts of innocent kids. Perfect. No problems there."

"But you and your parents didn't kill those innocent kids, or commission it. And the monsters who did those things are all long dead, beyond punishment. And you didn't even know your great uncle had them. Destroying them won't help those kids."

"But selling them makes us a sort of accomplice after the fact. Maybe more. Who do you think would buy such books? Someone with a sick, sociopathic mind. Hell, word of the sale might prompt people to make more."

"That's not—"

"Look, I don't want to talk about his anymore. You ready for the second?"

Jim opened his mouth and started to speak, but then he shut it again. Finally, he said, "Fine," and stood up. They switched sides of the court and began to play again.

The second set went poorly for Bart. He won the first game, then lost the next six in quick succession. His serve, in particular, deserted him. Jim hit many easy winners on Bart's balloonish second serves. They packed up their gear in silence, and when they got inside Bart's car to leave, he turned the radio on at a fairly high volume. After a few blocks, Jim turned the music down.

"I know it's a sensitive topic, but just hear me out. This once, let me say my piece, and then I'll never mention it again, if you like."

Bart turned right as the light turned green. "Okay, just this once, but keep it brief."

"Are you familiar with the book *The Protocols of the Elders of Zion*?"

"Nope."

"Well, it's a fraud, probably written by some of the Tsar's men, supposedly exposing the secrets of the Jews, and it's all the classic anti-Semitic stuff, their Satanic roots, their plans to take over the world, their control of the media, all that ridiculous shit. And as a companion to that, there's Hitler's *Mein Kampf.* Or there's *The Clansman*, which was the basis for *The Birth of a Nation*, which I know you saw in that film studies course we took last year. Or more recently, there's the white supremacist, black-

and Jew-hating 1970's book *The Turner Diaries*. And let's move on. *The Communist Manifesto*. Any number of Holocaust-denying books. Or let's throw out some less serious, but still absurdly wrong books—Von Daniken's *Chariots of the Gods?* and the like, or the whole host of Intelligent Design books. All of those books, in varying degrees, are fucked up. So my question is, if you were in charge, would you destroy every copy of them?"

Bart glanced over at his friend, then refocused on the road. "I see what you're doing here, and no, I wouldn't. I concede that point. Destroying books like that is counter-productive— in a sense, it makes martyrs of them. It gives them power, respectability of a kind, by saying, in effect, this is dangerous to society, we must destroy it. That only encourages the crazy conspiracies of already paranoid groups. It's better to leave them out there and counter their positions with your own, more reasonable opinions or facts. But none of these examples reflect on my family's situation. My uncle's books weren't about offensive political or social systems or opinions—well, the witch hunter's one used to be, but no one's taken it seriously for hundreds of years. It's not their ideas, it's the books themselves. I mean, why are we talking about this? *The Wizard of Oz* was a great children's book, but not when its very structure and makeup is from tortured babies."

"I'm not condoning what they did, or saying make more. And I'm not advocating selling it to latter day devil worshippers or some cult or something." They were on Jim's block. Bart pulled up outside Jim's apartment building. "By all means, use some of the cash for charity, do some good with the money. I'm just saying, don't let your moral outrage and emotion cause you to do something rash. That's all." Jim gathered up his tennis equipment.

"Okay, I will. Thanks for playing. I'll talk to you later."

"Later." Jim got out of the car, and shut the door behind him.

Bart waited until he saw Jim open his door, and then drove off. At the light, he saw the car in front of him was a Passport. Anal passport—that was a new one.

* * *

Christina Aquino was in her late 50's and conservatively dressed. She was the type of lady that Bart's mother referred to as a "handsome woman," an expression he always found curiously masculine. She led him into her office and asked him to sit down, motioning to a sturdy yet plush seat in front of a wide oak desk. Bart did so, and found the chair to be very comfortable. He glanced around, taking in the environment. He knew beans about antiques and interior decorating, but even he could tell that the furniture was tasteful and expensive. The oil painting on the wall—a portrait of an old noble man in a forested mountain scene—also looked both aesthetically pleasing and commercially valuable. Which made sense. He sighed and thought to himself, for probably the ninetieth time, "Am I doing the right thing?" The books, he saw, were near the corner of the desk, sitting peacefully. He spared them a glance, then looked away. The body and blood of innocents, literally.

"Well, Mr. Duckett, our experts looked over your books, and confirmed their authenticity. They were all amazed—everyone thought that the Books of Pain were all destroyed long ago. And in such good condition, too, nothing short of amazing." Aquino's smile was quite winning, quite sincere.

Yes, Bart thought, it is amazing—amazing that such a sweet-looking old lady is impressed by the torturous deaths of little children.

"To get down to brass tacks, my group thinks your asking price of $1,000,000 per book to be very fair. So, I'm authorized to give you that. Do we have a deal?"

Bart closed his eyes for a moment, pondering. Get thee behind me, Satan! Was he doing the right thing? Or was he letting his soul be bought for a large price? Finally, he groaned softly and said, "Yes, we do."

"Excellent! Do you want the transfer to be done electronically, then? That would probably be easiest."

"Actually, my family and I would prefer checks, and if possible, several separate ones, made out to my family and to several charities." Bart took the piece of paper out of his pocket and handed it over. "As it says here, I'd like three separate checks of $100,000 each to myself, my mother, and my father—all of our names are listed here—and then three individual checks of $900,000 each to these various charities—UNICEF, ALS, and Mosquito Nets for Africa."

Aquino stared at the list, and then locked eyes with Bart. "You realize if you write the checks in your name you'd get a huge break on your taxes, right?" Her expression was one of deep shock.

"We know…we just want to do it this way, if that's all right."

"And you did mean $900,000 to the charities, and $100,000 to yourselves? You sure?"

"Yes, just like it says, please."

Aquino sniffed and shook her head, but reached into a drawer and produced a checkbook. "As you wish."

As she started to write out the six checks, Bart slumped in his seat and rubbed his eyes. She hadn't said one word about the nature of the books. As if they were regular old antiques. She must be sick. And he was helping her. Jesus.

"There you go," she handed over the checks, and he scanned them one by one, putting them carefully into his wallet. His hands were shaking slightly—he'd never held checks for anything over $1000 before. He folded his wallet carefully and slid it awkwardly into the front pocket of his jeans.

"On the behalf of my group, then, thanks for selling those books to us, Mr. Duckett. If you'd like you're welcome—"

"Sorry to interrupt, but I'm in a bit of a hurry. So thanks, but I must be going." Bart stood up, and turned around quickly, and walked out just as Aquino managed a puzzled goodbye to his back.

As he walked back to his car, he noticed, almost subconsciously, that the two vehicles sandwiching his in the lot were a Venture and a Rodeo. Bart smiled and then laughed. And then frowned, as he guiltily remembered what was burning a hole in his pocket.

* * *

The final room in the Torture Museum was Torture Today. Abby crossed into the room and was struck by the difference in the exhibits. Instead of simple wood and metal devices and machines, many of which were worm-eaten and rusty, the ones in this room were intricately complicated and looked like they'd been constructed yesterday. Stainless steel, rubber, dials, and most with ominous-looking electrical cords snaking around them. And instead of woodcuts or drawings, there were photographs of the devices in action, and a small video room in the corner.

Abby looked at each exhibit thoroughly, mouth agape. She was shocked by the ingenuity of these tools—someone had really put thought into them, really knew the best ways to cause agony. Such a perversion of intelligence, hard work, and empathy.

At the exit was a table with a large hotel registration-style book sitting on it. A pen was tied to the book with a cord, and the word *Comments* was printed on the black leather cover. Abby opened up the book and read some of the previous entries at random.

"What a turn on," said one. "I hafta jerk off now!" A crude little stick figure demonstrated this.

"This is sick!!!!" said another. "U R insane. I'll laugh when U burn in HELL!!"

"Fuck you Liberals! TERRORISTS ARE TRYING TO KILL US OR HAVE YOU FORGOTTEN 9/11?"

"For the most part, an interesting art collection. But the theme was a tad morbid. Maybe balance it out with some nice still lifes, or pastoral scenes." This in spiky letters, in black Sharpie.

As she kept flipping through, Abby noticed two types of comments were the most common. The first was a variation on, "Gross! Have you no decency? Think of the children!" (This despite the prominent age warnings at the entrance to the museum). The second was, "Disgusting, but worthwhile. We shouldn't forget that these things happened, no matter how terrible they were." She kept reading.

"People suck!" said one, written in red ink in a neat cursive hand. "Those Pain Books were the worst! I'm gonna have nightmares!" Abby nodded in agreement with that one. She'd spent five minutes staring at those, horrified, yet transfixed. What they'd done to those children! Not wasting a single part of their bodies, like Native Americans with bison carcasses, only taken to an obscene degree. It was almost poetically fiendish.

Abby picked up the pen, thought a moment, then added, in her block printing, "Disturbing—as it should be. Every police officer, minister, armed services officer, and politician should have to look at these things."

A few steps away was a large Amnesty International box, with pamphlets on one side and a wide slot on the other. She'd seen their symbol throughout the Museum, they were one of its sponsors. Abby rummaged in her purse, and pulled a five-dollar bill out of her wallet and dropped it in the donation slit. Then, shivering slightly, she walked out.

Roger
Hollee Nelson

My brother was nine and I was five when he ripped the head off of Sir Waffles, my favorite stuffed dog, because I wouldn't share. When our mom grounded him—a week of no TV, no outside—my brother waited until we were all asleep and then climbed out the window. He took Sir Waffles' disembodied head with him, stuffed in one of the pockets of his cargo pants like a sad, floppy trophy. Our neighbor found him the next morning, curled beneath her azalea bushes. Nobody had even known my brother was missing.

The second time, he was gone for three days. He was twelve and suspended for fighting in school. He'd held another boy down on the playground and force-fed him a cashew butter sandwich. The boy was allergic. Our parents were livid. My brother waited again until we were all asleep before shimmying down the drainpipe.

In the morning, when we found his bed empty save for a note that read *I HATE YOU ALL*, our parents sighed. They spent three days combing the city and left me home alone with our neighbor's daughter, five years older, who didn't mind what I did as long as it wasn't with her.

I spent each day in my brother's room, cleaning, putting away the toys and the books and the clothes he'd left on the floor, arranging everything so it would be nice for him when he got home, so he wouldn't be angry anymore, so maybe he'd play Ninja Turtles with me when he was ungrounded.

They found him camped out in an abandoned apartment behind the 7-Eleven on the third day. He'd broken a window to get in and had eaten nothing but stolen granola bars and beef jerky. He screamed and bit like an animal when they hauled him away—or so I overheard my aunts say at the family picnic.

Our parents called him selfish. They'd had to postpone a dinner party for our father's coworkers in order to search for him, my vagrant brother. Did he not know how bad he made them look?

Four years later, he was sixteen, and our parents, tired of chauffeuring their children when they could be golfing or sunbathing or whatever it was parents did, gave him free access to the car in exchange for driving me to and from soccer practice. I would hear him before I saw him, rock music so loud it rattled my teeth from around the corner.

Once, he was late getting me by almost an hour. When he finally screeched up, the car reeked of sweat and something I couldn't place, something like potting soil and iron. A green Milk-Bone crunched into the floor mat beneath my cleat. A bottle of antifreeze, three-quarters empty, rolled around in the back. My brother's skin was oil-glossed, his yellow hair stuck to his forehead. He wore a different t-shirt than the one he dropped me off in. His nails were dirty.

I asked what he'd been up to, but he didn't answer. He didn't wait for me to put on my seatbelt either; when he swerved out of the parking lot, the tires squealed and my head cracked against the window.

"Shut up," he said, even though I hadn't even said *Ow*.

He didn't take the right way home. I didn't notice at first. I was twelve. There's an implicit trust that comes from being twelve and in a car; you just assume whoever's behind the wheel has it all under control. It wasn't until he fishtailed onto Route 50 that I realized something was wrong.

I asked where we were going, and he only told me to shut up again. His legs kept jumping. The car would slow, accelerate, slow, accelerate with every bounce.

In my most reasonable voice, I said, "We're supposed to go straight home."

"Shut up," he said. Then: "Fuck home."

We ran out of gas a little past Grafton. Parkersburg was two hours in the rearview mirror. When the car sputtered and died, my brother sat very still. Then he got out and started walking. It was dark. He stuck close to the tree line on the outside of the guardrail and didn't look back.

The police found me balled in the passenger's seat, sobbing, over an hour later. They found my brother, dirty and hungry, two days later with ripped jeans and a dog collar in his back pocket. The address on the tag was three blocks away from our house. Three days prior, my brother had fought with the boy who lived there over a game of pickup basketball. They never found the dog.

Then my brother was twenty-two, and a young girl stumbled into the police station with bare feet and a ripped dress. She'd gone on a date, she said. He seemed fine at first, she said. It wasn't until they went back to his place, when she said she was sorry, but she wasn't like that, that she realized something was wrong.

She had purpled fingerprints on her throat and a cut on her lip and she was lucky, they said, because it could have been much worse if she hadn't been able to claw her way out and run. When they asked her who had done this, she said he said his name was Roger. She showed them my brother's Facebook photo.

He was three states away and driving a different car when they found him two months later.

We should have known then, my family and I, and maybe we did. Maybe we just didn't want to. Maybe we wanted to believe in the reformatory power of the American prison system. We visited him once, shortly after he went in. The prison smelled like disinfectant and sweat. Everything was grey. My brother, small in his orange pajamas, looked unrested and sallow on the other side of the table. He picked at his cuticles and wouldn't look any of us in the eye. In the parking lot after, warmed by the sun, my father draped his arms around my mother and I, gave us each a squeeze.

"It's so hard," my mother said, "seeing him like that."

My father nodded. So hard. Too hard. Easier to let the months lapse, to remind themselves that they needed to visit next week or the week after and to never follow through. My brother would call sometimes, usually on Sundays, and I would tell him about school and he would tell me how he missed his car, his jeans, his bed. Our parents were conveniently never home.

Finally, they released him on an unseasonably warm spring day, called him reformed and corrected, and our parents, remembering they had a second child, one now allowed in public, threw him a party. He had a beard and biceps—two things he'd never had before—and they blew up balloons in his honor. Welcome home, they said. We've missed you so much.

He didn't disappear for a while after that. He stayed with me most of the time, and he seemed okay. He started working as a janitor at the hospital, and we played Mario Kart on the weekends.

"You know," he said one night when we were in the middle of a game, "you're the only one who ever gave a shit about me."

"That's not true. Mom and Dad love you," I said, but the words sounded hollow even to me.

My brother shook his head and mashed the buttons on his controller. He said, "You're the only one who never gave up on me, not when we were kids, not when I was in the clink, never. Means a lot. I won't forget it."

I didn't know what to say. My brother had never been the sharing type, and I was touched. I patted his knee.

"I'm just glad you're doing better now," I said.

A month later, we had a cookout. It was my brother's birthday. Our father grilled and our mother hovered and my brother and I sat in the shade of their big oak tree and drank chilled beer.

"How nice is this," our mother said as we sat down to eat, "all of us together like a family again."

"Nice," our father and I agreed.

My brother was quiet. He ate forkfuls of potato salad so quickly that taste was surely impossible.

After our mother cleared away the plates, our father leaned back in his chair and asked my brother when he was going to get a real job.

"You're twenty-seven now, son," he said. "Can't be sweeping the cancer ward forever."

My brother's face darkened. He cracked his knuckles in his lap, a new nervous tic I'd noticed in the last few months.

"Soon," he said.

"The guys at work keep asking me," our father continued, "when my felon son is going to make something of himself."

My brother stiffened beside me.

"Dad," I said.

Our father held up his hands. "I'm just saying."

That night, wobbly and weak-limbed from the beer, we slept in our childhood bedrooms. I woke sometime after midnight to my brother rifling through my nightstand.

"Roge?" I mumbled, squinting in the darkness.

"Shh." Keys jingled. "Go to sleep."

"What are you doing?"

"I gotta go," he said.

I tossed back the covers and sat up. The house was deathly quiet around us, and my skin prickled. Our father always, always snored.

"What's going on?" I asked. "What'd you do?"

My brother paused in the doorway. He had my keys, and he looked sad.

"I thought you were different," he said, and then he was gone.

I chased after him, but he was faster. The front door slammed, my engine turned over. I froze for a moment, then dashed for my parents' bedroom.

"Mom!" I cried. "Dad!"

They didn't respond—couldn't. In the fading arc of headlights through the blinds, I saw two empty glasses, two gibbous moons where sleeping faces should have been.

A wretched banshee cry ripped itself from my body, and I wailed until my voice cracked, until bile arced like hot lava up my throat, until the neighbors caught on and called the police who found me shivering on the floor, heaving, clutching my father's cooling hand to my face.

"What happened?" they asked. "Who did this?"

But I couldn't answer. How could I say *We did*? How could I say, *Every minute of every day, we did*?

Walking on Knives
Matthew R. Davis

As the car arrowed in towards the curb, Zara huddled inside her coat and wondered again: *is this really such a good idea?*

She looked at Ben as he brought them to a halt, but his expression revealed nothing in the near darkness. Maybe he was practicing his role for the game ahead; if so, he might have missed his calling as an actor, for she barely recognized him. She couldn't tell if he was as nervous as she, or if his poker face hid a capering lust she'd not seen in months.

"I guess this is our stop," Zara ventured.

Ben placed one hand on hers, his wedding band cool and firm against the back of her finger.

"Here we go, baby. Remember how we discussed it. You get out and walk, I do a lap around the block, and then I pick you up again."

"Only then, you won't know me."

"We'll be strangers," he confirmed. "For a little while, anyway."

Zara sent him a wan smile as she unlatched her seatbelt and reached for the door handle, trying not to think that for some time now they'd felt like strangers who happened to share a house.

"Just don't be too long, okay? I don't want every freak in the area zoning in on me. And what if someone I *know* sees me like this?"

"At this hour, in this part of town? Zara, you'll be out of the car for maybe a minute. No one is going to see you and know who you are."

"I know who they *will* think I am."

"Yeah, but that's kind of the point, isn't it? You aren't *you*."

A dubious comfort. Zara pushed the door open with her leg, and a nearby streetlight gave her stockinged calf a subdued sheen. Stepping out, she turned and bit her rouged lip.

"All right, Ben. See you in a minute."

"And don't use my name." He gave her his special smile— the one that always lightened her heart, the first thing she'd come to love in him. "Remember, you won't know me. Not until after. See you real soon, lover."

Ben blew her a kiss as she closed the door and stepped backwards onto the footpath— a relatively easy task that she'd always taken for granted. But she'd never attempted it in stiletto heels before. By the time she'd tottered to a halt and made sure she wasn't going to fall face-first into the gutter, their crimson CR-V was off down the road. The game had begun.

Okay, so where are we?

Swallowing her nerves, Zara folded her arms and looked around. Across the road, a threadbare strip of parkland loomed, teeming with the lurking rapists of her imagination; on her side of the street slept a row of shabby shops. Well after midnight in a part of town she'd think twice about venturing through in broad daylight, and here she was, alone and barely dressed.

The black knee-length coat was barely enough to preserve her dignity, and beneath it, she was clad only in what Ben had bought her two days ago: revealing red lingerie, all sheer and saucy lace, complete with suspenders and stockings. Looking in the mirror after trying it on, she had spluttered at the thought of ever wearing it outside the bedroom...and yet here she was, tottering down this eerily silent street, watching the tail-lights of the CR-V disappear as Ben took a left turn to circle the block. Here she was, dressed as a prostitute for some sexy cosplay, when lately her idea of a good time was curling up with some ice cream to re-watch *The Little Mermaid.*

And now it's me walking on knives, she thought, leaning down to rub at her tightly flexed calves. *But like her, I'm doing it for love. Also for hot, dirty sex...but mainly for love.*

Zara passed a hairdressing salon that looked about as hygienic as the average public toilet and felt judged by its blank glass eyes, as if it were regarding her rich red hair with envy, keen to shear it from her scalp. She shuddered and turned her gaze back to the footpath. The corner Ben had taken seemed to be flying towards her at a rate as unseemly as her racy attire.

If he hasn't come back by the time I reach that road...

She'd do what, exactly? Hang around under the streetlight awaiting his return, feeling as raw and exposed as a herbivore at a watering hole? She already felt watched, stalked, and now she realized why: behind her, the still night air was giving way to the growing grumble of an approaching engine, and it wasn't the quiet purr of the CR-V.

Zara walked on, not looking back, and fervently hoped that the driver didn't pull over. Not that she could really blame him if he did.

What if it's the police? Oh, Ben, you and your stupid ideas!

The car loomed towards her tense back— close now, closer— its headlights throwing her shadow face-first onto the ground before her—

And cruised by without slowing.

She let out a sigh of relief, but when the sound of the engine faded, the desolate silence returned. Where she lived, the night air was always humming with the to and fro of local traffic, the buzz and bustle of urban life. This hollow quiet was too much like the anticipatory hush of bloodthirsty spectators.

Zara was still alone when she reached the corner, cursing Ben as her taut legs led her around the curve and up the next street.

How long does it take to do one lap of the block? What the hell is he playing at, leaving me out here like this?

But then what was *she* playing at, getting worked up in entirely the wrong manner? This was supposed to be *fun!* She took a breath, focused on the fantasy.

Here you are, a respectable young businesswoman, walking through one of the more insalubrious parts of town, wearing little enough under your coat that you could be propositioned or arrested at any moment, and your man is on his way, hungry for your sex.

A quick shiver surprised her, dirty and delicious. She was tuning into the right wavelength now, wanted to be rash and daring, to open the coat and expose herself to the night air. When Ben pulled up alongside her, she might do just that.

See something you like, sugar?

By now, Zara had made her way to the midpoint of the street. Up ahead, she could see the corner where Ben would have taken another left turn. Across the road, a rank of trust houses gave her a steely glare, daring her to judge; on her side of the street, a darkened real estate office wore spray-painted tags like prison tattoos. Just up ahead and to her left was the derelict community center.

Zara was surprised that the ruins hadn't been torn down to make way for yet another fast food outlet or bottle shop. The wreck had once been an indigenous community and health center, but one night, a couple of morons had tossed a molly through one of its windows, and what remained now was a blackened hulk. The facilities were moved to a new building during the arsonists' trial, and the old one sat here and festered like a rotting tooth in a dirty mouth.

Ben better be back before I have to go past that place, Zara thought with a shudder. The old community center gave her the creeps, slouching there like a scorched skeleton. Perhaps it was because the place now stood as a monument to human malice.

Speaking of which, surely it had been over a minute since Ben had left, maybe even two. Where the hell was he? Had he driven off and left her walking the streets alone as some sort of humiliating revenge? It didn't seem possible. Ben had a hot temper, but he'd never shown any propensity for cruelty. Besides, what could she have done to anger him so?

Relax. He loves you. Trust him.

But then she heard a laugh nearby, and relaxation became impossible.

Two figures had appeared around the corner at the end of the street, heading straight down the footpath toward her. They walked under a streetlight, confirming what the laugh had postulated: a pair of coarse young men, and they sounded drunk, high, or both.

Oh, fucking hell! Not NOW!

Zara's arousal was ancient history. Why did Ben have to choose *this* area for their little role-play? Slumming it was all well and good in theory, but the reality of this seedy environment was hardly reassuring to a woman dressed like she was gagging for some action. She patted her coat in search of her phone, grimacing as she remembered that its pockets were purely decorative and that she'd left the mobile in the console of the CR-V.

She had reached the community center now, and the two men were maybe twenty meters away. She was between streetlights, and couldn't tell if they'd seen her—maybe they were too distracted, the click of her heels drowned out by their boisterous laughter. Keeping her eye on them, Zara slipped onto the dirt driveway of the community center.

The earth made much less noise beneath her shoes than the cement, but with each step her heels threatened to punch deep into the soil and mire her. Waiting just ahead was a large stand of trees that she intended to use for cover, but she was still grimly stabbing her way toward them when the two men came into sight on the footpath, almost level with her position. To her dismay, they were only twenty feet away now—and worse, they were *looking* for her.

"There she is!"

"Heyyyyyy!"

"Hello," Zara replied, keeping her voice neutral and folding her arms, waiting to see how the situation developed, waiting for the CR-V to cruise by *right now*. The two men on the footpath were young, off their heads, strangers—little more than loopy mouths grinning out of black hooded jumpers. They differed slightly in height but otherwise could have been twins in uniform, and to take the edge off their potential threat, Zara thought of them as Tweedledum and Tweedledee.

"Whatcha doin'?"

"I'm just taking a walk, that's all."

Dum muttered something, and they both spluttered with laughter. Dee managed to say, "Hey, are you, like…lookin' for business?"

"No!" Zara snapped. "I'm not a…not in that line of work."

"Aw, we didn't mean nothin'." Tweedledum stumbled forward a couple of steps, just enough to take him off the footpath. "It's just that, uh, it looks like you're not wearin' anythin' under that coat…"

Ah, fuck, Zara thought, but what she said was, "Look, I'm meeting someone, okay? Off you go, and have a good night."

"Awwwww!" Dum whined, taking a couple more unsteady steps. Dee followed, faceless but for the grin that floated in the shadows of his hoodie. "Just a quick look? I'll show you mine if you show me yours!"

Dum made a display of fumbling for his zipper as Dee laughed and slapped him on the arm. While their attention was distracted, Zara turned and began stalking as quickly as she could toward the community center. Curse these heels! Without them, she could easily have outrun this pair of idiots. If she stopped to remove them now, the men could be on her in seconds.

And then I'd have to use them as weapons.

"Hey, where you goin'?"

Her flight had been duly noted by the wasted couple. Looking back, she saw them shambling after her, waving their arms.

Well, at least they weren't running. Zara turned her attention back to the driveway and saw that it led into a large rectangular parking area just ahead. Reception was on the other side, perhaps twenty seconds away in these ludicrous shoes. Once inside she could barricade the door, find some place to hide until her pursuers left her alone. They were taking their time, either confident of eventual capture or taking the episode none too seriously, and Zara knew that she was going to make it.

She was halfway to Reception when she looked back, and moonlight flashed at her from a reflective surface across the lot. She realized that a car was parked on the other side, its dark red hue shading into the night. Only its windshield had given it away, and she recognized its shape with a surge of both relief and confusion.

"Ben?" she cried. "*Ben!*"

"*That's right, baby!*" one of the guys behind her yelled. "*Ben Dover!*"

The two loons sprayed more howls into the air. Glancing back, Zara saw that this latest fit of laughter had slowed them to a standstill, giving her an even bigger lead. Now she was stepping up onto the Reception porch, reaching for the door with one desperate hand. The lock had been smashed, and she slipped shadow-swift into the darkness.

Closing the door behind her, Zara looked for something with which to barricade it. The reception area was a mess of broken beams and cinders, its charred walls lent some vague light by the pale moon shining in through gaps in the boarded-up windows. She grabbed a length of crumbling wood and hauled it across to the door, but it was obvious that she would need more to keep the men out.

Ben must be nearby. Find him!

She could see holes gaping in the far walls, maws the shape of open doors, and carefully picked her way to the nearest. The next room looked much like the first, a blackened shell. There was nothing that could be salvaged for a weapon or barricade.

"Hey, sexy! You really don't wanna go in there!"

Her pissed-up paramours had not given up just yet; now one of them was knocking on the Reception door. Couldn't Ben hear them?

Where IS he?

"Ben! Are you in here?"

Her words were still ringing through the desolation when something moved beyond the next door. It could have been swift footsteps crunching through the debris.

"Ben…?"

Zara hurried to the opposite door and yanked it open. The top tore free of the jamb, but the bottom wedged against a pile of slag. Cursing as she forced her body between the crumbling door and the all-too-solid frame, she saw that the room ahead appeared to be empty, but a shaft of moonlight pierced the ceiling, and along its soft, cool ray, Zara could see a cloud of ash particles dancing like disturbed bees.

Whoever was in here with her, she'd just missed them.

Surely Ben would have answered her call. Trying not to wonder who else it could be, Zara hurried across the room. The hovering cloud of ash caused her to break out in a hacking cough and ensured that her coat would need a hell of a good clean when she got home. She'd be lucky if Ben even let her back in the car in this state.

What the hell was he *doing* here, anyway? When she found him, she'd want answers, and they had better be good ones. Either way, she could see this saucy scheme ending in another argument rather than the titillation they'd intended. Zara sighed and wrote the night off as a dead loss.

The black line against the far wall proved to be another door. She grabbed the desiccated edge and swung it open to reveal a deep-throated corridor. The floor was littered with charred wooden sleepers, so at least Tweedledum and Tweedledee would find their progress hampered if they suddenly appeared through the other door at the left end of the hall. Looking to her right, Zara saw a cement staircase leading upwards. A girl was sitting on the fourth step, watching her.

Zara jerked backwards and gasped, choking on ash. The girl eyed her for another second or two, then rose to her feet without a sound. She tucked something into a pocket, tossed a flapping black object into the darkness, and hurried upwards. The scorched cement slapped beneath the stranger's shoes as Zara picked her way toward the steps.

Who the fuck was that?

This derelict was proving to be a rather popular hangout tonight. Then again, who was to say that it didn't have regular tenants? Perhaps the girl was squatting here. Zara hadn't been able to make out much of the stranger in the dim moonlight, but she had appeared quite young—an impression of fishnet stockings, of dark clothes and darker hair, the glittering eyes of a night-stalking cat as it slunk across the path of a moving car.

Now at the staircase, Zara lifted one foot and placed it on the bottom step. Gazing upwards, she realized that her stiletto heels were going to be a painful encumbrance: the cement rise was littered with shards of soft black wood and lumps of broken concrete. But maybe Ben was up there. Biting her lip, Zara leaned forward and began undoing her shoes.

From her left came a dull thud, then a bellowed curse.

By the sound of it, her pursuers had managed to gain entrance via another door and were working towards her from the far side of the building. Any moment now, they would be opening that door at the left end of the passage, and they would see her. She slipped off her second stiletto and made ready to run.

Someone tried the handle of the door to her left…again…thrice. Whoever it was, they lost patience fast. When the door failed to open, it was subjected to a brutal blow that smashed it from its weak hinges. Through the swirling ash, Zara saw the black figure stride into the corridor.

He was neither of the young men from outside – too tall and broad. His face reflected none of the moon's meager light, and nor did his teeth, eyes, or clothes. He was pure ebony, breathing hard and heavy as he limped through a cloud of stirred ash, a monster ripped from the dark fabric of childhood dreams. He paused as he spotted her, one finger stabbing at her like a blow.

"WHORE!"

Any reservations Zara had about heading upstairs vanished in a heartbeat when that guttural voice lashed across the corridor. Clutching her stilettos, she began running upward as fast as her sore feet would take her. She heard him growl deep in his throat and give chase, loping over the shattered sleepers.

Her coat quickly proved to be a burden—buttoned, it hampered her hammering knees and slowed her progress. At the first and only landing, she took the opportunity to undo the two buttons with trembling fingers, the coat flapping behind her like a vampire's cape as she raced up the second half of the flight. Now she was running into the unknown almost naked, but staying ahead of the beast below was her main concern.

Zara burst onto the second floor and found herself in another long hallway. The ceiling was almost intact here, and only the window at the far end of the corridor provided any pale light. Against this, she saw the silhouette of the fleeing girl receding down the hall.

"Wait!" she gasped, not even recognizing her own desperate, ash-choked voice. *"Help!"*

The shadow ducked to one side of the window, and Zara heard a door slam. Behind her, she could hear the harsh breath of her pursuer echoing up the stairs, brutally sexual in its raw exertion, and the grim possibilities inherent in that breath sent her racing down the hall after the girl.

The corridor did not reward bare feet, strewn with debris as it was. Grit made for uncertain footing, and she almost lost her balance more than once. The man came off the stairs behind her, his heavy tread thumping against the groaning floor like her heart against its cage of ribs.

Where had the girl gone? She'd slipped through one of the many doors along this corridor, but the veil of darkness had denied sight of the correct one. Pale light gleamed through the window ahead, and Zara could see three more doors between her and the end of the hall.

Pick one! Quickly!

Zara plumped for the nearest and prayed it was unlocked. She hit it with her shoulder and grabbed the handle at the same time, feeling her hope of security die away as the loose door jostled in its frame. She wrenched the knob with a sweaty palm, felt it give. Then she was inside and slamming the door.

A ragged hole in the ceiling showed that she was alone with burned chunks of timber, the twisted remains of furniture. None of it would give her a place to hide, there were no other exits, and the door would not lock. Terror clutched her heart, possessive, undeniable.

The man's footsteps neared the door and came to a halt. He had seen her enter this room. Zara backed up against the wall to the side of the entrance, trembling hands clutching her shoes against her stomach. Gripping a stiletto firmly by the toe, she tried to slow her breathing, to calm her nerves, but it was a pointless exercise: as the hunter huffed and puffed just outside the room, her jackrabbit heart raced ever faster.

Time lay motionless, for a second, for an hour.

Then the door exploded inwards, and she flinched back as he lunged into the room.

Now!

With the barest scintilla of light to guide her, Zara aimed for the center of his dark head and let loose. Her arm rolled fluent and fluid like a cricketer swinging at a full toss, knowing that they were just about to hear the full crack of the ball hitting the sweet spot. But there was no crack, just an anonymous thud as the steel heel of her stiletto struck the silhouette of the man's head. He stiffened and choked, twitching, and she tried to pull back the shoe for another blow.

That was when she realized that the heel had pierced his eye and was embedded deep within his brain.

* * *

As Ben accelerated down the road, he watched Zara shrink in the rearview mirror. She looked so different huddled in that short coat, her lustrous red hair down and proud, and he began to see her as something other than a wife fulfilling an obligation. She looked like a stranger, a sexy stranger, and his fingers twitched on the wheel. This was going to work.

It wasn't that he'd lost his desire for her—Zara was as beautiful as ever, maybe even more so. But their respective careers demanded long, unpredictable hours that had drained the passion from their short marriage like needy children. Neither of them had much time or energy for sex, and when they did, the results were perfunctory and unsatisfying. This had made them edgy, uncommunicative, and being apart so often only reminded him that they'd met and married fast, with so much yet to learn about each other. Perhaps little games like this could help them see each other afresh, strip everything back to the core of passion that had dominated the first months of their courtship. He rounded the corner, imagining the two of them rutting with a frenzied passion he could only wistfully remember, and pulsed with need for the woman he loved but barely knew.

Distracted by the fantasy, he didn't notice the girl until he was almost on her.

Christ!

The CR-V's brakes were in peak condition and made barely a sound of protest as the car lurched to a sudden halt. Gasping, Ben saw the girl turn in his headlights and squint towards him. He was trying to take in her appearance—fishnet stockings, dark hair and flashing eyes—when she stepped out of the glow and walked toward his passenger side window. Zara had left it down for fresh air, and before he knew it, this stranger was leaning into his car.

"Hell of a way to get my attention, baby." Up close, she looked so young, but there was something in her demeanor, an intelligence that suggested experience beyond her years. "So, you lookin' for a little love?"

Ben realized what she was about, on tonight of all nights, and the irony of his situation struck him momentarily dumb.

"Don't be shy."

The girl shocked him again by opening the passenger door and sliding towards him. Of course Zara had left it unlocked; she was coming back soon, wasn't she?

"Hey, what the *hell*— "

"*Sssh*. Here, let me make it easy for you."

The girl was right in his ear now, her raven hair brushing his cheek. Her ashen scent made him light-headed, giddy, and when her slim fingers slid up his thighs, over his pockets, they narrowly missed the bulge that had been summoned by his yearning for Zara.

"Get off me!" he spluttered. "This is *not* happening."

She dodged the warding-off elbow he thrust in her direction and whispered right into his brain.

"Why not? I'm sure you can afford me, honey. Why don't you check?"

She pulled away, and out of instinct, Ben's hand fell on his pocket, only to find it empty, the comfortable weight of his wallet missing.

"Hey!"

The girl's Cheshire Cat grin was already halfway out the door. Ben threw the car into park, fumbled his belt off, and lunged across the passenger seat. She grabbed the edge of the door and slammed it shut, bringing his lunge to an abrupt halt as his head thumped against the window. His brain exploded into white light, *pain*, then melted beneath the crimson corrosion of blind rage.

"You little slut!"

She was off, fleeing over the footpath towards some derelict building. He slid back into the driver's seat and shoved the stick back into drive, aimed after her, raced over the footpath into the car park beyond. Ah, the old community center, or what remained of it. Who was going to help her in there? No one— but perhaps she meant to hide, and she was almost at the front door.

He pulled up in one of the parking bays and killed the engine, fuming. He *had* to get that wallet back. How the hell would he explain its absence to... *Zara!* She was out there, alone, and next to naked. Christ, he'd better make this quick.

He hurried across to the Reception door, and it groaned open at his touch. The chamber beyond was in a state of utter decrepitude. Deeper holes in the darkness were doors to lead him further in, and he headed for one at random, thrumming with fury. He had to find that light-fingered harlot and get his wallet—and his pride—back where it belonged.

However, letting his anger cloud cool rationality had been a bad idea. Soon he had no idea where *he* was, let alone the girl. He stalked through room after room, all of them ruined, empty, and found nothing. The disturbed ash was making his throat itchy, clogging his grumbling voice. Minutes had slipped by, and Zara was no doubt beginning to worry. The fact that she was out there unprotected added to his woes, which in turn made him angrier; every distant noise sounded like her voice calling to him in fear, reminding him of his responsibility, of his weakness, of what he stood to lose.

He was crossing yet another barren room, beginning to think he should just cut his losses and go fetch Zara, when he tripped over some unseen obstacle and crashed hard to the floor. A bright bloom of pain lit up his foot, and he cursed at the top of his lungs, choking on the ash that now coated him top to toe.

How the hell am I going to explain this? Oh, that little bitch!

His right foot was a constant ache, but he made himself walk on it anyway. The pain worsened his mood, made it foul and furious. He felt like crushing anything that hindered his progress towards the next door. Nothing did, but when he turned the handle, the portal proved to be immovable. Part of him was grimly pleased as he tried the door twice more: now violence was the only option. Supporting himself against a wall, he raised his left foot and propelled it forward. His anger felt validated when the wooden panel crashed to the floor, defeated.

Limping through a swirl of grit, his eyes flew straight to the shadow at the other end of the passage, finding just enough detail in its contours to recognize it as female—she was lurking at the foot of a staircase, lingering just to taunt him all over again. Rage blossomed across his brain like a blood-black bruise, and now it was throbbing worse than his poor foot, and he stabbed at her with a fierce finger and yelled the first thing that came into his head. It didn't even sound like him anymore. The girl immediately took flight, up the stairs and into deeper darkness.

For just one moment as he began to give chase, he thought it might have been Zara, but his anger quickly and brutally dismissed the notion. She had no reason to be in here, and anyway, there was no way she would have been able to fly upstairs like that: her high heels would have made it impossible. She would have lost her balance, fallen, maybe even broken an ankle.

Not only are they impractical, he thought grimly as he stalked after the thieving whore. *Those shoes are downright dangerous.*

Christmas Shopper
Rudy Kremberg

Nelly didn't believe in heaven, certainly not in the biblical sense, and until the Saturday before Christmas, the existence of hell had always seemed just as improbable. That was the day she finally did her shopping.

She'd been putting it off, as she did every year. But this year things had been even more hectic than usual at work, what with the looming presentation the firm was counting on to stay viable. Then there was Tom's nagging insecurity to deal with— the status quo wasn't enough anymore, and it was either say yes to his proposal or move on. Not that she wasn't emotionally ready to tie the knot or move on. She just couldn't find the time for either.

But the Christmas shopping couldn't wait any longer. And now that the Wondermart down the street from the office was having a sale—the *Better Than Black Friday Pre-Christmas Shop Till You Drop Super Sale Event!*, to quote the ads—all of her excuses were null and void. Of course, it helped that she knew exactly what to get her family: a sweater for her father, a blouse for her mother, a toaster oven for her sister and her sister's husband, a video game called Jungle Explorer for their boy.

As for Tom, she hadn't gotten around to deciding. She was confident the right thing would occur to her, though. It always did. Her boss had said so himself after she'd done a run-through of the presentation.

Pulling into Wondermart's crowded parking lot on Saturday morning, her SUV almost nicked a van that cut in front of her—the driver honked his horn at her as if she were at fault, and she honked right back. She had to drive around the lot three times before she found a vacant spot, braking repeatedly for shoppers and their carts, nearly mowing down a family that materialized in front of her without warning.

The free spot happened to be next to the van. Her gut instinct told her to stay away, that she'd be asking for trouble if she parked beside it. Normally she would have heeded that instinct, but not this time. She wanted to get the shopping over with as fast as humanly possible.

The store was the size of two football fields, and two things hit her as soon as she'd followed the lineup inside: it was so crowded she could barely move, and it was hot. She smelled sweat and bad breath, felt shoulders and elbows pushing against her from all directions, heard shoppers complaining and babies crying. And "The Little Drummer Boy," her least favorite carol, was coming out of the ceiling.

She made a beeline for the carts, discovered she didn't have coins, fought her way to a cashier for change, then back to unlock a cart. Her strategy was to advance from there through the middle of the store, starting with the men's clothing section and ending up in entertainment and electronics. That was where she'd find Jungle Explorer. And something for Tom, surely.

By the time she was halfway to the sweaters, she was drenched in sweat, dehydrated, a little dizzy and nauseated, her heartbeat racing and her patience hanging by a thread. She found herself thinking about work, fearing that this shopping excursion would cause her to fall behind schedule. She tried without success to shut the thought out of her mind, to disregard the incessant drone of "The Little Drummer Boy." Pushing on through the crowd, she eventually made it to the sweaters.

The best size for her father was sold out, so she grabbed the next one up. The blouses were straight ahead, and the pickings were even slimmer. Forget the pink silk her mother preferred; she had to make do with a puke-colored synthetic blend.

The toaster oven she wanted was sold out, too. She had to splurge on a more expensive model. Dropping it into her cart, she had another dizzy spell but managed to stay upright.

On to the video games.

She spotted a single copy of Jungle Explorer, the only one left, and charged into the thickening crowd, using the cart as a battering ram. She was closing in on the item, thinking of the looks she'd get from her nephew if she disappointed him, when somebody else's cart bumped hers aside and rolled over her toes, distracting her for a crucial moment.

No sooner had the pain in her foot reached her brain than a hand snatched the last Jungle Explorer. She didn't see whose cart it was; the shopper was instantly engulfed by the crowd.

The only game still available was something called Zombie Invaders, so she settled for that.

Which left Tom. What to get him?

She wasn't going to be sucked into a wild-goose chase, she swore. Last year he'd had the nerve to tell her Christmas shopping was more a gal's thing than a guy's. She'd called him sexist. If she didn't find the right present for him this year, she wouldn't lose sleep over it.

The electronics section was across the next aisle. Out of the crowd, parting it like Moses parting the Red Sea, a uniformed store employee wheeled a dolly laden with small boxes labeled Celina and, below that, Voice-Activated Smart Speaker. He unloaded the boxes into a depleted bin marked *20% OFF*.

Smart speakers—weren't they still pretty cool? Virtual personal assistants that answered your questions, turned your lights on and off, played your favorite music, did damn near everything except deliver your presentations for you. All you had to do was ask the questions and give the orders. No need to lift a finger.

Just what Tom needed.

At that point, she was eight or nine yards from the bin, and half the boxes were gone. She surged ahead, ignoring a cart that smashed into her hip. Five yards away, and only a couple of boxes remained. One of them vanished, and an arm was reaching out for the other. The arm of a thirtysomething woman in a red nylon parka. Nelly glimpsed the grim determination in her face.

Before the last box could disappear, she elbowed the woman in the ribs. If there was a grunt or a yelp or a swear word, the din that filled the store drowned it out. Regardless, the outstretched arm withdrew and the box was unclaimed long enough for Nelly to seize it.

She didn't get another look at the woman she'd elbowed. Not inside the store, at least—the crowd had swallowed her up, just as it had swallowed up the shopper whose cart had run over Nelly's foot. Nelly briefly wondered if they were one and the same person.

Back in the parking lot, after enduring the checkout lineup for half an hour, she unloaded her cart into the trunk of her SUV. She was desperate for a drink now, desperate for breathing space. Desperate to get away from this hell—it was still just a figurative hell so far.

She wheeled the empty cart to the cart station, then maneuvered her way back to the SUV. The van was still beside it, and the parking lot had become even more crowded. Cars were coming and going, making abrupt turns, forcing pedestrians to scurry to safety.

Her phone went off as she started the engine. Out of habit she took the call, and if she hadn't let her annoyance get the better of her—an air-duct cleaning service was promoting a Christmas special—she would have paid more attention to her surroundings. As it was, she didn't see the van backing out of its spot while she moved forward out of hers, and she was slow to notice that a woman wearing a red parka was walking across the traffic lane ahead of the SUV, on course for a collision. At the last second, just before Nelly swung the wheel and braked, the woman jumped out of the way. Staggering backward, she looked up, a hateful gleam of recognition in her eyes, and said something Nelly didn't quite catch. The C-word?

I don't need this, Nelly thought, accelerating out of the parking lot. When it was behind her, she heard what sounded like a scream, but there was nothing to see in her rearview mirror except cars and the faceless crowd. She drove away, didn't look back again. It wasn't until suppertime that she saw the news on TV.

There had been an accident in the parking lot at Wondermart. A van backing out of a parking space had hit a pedestrian, knocking her to the pavement and crushing her skull. The victim was a mother of five. Sobbing as the camera mercilessly closed in on his face, the woman's husband told the reporter she'd been shopping for Christmas presents for her family.

The reporter mentioned what witnesses had seen: the woman had stepped into the path of the van in order to avoid getting hit by another vehicle, an SUV.

The driver of the SUV might not have been aware of the accident but was being asked to contact police.

Nelly stared at the screen, numb with guilt and horror.

* * *

The dreams started that night. She was back in the store, caught up in the swell of shoppers storming the bin with the discounted smart speakers. Elbows and coughs and bad breath were in her face. "The Little Drummer Boy" was playing over the loudspeakers in the ceiling. Her windpipe narrowed, cutting off the air flow to her lungs. She felt as if she were going to throw up and at the same time pass out. As the crush around her tightened, she pushed and kicked her way to the main door at the front of the building. It had been left ajar, but before she could cross the threshold it slammed shut. She heard the lock click, tried in vain to force the door open, and ended up screaming for help.

Why should anyone help you? a familiar voice asked. It was the voice of the shopper in the red parka. Nelly turned to look at her.

Her head was crushed beyond recognition, a mass of blood-saturated facial tissue and brain matter and shattered bone.

Nelly screamed again.

* * *

She didn't contact the police. She was going to, but Tom talked her out of it. It would have served no purpose, he rationalized. The woman was dead and the police weren't going to bring her back, they'd only complicate Nelly's life. Besides, the accident wasn't Nelly's fault—the woman had carelessly stepped in her way. End of story.

After some hesitation, Nelly agreed with him. But she felt guilty.

* * *

She had the dream again the next night. And the next and the next.

It always ended the same way—she was locked inside the store, trapped with the mutilated dead woman and a horde of rabid fellow shoppers.

She couldn't get a decent night's sleep, felt tired and irritable at work.

Still, she followed the usual Christmas routine, wrapping the presents she'd bought, taking them to her parents for the family gathering on Christmas Eve, watching the Pope's midnight mass on TV—since her sister's wedding a decade ago, this annual ritual was the closest she'd come to attending church. Tom joined her on Christmas day. He was delighted with the smart speaker.

It was going to make his life not only easier but less lonely, he joked—now he had Celina to talk to when Nelly was too busy.

* * *

The holidays were filled with parties and dinners and phone calls, and Tom didn't get around to setting up the speaker until the New Year. Nelly received a call from him the same day.

"Something weird's going on," he said. "It's that smart speaker you got me."

She came over to his place, watched him double-check the speaker's internet connection.

"Can't find anything wrong," he said. "Now listen to this."

He turned to the speaker.

"Hey Celina, what's the weather going to be like tomorrow?"

Silence for a good ten seconds.

Nelly shrugged. "Maybe the voice recognition isn't—"

Tom held up his hand. "Here it goes. Listen."

The voice-activated speaker wasn't full range, but what came through was clear enough. Movement and voices in a crowded place. A baby crying. Car engines starting. Sudden commotion. A scream. Then silence again.

Nelly stood there, frozen.

"I know those sounds," she said in a flat voice. "I heard them in the parking lot at Wondermart. After I bought your present."

"The speaker must be picking them up on the net," Tom said. "Probably through a live mic somebody forgot to turn off. It just happens to sound like what you heard that day."

They listened some more.

"Hello?" Tom said. "Hey Celina, are you hearing me?"

No answer, just the same noises.

"I'll take it back for an exchange," Nelly said. She would have asked him to do it, but the store was only a two-minute drive from her office.

She told him about her recurring nightmare, almost couldn't bring herself to articulate the gory details. Holding her in his arms, he tried to reassure her that the dreams would stop and she'd get over the accident, she just needed time.

They packed up the smart speaker. Fortunately, she'd kept the receipt.

* * *

Pulling into the store's parking lot, Nelly found herself overcome by dizziness and nausea and shortness of breath. It was even worse than before. She powered down the window, let the cold air fill her lungs. When she felt well enough to resume driving, she turned the SUV around and escaped.

She couldn't ever go back, it dawned on her. She'd have a full-blown panic attack if she did. Might even die if she passed out and choked on her vomit.

Her sister had mentioned she'd be exchanging most of Nelly's presents—the sweater for their father was too big, their mother hated the blouse, and Zombie Invaders wouldn't run on her boy's computer. She kindly agreed to take back the smart speaker at the same time. That evening she dropped off the replacement at Nelly's place.

Before bringing it to Tom, Nelly tested it.

"Hey Celina," she said. "What's the weather forecast for tomorrow?"

The same thing happened: Celina's voice was nowhere to be heard, and what came through instead were the sounds of the parking lot, the commotion, the scream, then silence.

"Hey Celina," Nelly repeated. "What's going on?"

Still the silence. Finally, after another ten seconds or so, a voice.

I shouldn't be here.

It was a woman's voice, but clearly not Celina's. This voice sounded unfriendly and strangely fragile, like something broken that had been cobbled together and might break into pieces again at any moment.

Don't you know who I am?

Nelly opened her mouth to say she didn't, then realized she did.

It was the voice she'd heard in Wondermart's parking lot and her dreams. The voice of the shopper who'd been run over—whose death Nelly was at least partly responsible for.

She collapsed on the sofa.

You put me here, the voice said. *I'm going to make you pay.*

Nelly pulled the plug, returned the speaker to its box. This time she would ask Tom to take it back for a refund.

* * *

"You've been under a lot of stress," he told her that night, massaging her neck and shoulders. "On top of that you're obviously feeling guilty about the . . . accident. Even though it wasn't your fault, as we agreed."

"But it was," she said.

She thought of the phone call from the air-duct cleaning service. If only she hadn't let herself get distracted—

"You need to dial down your stress," Tom advised her. "Cut back on your workload. See a therapist if the guilt doesn't let up."

He continued to massage her neck with one hand, slipped the other under her panties. She moaned, then kissed him.

"I don't want to be alone tonight," she said. "Maybe you're right about getting married. Or at least living together. Maybe it's time."

He smiled and kissed her back. "That's what I've been waiting to hear."

He'd stay the night after he brought over a change of clothes from his place, he told her. He didn't expect to be gone longer than an hour.

"Make it faster," she urged him.

He said he'd hurry.

* * *

An hour later he still wasn't back. He didn't pick up when she called after an hour and a half, or when she tried a second time, or a third. Close to four hours later, his brother called her.

Tom had been in an accident. His car had veered off the road, crashing into a lamp pole. He had died of massive trauma to his head, probably instantly.

A driver going the other way had reported seeing him as they'd passed each other, the police had said. The light from the lamp had hit his face, and the other driver had been struck by his startled, shocked expression—it was as if he'd seen a ghost. A second later his car had been in the other driver's rearview mirror, swerving into the pole.

It hadn't been possible to check Tom's expression after the accident. His face, along with the rest of his head, had been crushed.

* * *

"Did you do this?" Nelly screamed at the smart speaker. It was still unplugged, packed away in its box on the living-room floor. "I know you did, you bitch!"

No answer.

"How?"

Still no sound from the speaker, but in her head she heard that strange patched-together voice.

It was easy, it whispered confidentially. *All I had to do was get inside his head. Just like I'm inside your head now.*

Nelly moved the speaker into the closet. She'd keep it there, safely out of sight, until her sister returned it to the store for her.

* * *

She took time off for the funeral, forcing a postponement of the presentation. Her boss made a show of being sympathetic, said all the right things, but she could tell he was disappointed. Maybe even a bit pissed.

Tom's casket was closed.

* * *

Halfway into the rescheduled presentation, she found herself reliving the dream, face to face with the mutilated woman inside Wondermart's locked main door.

At first, she managed to convince herself none of it was real, that it was all in her mind. Then she saw the woman's blood smeared on her skin and clothes, could have sworn it was actually there. She screamed at the top of her lungs, didn't stop until her prospective client called for help.

The presentation was rescheduled again. It was canceled altogether when word came that another agency had won the account.

Soon there was more bad news: the firm could no longer afford its current overhead. That meant jobs had to be cut, half a dozen in the creative department alone. Including hers.

* * *

"You bitch, were you behind that, too? Did you get inside my head again?"

Again, no answer. The speaker was where she'd left it, in the closet, waiting for her sister to take it back to the store.

"What do you want from me?"

In her head, that familiar voice:

I want you to suffer.

* * *

The therapist didn't think Nelly was hearing the dead woman's voice. Guilt was making her believe she was hearing it, he told her—she'd readily admitted nobody else had heard it, at least not in her presence. The therapist encouraged her to keep using the smart speaker. *Confront the issue head on,* he said. *Take the bull by the horns.*

Nelly started looking for another job, meeting other men. She even reconnected the speaker, albeit reluctantly. And for a while it worked the way it was designed to.

But the nightmares wouldn't end.

* * *

"What'll it take to make you stop?" she snapped at the speaker after another gruesome dream had disrupted her sleep. "How do I get you to leave me alone?"

You can start by apologizing, the woman's voice answered. *For what you did to me.*

So Nelly said she was sorry. And she was. But not really for the woman, truth be told. No, she was sorry about what she'd brought upon herself and Tom.

The woman seemed to have read her mind.

For what are you sorry, exactly? I want to hear you say it.

"For what happened in the parking lot."

Spell it out.

"For forcing you into the path of the van."

For killing me. Say it.

"For killing you."

That's better. But an apology is just for starters, like I said.

"What else, then?"

A couple of things. First, I want you to help my parents. They're old and my mother's sick. The Christmas present you stopped me from buying was supposed to help them. So I want you to buy one of those talking speakers for them. I want you to set it up and teach them how to use it. Be there for them when they need you.

The woman recited their names, an address and a phone number. Nelly wrote it all down.

"If I help your parents, will you promise to leave me alone?"

Just do this. Then we'll get to the other thing.

She wouldn't say more.

* * *

The woman's parents lived in a subsidized low-rent apartment complex. They were in their late seventies, like Nelly's parents, and the mother had known who she was even before she'd introduced herself—her dead daughter had told her, she claimed. After Nelly set up the smart speaker she'd ordered online, they served coffee and showed photos of their late child, their other children and grandkids. The children's families had moved out of town, Nelly learned, though they all got together every Christmas.

"My daughter wasn't ready to leave this life," the mother said, gazing at one of the photos. "She needs to make peace with it before she can move on to the afterlife. In the meantime, she's stuck halfway in between. That's what she told me."

"She really talked to you?"

The mother nodded, pointed at a nearby radio. "Sometimes I hear her inside there. She's lonely. Lonely and mad, but mostly lonely. Even though she's got other...victims of Christmas to talk to."

"Victims of Christmas?"

"Uh-huh. Suicides and heart attacks, especially. She says they're stuck just like she is, they can't get free until they sort things out with the living world."

Her husband didn't contradict her, just listened solemnly. When she was out of earshot, he explained to Nelly that she was suffering from dementia.

Nelly wondered if she wasn't losing her marbles, too.

* * *

She tidied up their apartment, brought them groceries from the neighborhood supermarket. She'd do the same every Saturday, she promised, knowing full well it would be impossible to find openings in her schedule.

That night she had the bad dream yet again. She woke up in a cold sweat.

"When are you ever going to make it stop?" she railed at the speaker.

I told you there were a couple of things I wanted you to do, the cobbled-together voice replied. *So far, you've just started on one and I'm not convinced you'll see it through.*

"What's the other thing?"

It's too early to think about that. Focus on helping my parents for now.

Nelly adjusted her schedule and continued the weekly visits.

Winter ended, spring ran its course, then summer and fall. She found a new job and a new boyfriend, carried on with the therapy even though it didn't stop the dreams, didn't change much of anything. Before long she got her first promotion, and soon after that, her boyfriend was complaining they didn't spend quality time together. By November she was so busy that she shortened her visits to the woman's parents and was tempted to skip them. The caretaking had become a burden, and she was growing increasingly resentful. But she forced herself to go through the motions, missing deadlines at work and upsetting her boyfriend.

Meanwhile she kept dreaming she was stuck inside Wondermart with the dead woman, screaming for help.

By December she was seeing the woman's crushed head not only in her sleep but whenever she drank her morning coffee. And talked with clients, delivered pitches, ate dinner or tried to make love.

As if that weren't enough, the woman was becoming more real, pressing against Nelly in the crowded store. Nelly could feel the moist warmth of her blood, the jagged breaks in her skull, the softness of her exposed brain tissue.

And other dead people were joining the woman, turning the dreams into a version of Zombie Invaders. Bloated corpses with slashed wrists, gaping gunshot wounds, foaming mouths. Their sickly pale faces were frozen in pain and despair.

Nelly was losing her sanity—that was the first possibility. The second, which was beginning to seem more likely, was far worse.

There actually was such a place as hell. And she was trapped inside it.

* * *

The situation came full circle just before Christmas, on the first anniversary of the accident.

It's time to talk about that other thing I want you to do, the voice said after Nelly had complained she was at the end of her rope, that she couldn't help the woman's parents anymore if the visions and nightmares didn't stop. *Today's the day I want you to start doing it. Want to hear what it is?*

"I'm listening."

You might not be able to handle it, I should warn you. Which is kind of the point.

"It can't be worse than what you've already put me through," Nelly said.

The voice gave no assurance that the other thing wasn't going to be worse, didn't respond at all for what seemed an eternity. Nelly waited with a mixture of impatience and dread.

I've got a much bigger family than you do, the voice finally spoke up. *Five kids, three brothers, ten nephews and nieces, not to mention my husband, my parents, my uncles and aunts and my in-laws. So many people to think of at Christmas that I never had time to think of myself.*

Now there was an unmistakable hint of malice in the tone, of relish at doling out this ultimate punishment.

"Just tell me what you want me to do."

I think you already know.

An image flashed before her mind's eye: shoppers crowding all around her, pushing her out of the way, coughing in her face and rolling their carts over her toes, the air getting hotter and stuffier, sweat drenching her clothes under her winter coat, "The Little Drummer Boy" playing in an endless loop as dizziness and nausea set in.

"You really want me to . . . for your whole family this Christmas?"

Not just this Christmas.

"How many Christmases?"

Every Christmas. Until you die or they die. The voice paused, perhaps to savor the moment. *And you always have to do it in person. At Wondermart, no earlier than the Saturday before.*

Nelly opened her mouth to protest, but her own voice had deserted her. The dizziness and nausea intensified, her breathing became labored. Somewhere inside the smart speaker, a Christmas carol was playing. "The Little Drummer Boy," if she wasn't mistaken.

Well, are you ready to start?

She managed to nod. Just before she passed out, she thought she heard the door to hell slamming shut and locking behind her.

Like Abigail Winchell
Christina Delia

I was feeling the pressures of housewife drudgery, Bad Mommy Syndrome (the twins had taken to alternately hitting and biting their friends on playdates). Jeff was working later hours at the office. Was he having an affair with his secretary?

"This isn't the 1950s," said Patty Stern wryly at book club. "He's probably screwing a co-worker. Or a woman who works in a nearby office. Or a man who works in a nearby office."

It really affected me, the things she was saying about my life, my marriage. Just announcing this, as if over a loudspeaker. All these Book Clubbers, these Quiche Eaters lowering their eyes in pity. Botoxed immobile masks they called faces.

I knew everything about these women: moles removed, rehab clinics entered, the accumulated miscarriages. All those popular names never used, never uttered, never printed on the birth certificates. No Ivys, no Jaxons, no Theos to call their own.

Would I dream of saying anything to hurt any of them? Not me.

Go ahead and shame me like I've never been shamed before, I wanted to say, but instead I said, "Hmm." I stuffed my mouth with flaky, greasy sausage quiche, and I just *know* I'm going to get fat again. Who puts sausage in quiche, anyway?

I hated book club, and I hated these women. We were reading Patty's choice this week, *Courageous Claudette,* about a woman who dreams of becoming a ballerina, loses her limbs in a fire, and never realizes her dream. At the end of the book, she gets to sit in the audience of a professional ballet recital.

"That's how life IS," Patty said. She was chewing her trail mix, careful to remove the raisins. They stared up at me from her waxy paper plate, like beady snowman eyes. I thought about what it would be like to watch Patty's face melt off come spring. She took a sip of "vino"; rosé from one of the plastic, stemless wineglasses Dina Fletcher-Porter bought on the Internet. *So convenient and less room for accidents,* Dina Fletcher-Porter had reported on her Mommy Blog.

Every one of these women had a Mommy Blog, or a home jewelry business, or a timeshare in LBI. What did I have?

Beautiful, bratty twins, and an equally attractive, selfish husband. We were a pretty Christmas card, like the kind I had to design by myself every fall, using an online coupon code and a snow family template.

"I thought the title was perfect," said Bethany Ruez. "Claudette IS courageous."

"You obviously didn't bother reading the book," Patty snapped. "Don't come next week. We don't need your insights."

I saw Bethany's face fall, the tears well up. How she had thought she belonged, and how she obviously didn't. It was like high school...no, it was like grade school. Like *Lord of the Flies*, a book I had read years ago and actually enjoyed.

It was so primal.

When I got home, the twins were sleeping, dull redheaded angels. Jeff too, was asleep on the couch, Nelson at his feet. The dog prefers Jeff, the twins prefer Jeff, and quite frankly, I prefer Jeff to me.

Patty had offered me rosé, but I had declined. I don't drink. I don't even take cough medicine. Most days I was so preoccupied, I'd forget to take my multivitamin. I was somewhere between wanting to live, and wanting to die.

That's how life IS, I imagined Patty would say.

I thought about how I had never finished junior college, and had no marketable skills. I was really feeling sorry for myself, when for some reason, I had the urge to go down to the laundry room.

It was such a cute space. Salmon pink walls, white wooden letters spelling out LAUNDRY, and with strategically placed hooks in between.

"Smart," said Dina Fletcher-Porter, when I had given the book club ladies the grand tour.

Smart? I wanted to scream. *It's a laundry room!* But I had thanked her politely, as the other women oohed and aahed, and Angie LaPlaca added the witty bon mot of, "I like pink!"

I was thinking maybe some of my innards are pink.

That's when I took the permanent Sharpie marker I saw on the revolving laundry stand and drew her. First, the face; a big, round circle. Next, I scribbled a wiry frizz of black hair shooting out from all points of the circle. The circle was definitely her head. No smile. I would make sure she never smiled. Why should she?

The body I sketched was a little plump. The clothes started out adhering to current trends: for some reason, I gave her a cold-shoulder top. Then I thought of *Jane Eyre*, which we had read in book club last year, and also gave her a petticoat. No skirt or dress necessary. Better to show what was underneath, like an elegant variation of that dream where someone takes a math test in their underwear. She was finished, she was dressed. A cold-shoulder top *and* a petticoat.

She could be a time traveler. She could be from anywhere.

Unlike *Courageous Claudette* in the book, I made sure my creation had legs and arms.

"What do I call you?" I asked the wall.

"I'm Abigail Winchell," the wall replied. "And *I* call *you*."

That's how it was from then on. The days seemed less monotonous. I finally had someone to talk to, someone who approved of me.

Abigail Winchell and I became fast friends. Probably because we had so much in common. Namely, sometimes I wore a cold-shoulder top, too.

We spoke about the things that gal pals discuss: celebrities, mothers-in-law, household hints. Abigail Winchell doesn't like Jennifer Aniston's new haircut. This is weird, because I saw Jennifer Aniston on a magazine cover recently, and I don't believe she has a new haircut. Yet Abigail Winchell keeps instilling it in me:

I don't like it, I don't like it.

She tells me things. Like who is to be trusted. Turns out that no one is to be trusted, except for her and me. We're like a secret club of women who reside in walls. She literally lives in mine, and I might as well only exist in sheet rock, in plywood. I have so much trouble breathing at a normal pace sometimes. God, I just wish my heart would stop.

"That's silly," scolds Abigail Winchell. "You've sacrificed enough, and now it's someone else's turn."

Not my twins. We both immediately agree on that. But Jeff is cheating on me. Abigail Winchell told me so. It gets worse: turns out he's cheating on me with multiple women from my book club: Patty Stern, Dina Fletcher-Porter and Angie LaPlaca.

They make Bethany Ruez watch.

"Filthy pigeons," Abigail Winchell says. "He's going to give you venereal diseases, and then you won't be able to have any more children."

"I wasn't planning on having any more children, anyway," I say slowly.

"Because of him," Abigail Winchell says.

"Because of him," I repeat.

"What about your dreams?" Abigail Winchell asks me.

"I don't have any," I say.

"I do," says Abigail Winchell. "My dreams are bold. You and Jeff have a joint savings account?"

"We do."

"Life insurance?"

"I don't want to hurt Jeff," I say.

"I do," says Abigail Winchell.

She tells me her plans every time I fold towels, or lift the stains from the twins' peewee football uniforms, or iron. I can't hear her anymore, I just can't. I take the iron, press it into my thigh, and scream.

Jeff makes me see a pretty, female psychologist, and I wonder if he's going to sleep with her, too. Strangely, he doesn't ask me about my Abigail Winchell wall. It's like he can't see her. Or like he doesn't want to.

On the Fourth of July, which she is calling my Independence Day, Abigail Winchell instructs me to burn down Patty Stern's house with all of the ladies in it, sporting their red, white and bluest.

I was thinking maybe some of my innards are red.

I am picturing these women, my frenemies, as Patty would say. (*We're all frenemies here!*)

And laugh, and laugh.

All these burning ballerinas, flesh falling off the bone, like Patty's specialty pulled pork.

She gives it a lavender rub.

I don't like it, I don't like it.

I know what I have to do.

I go to Patty's house. Bring a tray of brownies. She eyes them with amusement, "You're clearly not a chef...I guess you can be my sous chef."

I thank Patty for her kind offer, but assure her that Jeff would say I'm not even an adequate sous chef.

"Maybe his next wife will be," she says. And laughs.

Angie LaPlaca admires my cold-shoulder top (*I like pink!*) They all agree the choice of pairing it with a petticoat is a bold, yet baffling fashion statement.

"Retro," says Dina Fletcher-Porter, looking over at Bethany Ruez like, *Did she just lose her mind?*

I did, I really did. They say when you lose your mind you have no idea, but I am fully aware. I'm insane. You'd have to be to keep living this kind of life.

No one liked the brownies. Of course they were just normal brownies. I wouldn't hurt any living thing. Not even a bug. A spider crawled across my hand on the drive home, and I didn't say anything, didn't even move.

I know what I have to do. I go home and get Jeff's sledge hammer from the garage.

Goodbye, Abigail Winchell.

The wall is gone. Where there was Abigail Winchell, there's a hole. Where there was me, there's a hole. There always was. Just no one knew. No one knows.

When the women from book club come over, they will say, *Ooh, you're building an addition?*

They won't know the sacrifice I made for them, for everyone else.

About the Authors

Jeremy Billingsley ("My Father's Home") works and lives in Northwest Arkansas. He teaches creative writing and English at the college level to both graduates and undergraduates. This year, along with this story, he has short stories coming out in Soteira Press, Hellbound Books, and Tell-Tale Press. He has published numerous short stories and two novels. He's currently working on an autofiction novel and another novel about death. Follow him on Twitter @JeremyBillings1 and on Goodreads.

C. W. Blackwell ("Drifter") was born and raised in Santa Cruz, California where he still lives today with his wife and two children. His passion is to blend poetic narratives with pulp dialogue to create strange and rhythmic genre fiction. He writes mostly crime fiction, dark fiction, and weird westerns. His fiction has appeared recently in *Switchblade Magazine, Mystery Weekly Magazine, Pulp Modern,* and *Aphotic Realm.* Follow him on Facebook @cwalkerblackwell and Twitter @CW_Blackwell.

Barrie Darke ("The Wolf Gang") has had several plays performed, and has worked with the BBC, but prose was always the main thing. He lives and writes in the Northeast of England, and teaches Creative Writing in a basement. He has also worked in a prison, where he learned more than the students. He has had around 50 short stories published in the UK and the US, and recently self-published a novel, *Dragon Clouds,* available as an e-book in Amazon's Kindle store. Follow him on Twitter @barriedarke.

Matthew R. Davis ("Walking on Knives") is an author and musician based in Adelaide, South Australia, with over fifty dark short stories published around the world thus far. He's judged for the Aurealis Awards and the Australian Shadows Awards, and his work has been shortlisted for both. He plays bass and sings in Blood Red Renaissance (on indefinite hiatus) and icecocoon, occasionally performs spoken word shows with punk poets Paroxysm Press, and dabbles in video editing, graphic design for posters and album covers, and composing for short films. His debut collection of horror stories, *If Only Tonight We Could Sleep,* was released in January 2020 through Things in the Well, and he's signed with a publisher for his first novel. Find out more at matthewrdavisfiction.wordpress.com.

Christina Delia ("Like Abigail Winchell") writes fiction and plays in New Jersey. She holds a BFA in Writing for Film and Television from The University of the Arts in Philadelphia. Her work can be found in the anthologies *Random Acts of Malice: The Best of Happy Woman Magazine*, *In One Year and Out the Other* (Pocket Books edition), *Forgotten Philadelphia*, and *Uncle John's Bathroom Reader Presents: Flush Fiction*, among others. Her play "The Mirror Had Other Ideas" is currently being performed in The Secret Theatre's Act One: One Act Festival in Long Island City, New York. Christina's story "Stuffie" is forthcoming in the horror fiction anthology *What Monsters Do for Love* (Soteira Press.) She is the proud mom of Juliet.

KC Grifant ("Maternal Bond") is a New England-to-SoCal transplant who writes internationally published horror, fantasy, science fiction and weird western stories for collectible card games, podcasts, anthologies and magazines. Her writing has appeared in *Andromeda Spaceways Magazine*, *Aurealis Magazine*, the *Lovecraft eZine*, *Unnerving Magazine*, *Frozen Wavelets*, *Tales to Terrify*, *The Macabre Museum* and *Colp Magazine*. Her stories have haunted anthologies including *We Shall Be Monsters*, *Beyond the Infinite: Tales from the Outer Reaches*, *Trembling With Fear*, and the Stoker-nominated *Fright Mare: Women Write Horror*. In her spare time, she consumes too much coffee and chases down a wild toddler. For more information, visit www.SciFiWri.com or amazon.com/author/kcgrifant. You can also say hi on Instagram or Twitter @kcgrifant.

Liam Hogan ("Cuckoo") is an award winning short story writer, with stories in *Best of British Science Fiction 2016*, and *Best of British Fantasy 2018* (NewCon Press). He's been published by Analog, Daily Science Fiction, and Flametree Press, among others. He helps host Liars' League London, volunteers at the creative writing charity Ministry of Stories, and lives and avoids work in London. More details at http://happyendingnotguaranteed.blogspot.co.uk or tweet to @LiamJHogan.

K.N. Johnson ("Accessory")'s story "Frigid" won Mythraeum's Pygmalion contest for its haunting take on an artist obsessed with ice and one woman. "Frigid" was developed into a short film by Loste Films. Johnson's dark non-fiction appears in *Proximity Magazine* and *Incandescent Mind* literary journal. Her short fiction appears in anthologies such as *A Haunting of Words*, *Below the Deck—Tales from the Cellar*, *Polterguests*, *Terra Nullius*, and *On Fire*. "Specter Hill" features the mysterious lights of Indiana forests and will appear in From the Yonder in 2020. Johnson earned her AA in Creative Writing; her fascination with human psychology has inspired her return to school for her BS in Psychology. She spends her days as a research specialist for healthcare studies and weekends with her family, cats, and true crime films and podcasts. She enjoys responsible legend trips and takes way too many photos during ghost investigation adventures. Follow her on Facebook @knjohnsonauthor.

Thomas Kearnes ("His Death Brings No Respite") graduated from the University of Texas at Austin with an MA in film writing. His fiction has appeared in *Gulf Coast*, *Foglifter*, *Berkeley Fiction Review*, *Timber*, *Hobart*, *Gertrude*, *A cappella Zoo*, *Split Lip Magazine*, *Cutthroat*, *Litro*, *PANK*, *BULL: Men's Fiction*, *Gulf Stream Magazine*, *Wraparound South*, *Night Train*, *3:AM Magazine*, *Word Riot*, *Storyglossia*, *Driftwood Press*, *Adroit Journal*, *The Matador Review*, *Pseudopod*, *Underbelly Magazine*, *Black Dandy*, the *Best Gay Stories* series, *Mary: A Journal of New Writing*, *wigleaf*, *SmokeLong Quarterly*, *Pidgeonholes*, *Sundog Lit*, *The Citron Review*, and elsewhere. He is a three-time Pushcart Prize nominee and three-time Best of the Net nominee. Originally from East Texas, he now lives near Houston and works as an English tutor at a local community college. His debut collection of short fiction, *Texas Crude*, is now available at Lethe Press, Amazon, and Barnes & Noble.

Rudy Kremberg ("Christmas Shopper") is a Toronto-based writer whose short stories have run the gamut from mainstream drama to dark fantasy/horror. His work has been published in Canada, the United States, Great Britain, and New Zealand, appearing in genre magazines (*Interzone*, *On Spec*, *Disturbed Digest*, the British Fantasy Society's *BFS Horizons*, to name just a few), anthologies (*Shivers: Canadian Tales of the Supernatural*; *The*

Wordscape, *Canadian Children's Annual* and *Northern Frights* series), literary journals (e.g., *Queen's Quarterly*, *The Roswell Literary Review*) and a host of other publications, ranging from *Storyteller* to *Knave* to *The Tampa Tribune*. His fiction has also been adapted for television (the horror series *The Hunger*) and broadcast on CBC Radio. His nonfiction credits include articles in general-interest consumer magazines, corporate newsletters, and trade periodicals, covering topics as diverse as information technology, medical research, and gourmet cheese.

Scotty Milder ("Seven Days of Dog Walking") is a writer, filmmaker, and film educator living in Albuquerque, New Mexico. He received his MFA in Screenwriting from Boston University. His award-winning short films have screened at festivals all over the world, including Cinequest, the Dead by Dawn Festival of Horror, HollyShorts, and the H.P. Lovecraft Film Festival and CthulhuCon. He has developed screenplays with independent producers and major Hollywood studios, and his low-budget feature film *Dead Billy* is currently available on Amazon, Google Play, and other streaming platforms. He is returning to writing fiction after a long hiatus. In the last year, he has had short stories appear in anthologies from Fantasia Divinity Press, DBND Publishing, Dark Peninsula Press, Soteira Press, AM Ink Publishing, and Gypsum Sound Tales. Visit his website at *www.deadbillythemovie.com* or *vimeo.com/trifectaplus*.

Bryan Miller ("Heart Skull Heart") is a Minneapolis-based writer and performer. His fiction has appeared on the *Drabblecast*, in *Intrinsick Magazine* and *Crimson Streets*, and in the anthologies *The Monsters We Forgot* and *Hellfire Crossroads*, among other publications. When he's not writing scary stories, he's touring the country doing stand-up comedy, which you can find on the *Late Late Show with Craig Ferguson* and Sirius XM Radio. Follow him on Twitter @realbryanmiller.

Hollee Nelson ("Roger") is a recent graduate from West Virginia University where she earned a B.A. in English. She aims to write stories that are a little bit spooky and a little bit silly. When she's not writing, she can be found baking treats, making hats, and championing goblin rights. Check her out @holleeban on Instagram and Twitter.

James Edward O'Brien ("Ring Rock") grew up in northern New Jersey in the US where he graduated from Dungeons & Dragons and punk rock to modernist lit and weird fiction. His short stories and poetry have appeared in the *Triangulation: Dark Skies anthology*, *The Literary Hatchet*, and on the *StarShipSofa* podcast. He lives in Far Rockaway, NY with his wife and three dogs. Follow Jim on Twitter @UnagiYojimbo.

Elin Olausson ("Uncle") is a bookaholic and a librarian, which means she's reading constantly (or wishing she was). Somehow, she finds the time to write, too. Her favorite genre is horror, which is ironic since she's scared of everything. Her stories frequently feature dysfunctional families, disturbed minds, and woods as dark as the ones surrounding the village where she grew up. She has published the short story "Scar" in *Black Apples* (Belladonna Publishing, 2014), and "Allfather" in the drabble anthology *Forgotten Ones* (Eerie River Publishing, 2020). Elin lives in Sweden and also writes LGBT romance under the pen name Elvira Bell. Visit her website www.elinolausson.com and follow her on Twitter @elin_writes.

Andrew Punzo ("In a Mother's Eyes") lives near Newark, New Jersey and works in New York City. His short fiction has appeared in Breaking Rules Publishing's *Horror* magazine, *Every Day Fiction*, *Tales from the Moonlit Path*, and other venues.

Lee Rozelle ("Mandibular Fixation") is the author of *Zombiescapes and Phantom Zones: Ecocriticism and the Liminal from* Invisible Man *to* The Walking Dead and *Ecosublime: Environmental Awe and Terror from New World to Oddworld*. Recently, his short fiction has appeared in HellBound Books' *Anthology of Bizarro*, *Dark Dossier Magazine*, *Steel Toe Review*, and the *Scare You to Sleep* podcast. He is a professor of English at the University of Montevallo.

Joseph Rubas ("In Control") is the author of over 300 short stories and several novels. His work has appeared in *The Horror Zine, All Due Respect, Nameless Digest,* and others. He currently resides in New York State.

Paul Stansfield ("Lemonade") was born and raised in New Jersey and graduated from Rutgers University. During his day job as a field archaeologist he excavated at various historic and prehistoric sites, and exhumed hundreds of graves. He's had stories published in such magazines as *Bibliophilos, Morbid Curiosity, Cthulhu Sex Magazine, The Literary Hatchet,* and *Horror Bites.* Currently he has stories available in several anthologies, including *The Prison Compendium* (EMP Publishing), *Cranial Leakage Vol. 2* (Grinning Skull Press), and *Hidden Menagerie Vol. 1* (Dragon's Roost Press). He is an Affiliate Member of the Horror Writers Association, and his personal blog is http://paulstansfield.blogspot.com. Finally, his hobbies include watching gross and gratuitous horror movies, drinking craft beer, and resisting the urge to strangle people who say, "I could care less" when they mean "I COULDN'T care less." Also, caring for his pet "Wiggles," the 30-foot tapeworm that resides in his intestines.

Louis Stephenson ("Itch") is a horror writer based in the Northwest of England. *A Nightmare on Elm Street* (1984) is the first horror movie he ever saw, and much like its director, Wes Craven, Louis' stories are inspired by his most terrifying nightmares, such as his works, "TUNNEL" and "bad.dreamer84" from the short horror anthologies *The Stuff of Nightmares* (2019) and Dark Ink's *Ghosts, Goblins, Murder & Madness* (2018), respectively. With the release of *Shadowy Natures,* he is making things personal with his disturbing tale, "Itch," which is inspired by Louis' real life, as he suffers from a severe form of psoriasis. In spite of this, he has a wonderful family and keeps his head high with making music, watching great horror movies, and eating cheeseburgers.

Thomas Vaughn ("Taking Out the Garbage") is an author of dark fiction who currently resides in Fayetteville, Arkansas. He is a fugitive from the debris field of rural Madison County. Thomas has published stories in numerous anthologies and magazines. When he is not writing fiction, he poses as a college professor who teaches classes in apocalyptic rhetoric. If you are interested in what he is up to, feel free to check-out his website at brokentransmitter.com.

***

Rebecca Rowland (Editor) is the author of the short fiction collection *The Horrors Hiding in Plain Sight*, co-author of the novel *Pieces*, and curator of *Ghosts, Goblins, Murder, and Madness* and the soon-to-be-released *The Half That You See*. Her stories most recently appeared in the anthologies *The Year's Best Hardcore Horror (vol 4)*, *Strange Stories, Movie Monsters,* and *Strange Girls* and in the magazines *Coffin Bell* and *Waxing & Waning*. A proud member of HWA and ALA, Rebecca accrued a hat trick of graduate degrees as well as an obnoxious amount of student loan debt, and as such, pays The Man as a librarian and ghostwriter but vacations as a dark fiction author and editor. Shamelessly judge her woefully rudimentary attempt at self-promotion at *RowlandBooks.com*.

Also By

DARK INK BOOKS

Available in Print - eBook - Audiobook

Ghosts, Goblins, Murder, & Madness
Twenty Tales of Halloween

Edited by Rebecca Rowland

Devil's Night, Day of the Dead, and Halloween have been celebrated around the world in one form or another, beginning with the Ancient Celts over two-thousand years ago. For some revelers, it's a time for guising, or dressing up in elaborate costume; for others, it's a time for practical jokes and mischief, and for some, it's a reverent occasion to acknowledge the thin line between earth and the spirit world.

Featuring twenty-one different voices hailing from five different countries and eleven states, *Ghosts, Goblins, Murder, and Madness* is certain to strike a chord with every horror aficionado.

Also By

DARK INK BOOKS

Available in Print - eBook - Audiobook

"Believe nothing you hear, and only one half that you see."

-The System of Dr. Tarr and Prof. Fether by Edgar Allan Poe

Poe's classic tale told of a state of the art hospital boasting a curiously experimental treatment, but things were not as they seemed. In *The Half That You See*, twenty-six writers from around the globe share their literary optical illusions in never before seen stories of portentous visions and haunting memories, altered consciousness and virulent nightmares, disordered thinking and descents into madness. Take a walk down the paths of perception that these dark fiction raconteurs have tunneled for you, but keep a tight grip on your flashlight: the course twists and turns, and once you're on route to your destination, there is no turning back. That which creeps about in the poorly lit corners of the human mind has teeth, and it's waiting for you.

Available everywhere March 2021